FINDING HER HEART

SAMANTHA HICKS

FINDING HER HEART

SAMANTHA HICKS

Affinity
Rainbow Publications

2022

Finding Her Heart
© 2022 by Samantha Hicks

Affinity E-Book Press NZ LTD
Canterbury, New Zealand

Edition 1st

ISBN:
ePub: 978-1-99-004963-7
PDF: 978-1-99-004964-4
Mobi: 978-1-99-004965-1
Print: 978-1-99-004966-8

Editor: CK King (Ravenseye)
Proof Editor: Alexis Smith
Cover Design: Irish Dragon Design
Production Design: Affinity Publication Services

ACKNOWLEDGMENTS

This year marks the fourth year of me being an author. I never thought I'd get one book published, let alone double digits. They say that when you love the job you do, you never work a day in your life. While that can be true, it is still a struggle to find the words and the motivation to write them. Nevertheless, this is a job I adore. Telling the love stories of the people in my head brings me joy. Every character is unique and have their own journey to take, and sometimes, no matter how hard I try, they are determined to go where they please.

None on this would have been possible without the wonderful people at Affinity and the community of authors and readers who all support each other and lift one another up. I am grateful to be a part of this team.

CK has done another brilliant job of making my words shine. With each book we work on together, I learn more. Her tips are invaluable to me and help me grow better as a writer.

Special mention to Finley, who despite being five years old now, still acts just like he did when he was a puppy. His companionship makes the dullest of days brighter.

DEDICATION

For Pappy
You can act as grumpy as you like, but we all know
you're a big softie.
Thank you for being an amazing dad.

TABLE OF CONTENTS

Chapter One	1
Chapter Two	18
Chapter Three	37
Chapter Four	43
Chapter Five	55
Chapter Six	70
Chapter Seven	75
Chapter Eight	83
Chapter Nine	90
Chapter Ten	101
Chapter Eleven	112
Chapter Twelve	121
Chapter Thirteen	141
Chapter Fourteen	151
Chapter Fifteen	163
Chapter Sixteen	172
Chapter Seventeen	191
Chapter Eighteen	200
Chapter Nineteen	214
Chapter Twenty	228
Chapter Twenty-one	236
Chapter Twenty-two	242
Chapter Twenty-three	254
About the Author	261
Samantha Hicks	261
Other Affinity Books	262

CHAPTER ONE

Ellis Davis sat at the desk in her home office, which doubled as the conservatory. She furiously tapped away at her keyboard, inputting figures and creating charts, racing against a deadline. Her client expected the report by the end of the day, and Ellis was only halfway done. No boss hovered over the self-employed actuarial consultant, but she would never disrespect her clients by going over deadlines. She prided herself on her ethics, and being tardy would only lead to loss of work.

A startling thump came through the kitchen wall. "Christ's sake. Are they not done yet?" She huffed out a breath and tried to find her place again on the screen. All morning, the new neighbours had been banging around as they moved in. Ellis was in no hurry to meet them. She kept herself to herself, not wanting to engage with the people on her street. She couldn't stand nosy neighbours. No doubt, all they ever did was gossip about everyone else. She didn't

1

have any proof of that, of course, but that didn't matter. She valued her privacy and was determined to keep it that way.

Another thud sounded. Ellis tore her glasses off in disgust and chucked them onto the desk. She leaned back and looked through the windows of the conservatory. She glanced over the dividing three-foot fence between her garden and next door's and caught a glimpse of a young, blond boy of about eight, kicking a football into the air. *Great, just what I need, a family living next door.* The previous neighbours had been an older couple. When the husband passed on, the wife moved into a care home. Ellis had liked the couple. They never made noise and kept out of her way, just how she liked it. *And now I have to put up with screaming kids. Just great.*

Ellis put her glasses back on and scanned the document on the screen, her brain trying to figure out what advice she was trying to relay. Normally, she had no problem maintaining the flow of statistics and mathematics in her head, but today it was a struggle. She blamed the noisy neighbours.

In the distance, Ellis heard the creaking of a gate but paid no attention. She zoned it out, along with the loud voices coming from next door. She carried on working for a few more minutes, until a woman's voice called out from the garden beside hers.

"Justin? Get back over here."

Ellis glanced over the top of her computer toward the bottom of her garden. The blond boy was sitting on her swing, going back and forth, and looking like he didn't have a care in the world that he was on someone else's property. Ellis gritted her teeth. They hadn't even fully moved in yet, and already she was pissed off with them. The swing had been on the property when Ellis bought it five years ago. She didn't know why she'd never taken it down. She supposed it gave her something to look at while she was thinking. The rest of her garden was barren, covered only in stone chippings. She wasn't a gardener, had no longing for plants, and grass was too much hassle to take care of. The week she moved in, she covered the area with stone and put the swing back up at the end.

And now the kid from next door was playing on it.

She pursed her lips and drew her brows down, not liking the gall he had to come over onto her property without asking. *A family with no rules.*

Ellis stood from the chair and went to the conservatory door. She stepped through, intent on telling him off, when she caught sight of a woman stood at the gate, glaring at the boy. Ellis blinked rapidly. The woman's long and wavy hair, the same shade as the boy's, cascaded over one shoulder. The jumper she wore was a mixture of bright colours and way too big for her small frame. One shoulder was exposed. Her face was make-up free, and Ellis guessed her to be about thirty-five. Although the woman glowered at the boy, her eyes were sparkling in the afternoon sun. Ellis surmised she wasn't much for disciplining her son and was probably just as disrespectful of other people's property.

"Come on, Justin. We need to unpack."

Justin jumped off the swing at the top of the arch and landed hard on the stones. Ellis grimaced, as stones flew up in every direction. She put her hands on her hips, angry at the wanton destruction this boy possessed. He jogged over to his mother, who clasped his shoulder and tugged him through the gate. She glanced up and spotted Ellis.

"Oh, hi. I'm sorry about my son. He's not very good at boundaries."

Her voice was soft, almost sensual, and Ellis swallowed hard. She hadn't been this affected by a woman in a long time, and she wasn't about to start now. She shook her head, scowling at the pair, then retreated inside. She didn't look up, as she sat at her desk and buried herself in work. *Perhaps it's time I get rid of that swing. And maybe get a lock for the gate.* The last thing she needed was that boy thinking he had the right to come over whenever he wanted.

Ellis worked steadily for the next thirty minutes. No more thumps came through the walls, so she assumed the moving lorry had left. She picked up her cold coffee, intent on finishing it off, when something banged into one of the conservatory windows. The noise caused her to jump more than before, spilling coffee over her paperwork and trousers.

"God, damn it!"

She shot out of the chair and slammed through the door. Lying close to the conservatory was a football. She looked up. The boy stood on the other side of the fence, his eyes wide. Ellis had been in enough meetings to recognise fear. In four hours, they'd already disrupted her day more than the old neighbours had in five years. She licked her lips and took a breath. Going off on a child wouldn't be prudent, despite how pissed off she was.

She picked up the ball and slowly approached the fence. The boy's eyes grew impossibly wider. "What's your name?" she asked him calmly.

"Jus...Jus...Justin."

"Justin. Nice to meet you. I'm Ellis Davis." Justin took a step back and glanced at his house as if he wanted to run away from the terrifying lady next door. Ellis inwardly smiled. She hadn't had the delight of scaring her staff in years. She missed the thrill. *He's just a boy.* She shook the glee away. "Justin, right in there is my office, where I work all day. I don't like being distracted or made to jump."

"I'm sorry, miss."

"It's okay, but please be careful next time."

The patio doors opened, and the woman stepped through, her gaze going back and forth between them. "What's going on?"

"Nothing," Ellis said, as politely as she could. She might not want anything to do with her neighbours, but that didn't mean she wanted to start a war. "Justin's ball came into my garden." She lobbed the ball over to him, harder than she intended. He managed to catch it just before it hit his face.

"Justin, I keep telling you, be more careful."

"I'm sorry, Mum. It was an accident."

Ellis felt a touch of empathy for the boy. Her earlier assumption about the mother's lack of discipline was wrong. It was clear she didn't put up with nonsense. "It's okay. No harm caused."

The woman looked up, her gaze friendly and warm. "Thank you. I'm Melissa, and this is Justin."

Melissa reached over the fence. Ellis stared at her hand. She hadn't touched another person in well over a year. She had no family to speak of, and friends were few and far between. Working from home meant she rarely needed to go out. Everything she wanted could be delivered at the click of a button. Her fingers trembled slightly, as she grasped Melissa's outstretched hand. She cleared her throat. "Ellis."

"Well, it's nice to meet you, Ellis. I promise this little tearaway will be on his best behaviour."

With that, Melissa turned around and took Justin inside, whispering in his ear. Ellis cleared her throat again and retreated into her home, a feeling of disquiet in her chest.

†

Melissa Cole stretched onto her tiptoes and shoved the glass pitcher into the top cabinet. *I'm going to have to ask Dad to loan his steps.* Being only five foot two was a hindrance. Craig had always been around to reach things for her. Now, simple things like going to the supermarket were a pain if the item she wanted was out of reach. *Yes, it was easier with Craig around, but I'd rather struggle than have him back with me.*

Melissa and Craig had split up nearly two years ago, due to his cheating. She was dumbfounded when his numerous affairs came to light. She'd truly believed they were soulmates. That betrayal had blackened her heart to love, except her love for Justin. He was her world. For the last two years, they had been staying with Melissa's parents while the divorce was finalised. That allowed time for their house to be sold and for Melissa to save as much as she could. She glanced around her newly purchased home, a smile stretching her cheeks.

This was the fresh start she needed.

The house was a lot cheaper than she'd expected. There were only two bedrooms but plenty of space downstairs, and the garden was big enough for Justin to run around in. Melissa understood the previous owners were an older couple. The décor they left was outdated, but the building was sound. She already had Pinterest filled up with ideas for decorating the place.

"Hey, Mum?" Justin yelled down from upstairs. "I can't get the Xbox to work!"

Melissa rolled her eyes. Her son was only ten, so she didn't expect him to do an amazing job of unpacking, but he had been upstairs less than five minutes, and the Xbox was the first thing he unboxed. *Typical boy.* She climbed the stairs and walked across the short hallway to Justin's room, opposite her own. She peered through the doorway. Just as she suspected, all his boxes were still stacked up on his bed. Justin was leaning over the TV, fiddling with the wires, his Xbox sitting proudly in front on his desk.

"Is it all plugged in properly?"

Justin glanced over his shoulder and shook his head at her, looking at her as if she were dumb. "Of course. I'm not stupid."

Melissa bit her lip. It was hard not to see Craig in him when he acted this way. She reminded herself Justin was growing, and puberty wouldn't be far away. *I'm going to have to get used to his attitude.* "Let me look." He huffed but stepped back. Melissa jiggled the wires, much the same way he had, and checked the wall socket was switched on. It all looked okay. She pressed the power button, but nothing happened. "It might have gotten broken in the move."

"I bloody hope not."

"Justin! Watch your mouth."

Justin blushed and looked to the carpet. "Sorry."

"I should think so. I won't tolerate you speaking to me like that."

He glanced up. "I'm sorry," he repeated earnestly.

"It's okay." She turned her attention back to the console, at a loss as to what to do. She couldn't afford a new one, and his birthday was months away. And then it hit her.

She hadn't switched on the main power supply yet. "Hang on." She headed back downstairs and found the fuse box in the cupboard under the stairs. She flipped the switch, and the cupboard light flashed on. *See, you don't need anyone but you.* She had been apprehensive about going it alone with Justin. All her life, she had lived with someone. She'd moved from living with her folks, to a roommate at university, then to Craig. This would be the first time she would be totally dependent on herself.

"It works," Justin yelled out.

"That's great, honey, but don't you dare think about playing it. You've got your stuff to unpack."

"Ah, man."

"Sorry. If you get it all done, we can have pizza for dinner."

"Yes!"

The sound of tape being pulled from cardboard wafted down the stairs, followed by frantic footsteps. She rolled her eyes. *No doubt I'll be up there tomorrow sorting it all out.* She smiled and turned back to the lounge. Her own mountain of boxes awaited her. *It's going to be a long night.*

†

Melissa carried the last of the cardboard boxes down the path to the small shed at the bottom of the garden. An hour ago, the sun had set on a long and busy day. She was tired, but happily surprised she'd been able to get everything unpacked and put away. Some things were not in their final resting place, but for now, everything had its home. All she had left to do was dress her bed. As suspected, Justin had his boxes unpacked in record time. He spent the rest of the day

8

on his computer and eating pizza. He had offered to help Melissa with her unpacking, but she declined. She got it done quicker without having to watch over him the whole time.

She closed the shed door and turned to go back inside. The light from the neighbour's conservatory caught her attention. It was nearing ten at night, but Ellis still sat bent over her keyboard. By Melissa's recollection, Ellis had been there all day. Every time Melissa made a trip to the shed, there she was. *I wonder what she does for a living.*

Melissa made her way back inside and into the kitchen to clear away the pizza boxes. Her mind drifted to her new neighbour. Melissa had never received such a frosty reception from someone before in her life. She recalled Ellis's stiff posture during their interactions. Her lips were set in a tight line, and the creases at the edges of her eyes stood out as she narrowed her gaze at Justin. Melissa didn't miss the slight frown when she offered Ellis her hand to shake. *Anyone would think I was diseased, the way she looked at me. I hope she isn't always so standoffish. The last thing I want is a grumpy neighbour. I'll have to try again, at some point, to make a good impression. It probably didn't help Justin had been in her garden, then kicked his ball over the fence.* Despite Ellis's stiltedness, her aura held an air of authority. Her jet-black hair was pulled impossibly tight into a ponytail, and her skin was so pale, Melissa wouldn't be surprised if she were a ghost. She wore a black polo neck and black jeans, both items clinging to her narrow frame. It was obvious to Melissa that Ellis hardly ventured out into the sun, and probably forgot to eat sometimes. Ellis was an enigma that Melissa found she wanted to solve. *It would be nice to make a new friend. Maybe I can pop over before I go back to work and invite her over for coffee.*

After clearing up the remnants of dinner, Melissa locked the doors, turned off the lights and made her way upstairs. She checked in on Justin, who lay on his back, snoring with his mouth hanging open. The move had been hard for him. He loved spending time with his grandpa, and kicked up a stink when mention of moving came to light. Melissa wasn't worried about him though. She worked long shifts as a nurse at the local hospital. Her parents were her primary caregivers and would have Justin overnight when she worked late or did a night shift. He'd be getting plenty of time with them.

She crossed the hall to her room, switched on the lights, and set about making up the bed. She sat on the edge of the mattress and let out a long, deep breath. *I'm finally done.* Her parents were coming by in the morning, she wasn't looking forward to her mother making suggestions about where everything should go, but she'd do her best. Her mother was usually right anyway. *She'll probably have the lounge moved around twenty times before they leave.* Melissa rolled her eyes at the thought.

"I really think it would look better if you put that chair in the bay window."

Melissa turned her back on her mother and rolled her eyes. Her parents had been in the house less than half an hour. Melissa had already conceded the angle of the dining table, which cupboard the crockery went in, and changing the living room rug from width ways to length ways. Her mother's "help" was wearing thin on her nerves. Justin had gotten fed up with the whole thing and retreated to the garden with his ball. There were only so many concessions Melissa would make for her mother. Moving her old reading chair was a point she wasn't going to lose. She generally read late in the evenings and liked to cosy up in front of the fire in the winter. Not only that, she also wanted to be able to look out the front window without having a cumbersome chair in the way.

"Mum, please drop it. I like it where it is."

Patricia huffed but nodded. "Fine."

At sixty-two, Patricia still held a youthful appearance. Patricia would never admit to the fillers and Botox regularly injected into her face, but Melissa knew. Patricia held a deep fear of growing old, so Melissa would never bring it up. It was nothing to do with her anyway, what her mother decided to stick into her face. Melissa herself might be tempted when she was getting up in years.

"Patricia," Melissa's father said from his place on the couch. "Leave her be. This is her house. Let her have it how she wants it."

Melissa smiled her gratitude at him. "Thanks, Dad."

Patricia huffed again but didn't comment further. "Are you sure living here is the best thing for you and Justin? It's a big house for just the two of you. How are you going to afford the mortgage?"

Melissa slumped into her reading chair and ran her hand through her hair. Her mother knew perfectly well she could afford the place. The sale of the house she shared with Craig had earned them a decent profit. She also worked full-time hours and picked up as much overtime as she could. Yeah, things were tight, but she'd rather struggle in her own place than always be reliant on her parents. With the child support she got from Craig, she'd be fine. She also didn't plan on being alone for the rest of her life. Eventually, she hoped to get back to dating and falling in love. She hadn't allowed herself that pleasure when she lived at home. The last thing she wanted would be a date meeting her folks. They were nice enough, but Christopher would interrogate, and Patricia would have them married off in a week.

"We've been over this, Mum, many times. I know what I'm doing. I want a fresh start with Justin and to move on with my life. I appreciate everything you two do for me. I'd be lost if you weren't prepared to have Justin for me when I work. However, this is what I want, and money isn't a problem right now."

"But what if you lose your job?"

"Then I'll get another one."

"It isn't that simple. There are thousands of people applying for the same job these days. You'd be lucky to find one."

"I'm a nurse, finding employment won't be hard for me."

"But how do you——"

"Enough!" Christopher raised his voice loud enough for Patricia to jump. "Leave her alone, Patricia. If you keep going on at her, she won't invite us around again."

Patricia's head lowered slightly, as she gazed at the carpet. "I just worry, is all."

"I know, Mum. I promise you; Justin and I will be fine."

One corner of Patricia's mouth lifted into a half smile. "Yes, you will. You're a strong, capable woman. You continue to impress us more and more every day."

"Thank you."

✝

Ellis poured the hot water into her mug, then stirred the coffee in. It had taken her well into the night to finally get her client's report just right. She had another full day ahead of her, researching an insurance company that wanted her to do market reconnaissance. They wanted to see if their policies were in line with current prices. Coffee was the only way she'd get through it without falling asleep. She was on her third cup already. *Maybe I'll see if I can get hold of a drip feed and send it straight into my blood.* She took a sip. The burn on its way down reminded her she hadn't eaten yet. *That'll have to be later, I need to crack on.* She was losing weight, too much her therapist said, but she never saw the point of cooking for one. She was happy living off fruit and sandwiches. Lucy, her therapist, wasn't happy at all. She said her diet would be okay if Ellis ate regularly, but Ellis would go all day with nothing but coffee. She knew she needed to get into a proper routine when it came to food, but work always came first. Once started, she would become consumed by her projects.

She took her coffee into the conservatory, moved a pile of papers out of the way, and set the mug down. She was about to sit when she noticed the boy from next door peering over the fence into her garden. *He hadn't better have kicked that bloody ball over here again.* Her hackles rose with the impending telling off. *I am not spending my time fetching his ball for him.* She wondered why he didn't just get it himself. Then she remembered his frightened eyes from yesterday. He was probably scared shitless to even try coming onto her property.

Ellis shook her head and went outside. Justin glanced at her and went back to looking in the direction of the swing. Ellis looked around the stones but couldn't see his ball anywhere.

"Justin?"

He looked up and took a step back. "Hi."

"Did you lose your ball or something?"

He shook his head vigorously.

"Then what are you doing?" *I don't have time for this.* Yet, she stayed where she was.

"I, uh, want to play on your swing."

Ellis glanced at the swing and back to Justin. Her first inclination was to tell him no. If he wanted to play on the swings, he should get his mother to buy him his own or take him to the park. Her resolve softened, as she looked into his hopeful eyes. There was a hint of fear still, but mostly they were the puppy-dog look she instinctively knew got him out of trouble whenever needed. She sighed. "Sure, go ahead."

His eyes widened and a huge grin spread across his face. "Really?"

Ellis shrugged. "Yes. But remember, I'm working, so keep the noise to a minimum." He nodded quickly and ran through the gate. He jumped onto the swing and started pumping his legs to take him higher. Ellis retreated inside and sat at her desk. For the next forty minutes, she tried concentrating on her work, but her gaze kept finding Justin on the swing. She noticed her cheeks were aching and realised it was because she was smiling. She straightened her lips and lowered her head, focusing on the computer screen and not the young boy giggling in her garden.

"Justin, what have I told you about going over there? Get back here now."

Ellis looked up at hearing Melissa yell from her side of the fence. As quick as she could, she rushed from the conservatory to the fence line. "It's okay. I said he could go on it."

Melissa eyed her and then glanced at Justin. "Really?"

"Yes." Fearing she was being judged, Ellis took a defensive stance, hands on hips, and nodded. "Why does that sound so odd?"

"It's just that yesterday…" Melissa waved her hand and smiled. "Never mind." She focused on Justin. "Nanny and Grandpa are going for fish and chips. Do you want to go with them?"

"Can I get a pickled egg for the ride home?"

"Of course."

Justin beamed and raced back over to his side of the fence. He looked back over his shoulder. "Thanks for letting me play."

"Any time." Ellis inwardly cursed herself. *Any time? He'll be over all the time now… Is that really a bad thing?* She was loath to admit it, but she had enjoyed listening and watching him have fun. *If he doesn't distract me too much, it shouldn't be a problem.*

"Thank you for allowing him to use the swing. He's loved them since he was a baby."

Ellis shrugged her shoulder. "It's fine. It's good it's getting some use, finally."

"Oh? Your children don't play with it?"

Ellis felt heat rise to her cheeks, embarrassed of what she was about to admit. Not that there was anything wrong with being a lonely old spinster, but she hated being judged. She supposed that came from years in the foster care system. Being shuffled from one home to the next had led her to believe there was something wrong with her and that the families she stayed with found her lacking. It was her greatest fear and was why she liked to keep to herself.

"Actually, I don't have any. It's just me here. The swing came with the property. I just never got around to dumping it."

Melissa wrapped her hands over the top of the fence panel and leaned a little closer, her eyes troubled for a moment. "Nothing wrong with being single. I am as well now." Her gaze was intense, but her words came out softly.

Ellis glanced up the garden to Melissa's patio doors. "So, it's just you and Justin?"

"Yep. We were staying with my parents after my divorce, but I'm finally pleased to have my own space."

Ellis refrained from asking what led to the breakup of her marriage. She had no interest in getting to know Melissa. She didn't mind Justin popping over occasionally to use the swing, but she drew the line at getting friendly with his mother. *Melissa, with her long blonde hair and blue eyes. And those god-awful geometric print jumpers she wears.* Ellis had seen two different ones already; she had no doubt Melissa's wardrobe would be filled with them. *She does look cute in them though. Colourful and vibrant. They bring out her eyes. Much better than my plain black all the time.*

"Melissa? You coming?"

Ellis caught a glimpse of an older gentleman standing just inside the patio doors. It was hard to get a clear image, as the sun beamed into her eyes. She assumed that was Melissa's dad.

"Yeah, I'll be right there," Melissa called back. She turned her attention back to Ellis. "I need to go. Thanks again for letting Justin play."

16

"You're welcome."

Melissa's smile was huge. She gave a tiny wave, then jogged up the path. Ellis stayed by the fence, watching Melissa's hair bounce around her shoulders. When Melissa waved again and pulled the patio doors closed, a flicker of a smile came to Ellis's lips.

Ellis made her way inside and sat at her desk. She stared at her screen but didn't see the words or numbers; it was all a blur. She took a few breaths. It dawned on her that Melissa was the outgoing type and would, no doubt, try her best to make friends. *God, what am I in for?*

CHAPTER TWO

"Good afternoon, Ellis."

Ellis grimaced at the computer monitor displaying Lucy's young face. She couldn't be more than thirty, and sometimes Ellis felt weird getting help from someone so much younger than herself. At forty-one, she should have her life together and not be requiring lessons on how to be a normal human being.

She was being hard on herself.

Ellis was successful and competent. Just because she didn't have friends, or the ability to enjoy long country walks on her own, didn't mean she was a failure. But still, not being able to find her place in the world was frustrating.

"Morning." Ellis loathed their weekly Tuesday appointment, but knew it was important for her mental health. She was stuck indoors most of the time, only venturing out for essentials and the occasional meeting. Ellis liked it that way, but Lucy explained she only liked it because it was what she was used to. Lucy had been trying to get Ellis out and about more often, but Ellis had always managed to beg off, much to Lucy's frustration.

"How has your week been?"

Ellis leaned back in the chair and rubbed her forehead. "Same old, same old. I picked up a new client. An insurance company wanted me to do some market research for them."

"That's interesting. I know you like to venture into new markets."

"Yes. It keeps me on my toes." Most actuaries Ellis knew only worked in one field. Being self-employed allowed Ellis to reach many different businesses. It kept her mind sharp and her work interesting.

"I know you don't like me asking, but how's your eating going?"

Ellis sighed and mentally rolled her eyes. Lucy always made her feel like she had an eating disorder when the truth was Ellis would simply forget to eat. "I wish you wouldn't keep asking me that."

"Ellis, you know as well as I do that you need good nutrition to keep your mind and body healthy. If you're not careful, you'll end up crashing."

Ellis refrained from mentioning that she'd almost passed out a few days ago after not eating for thirty-six hours.

"I can tell from your face that it hasn't been going well." Lucy shook her head, swaying her light-brown hair above her shoulders.

"I eat when I remember."

"That's not good enough. By next week's appointment, I want you to have set up a schedule where you eat at least twice a day. Set an alarm if you have to."

"Lucy—"

"It's non-negotiable."

"Fine. I'll try."

"Good." Lucy glanced down for a moment. Ellis assumed she was checking her notes. "Now, what else has been going on? Did you go for any walks?"

Ellis pressed her lips together.

"I see. Ellis, you need to start putting yourself first. I've been treating you for nearly two years, and I'm sorry to say, you're no farther along than when we started."

Lucy was right. Today was no different from any other day since Ellis went self-employed. Her isolation hadn't been so bad when she went to the office every day. At least there she could interact with people and get out from behind the same four walls. In the last five years, she had successfully managed to lock herself away from prying eyes and judgmental stares.

Ellis felt like crying.

"I don't mean to have a go at you, Ellis, I'm worried about you."

"I know. I did talk to the new neighbours a few days ago."

"Oh?"

"Yeah." Ellis grinned, as she recalled Justin's delight playing on the swing. "They moved in on Saturday. A woman and her son. The boy, Justin, likes my swing."

"You allowed him to play on it?"

"I know, crazy right?" Her smile grew wider. "The first time I met him, he had just kicked his ball over the fence. He looked so scared of me. I had to make a conscious effort to relax my posture and not frighten him any more than he already was. The next day, he was staring at the swing and asked if he could play on it. I shocked myself when I said yes."

"That's amazing."

"I, uh, actually enjoyed listening to him play. I thought it would annoy me, but it didn't."

"That's great. What's his mother like?"

Ellis cast her mind back to the brief conversation they had over the fence. *Cute, young, over friendly.* "She seems nice enough. Divorced. Wears these awfully bright-coloured jumpers. Very chatty."

"You're smiling."

Ellis's drew her brows down. "Sorry?"

"When you talked about her, you were smiling."

"Oh."

"There's nothing wrong with that, Ellis. You're allowed to like someone."

"I don't like her." Her words came out in a rush, and she knew Lucy would pick up on it.

"Ellis, calm down. I'm not implying anything here. You can be friends with someone without hidden meaning. Not everyone is out to get you."

Ellis closed her eyes briefly. Stacy's face coming to her mind's eye. Getting friendly with her assistant had been the single biggest mistake in her life. It was no secret at her firm that Ellis was a lesbian. What she hadn't expected was for Stacy to try and sue her for inappropriate behaviour in the workplace. The case had been baseless, and Ellis was vindicated. However, Ellis's bosses hadn't liked the publicity and let her go. That was the reason Ellis had started her own company and shied away from public view. She had been judged all over again, and despite her innocence in the matter, she had lost the respect of her colleagues.

"I know. I'm sorry."

"Don't apologise. I think you should try and be friendly toward her. Get to know her. You'll soon discover not everyone is a monster."

Ellis wasn't so sure about that. She hadn't been able to trust anyone in all her life, not completely. It had taken months for her to open fully to Lucy, and she still wasn't comfortable with it. *Do I want to get to know Melissa? What if it's a shit show? I'll have to move. Not that it'll be a problem. I've got plenty of money.*

"I can see your wheels spinning. Don't overthink. Just start small, saying hello when you see her, et cetera, and see where things lead."

It would be a huge step for Ellis. She didn't even say hello to the postman. Starting a friendship with Melissa was too daunting. *Maybe I can start with Justin. Kids are easier to get along with than adults.* If she could manage to hold a conversation with him and come out alive, talking to Melissa might be easier. "I'll think about it." Lucy smiled but the doubt was reflected in her gaze. Ellis couldn't blame her; she didn't think she would do it either.

"This can't be happening!"

Ellis looked up from her computer at hearing Melissa's voice coming from outside the front of the house. She could hear the frustration in her tone. Ellis pushed back from her desk and made her way through the conservatory and into the living room. She stopped at the front window and peered through the blinds. Melissa and Justin were stood by the side of Melissa's car. The bonnet was up, and Melissa was fumbling with her phone. *Car trouble.* Ellis turned away, intent on going back to work when Melissa's voice sailed over to her again.

"It's fine, Dad, we'll catch the bus."

Ellis chewed her lip. Her initial instinct was to ignore Melissa's problem, but Lucy's words came to mind. *It really would be neighbourly to see if I could help.* She took a breath and grabbed her jacket from the banister. She stepped outside, the chill morning air making her shiver. Spring was in full swing, but sometimes the mornings were still cold. She went down the path and stopped next to Justin, who was dressed in his school uniform. "Hey, Justin." He smiled but didn't greet her with words. Ellis turned her attention to Melissa. The bottom few inches of a nurse's tunic peeked out from under Melissa's coat.

"What's up?" Ellis asked.

Melissa turned around, clearly irritated, as she put her phone into her shoulder bag. "I think the battery is dead. Justin is late for school, and I need to get to work. Do you have any idea about bus timetables?"

Ellis shook her head. She hadn't been on a bus for over twenty years, not since she gained her driving license. She chewed her lip again and glanced at Justin. It wouldn't be fair to make them traipse all over town looking for the right bus stop when her car was sitting ten feet away. "I can give you a lift."

Melissa's eyes lit up for a second before she pursed her lips. "I can't ask you to do that. I know you're working."

23

"It's okay. I haven't started yet, and today's not very busy for me." She didn't know why she'd lied. Going out of her way to drop them off would take a good chuck of time out of her schedule. Gazing into Melissa's grateful eyes made the sacrifice worthwhile.

"Are you sure?"

"Positive. I'll just grab my keys."

Five minutes later, they were on their way to Justin's school in her two-year-old Audi. It was a sporty number, and Justin looked cramped in the back seat with his knees practically hitting his chin. Ellis gripped the wheel tighter, not used to being this close to anyone.

"Thanks for this," Melissa said. "You've saved my life."

"It's okay. What will you do about the car?"

"I guess I'll try and get a battery delivered at some point."

"I can do that for you." Ellis clamped her mouth shut. *What is it with you offering things suddenly?* She didn't have time to be chasing around for a neighbour she didn't even know. She chanced a glance at Melissa, who gazed at her through narrowed lids.

"You've done enough already. I don't expect you to do any more."

"I'm at home all day anyway. I can get the battery delivered later and have it fitted before you finish your shift." *Lucy would have a field day if she knew I was being* this *friendly.*

"I'm not sure."

"Mum," Justin whined from the back. "She said it was fine. If she does it, at least I'll get to school without catching crappy busses."

Ellis wasn't keen on the sarcastic tone of Justin's voice, but she didn't comment. Melissa seemed okay to let him talk to her like that, so it was none of Ellis's business.

"Fine, okay. Thank you, Ellis, that's really nice of you." Melissa fumbled with her keys and took off the car key. She placed it in the cup holder by the handbrake. "Thank you so much for this. I owe you one."

Ellis smiled, but it came off like a grimace.

A few minutes later, she pulled to a stop outside Justin's school. Melissa exited the car and pulled the seat forward so Justin could get out. "Grandpa will pick you up when you finish, and Dad will get you from theirs when he's done with work. I'll pick you up tomorrow after school."

"I know, Mum, you keep telling me."

"I'm sorry, I just want to make sure you know what's going on."

"What's going on is I'm late." Justin hiked his bag higher up his shoulder and ran toward the school gates. He didn't even say goodbye to Melissa.

Melissa climbed back into the car and let out a long breath. "It's just hormones," she muttered under her breath.

"Are you okay?" Ellis could see the strain in Melissa's features. Being a single parent who worked was taking its toll on her. Anyone with eyes could see that.

"Yeah." Melissa waved her hand. "The past couple of weeks in the new house has been an adjustment for us all. Living with my parents was easier. Justin is all over the place, staying in three different houses. It's tough on him."

"And that's why you don't mind that he talks to you like shit?" Melissa's eyes widened, and Ellis inwardly cursed. "I'm sorry, that was out of line." *Your social skills have seriously dived in the last few years.* She started the car, but Melissa's hand on her forearm prevented her from pulling away.

"It's okay. You're right. He does talk to me like dirt sometimes. He's a good kid, but in the last few years, he's gone through lots of emotional and physical changes. After everything he's been through, I don't mind allowing him the chance to vent his frustration."

"Even if it's directed at you?"

Melissa shrugged a shoulder. "He's my son. What else can I do?"

Ellis had no answer for that. She hadn't had a family of her own. She couldn't even keep her cat with her. One day he just up and left, presumably to find a happier living environment. Who was she to judge or advise Melissa on her parenting choices? *If he were my kid, no matter what he had been through, I would have torn him a new one.* It was a good job she wasn't a mother; she had no maternal instincts. To Ellis, everyone should show respect. She wouldn't tolerate that kind of behaviour from anyone, especially a child.

She pulled away from the curb and headed to the local hospital a few miles away. Silence filled the air. As she drove, Ellis tried to come up with something to talk about, but she was at a loss. Melissa seemed to be struggling just as much. Ellis glanced at her. Melissa's head was turned away, gazing out the passenger window. Ellis cleared her throat. "Um, how are you finding the new house?" In her peripheral vision, she saw Melissa turn toward her.

"It's great. I've been spending my days off moving things about to where I want them, and ordering paint supplies for redecorating. It feels like home already."

"That's great."

"I've met my neighbours on the other side of me. They seem nice."

I wouldn't know. I don't think I could even tell you what they look like. Lucy's right, I have become a hermit. Ellis hadn't minded before, but being in Melissa's presence was reminding her of the life she'd once had. She'd loved nothing more than heading to the wine bars with her friends and catching up over coffee in the local Starbucks. All of that had disappeared the moment the allegations came out. One by one, her friends stopped answering her calls. Eventually, Ellis stopped trying. Even after the accusations were dropped, Ellis refrained from contacting any of them. *If they couldn't support me when I needed them, were they truly friends? Nope.* She didn't need anyone. She was fine on her own. *Except now I'm locked away in my home with only my clients to talk to. I even avoid that if possible and email them instead. God, what have I become?* She didn't like this new version of herself, but she was unsure how to change. She looked over at Melissa. *Small steps. Start by opening up a little.*

"I haven't met them, your neighbours."

"Really? I thought you had been in your house for a while now?"

Ellis's knuckles turned white, as her hand tensed on the wheel. "I, uh, pretty much keep myself to myself. I'm not keen on socialising."

"That explains your death grip on the steering wheel."

Ellis made a conscious effort to relax her hand.

"You're uncomfortable, aren't you?"

Ellis nodded. "My therapist says I need to get out more, start making friends again, but I'm not sure I know how." She surprised herself with that admission. Her ears burned with her embarrassment.

"Well, helping me out today is a good start. I'll try not to overwhelm you with my gregarious nature, but I warn you, I have no boundaries when it comes to talking. I love a good natter."

Ellis found herself chuckling along with Melissa. "I'll keep that in mind."

At that moment, the hospital came into sight. Melissa directed her to where she needed to be dropped off. A minute later, Ellis rolled to a stop outside Accident and Emergency.

"Thank you so much for this," Melissa said, as she unbuckled her seatbelt.

"You're welcome."

"And you're sure you don't mind sorting the battery out for me?"

"Positive."

"Okay. Well, I finish at nine tonight. I can probably get a lift home from a colleague."

"I'll post your key through the letterbox when I'm done."

"Thank you again." Melissa reached over and quickly squeezed Ellis's hand. "You're a life saver."

Ellis nodded and clenched the hand that Melissa touched. *I can probably handle the talking, but I'm not sure I can cope with her touching me all the time.* She found it weird and uncomfortable. *Maybe in time, I'll get used to it.* She watched Melissa exit the car, then jog through the automatic doors of the A&E department. Ellis took a shuddering breath and pulled away. The car ride had been devastatingly painful, but she was pleased she had taken the first step in trying to connect with someone other than her clients. *That alone should keep Lucy off my back for a while.*

†

Melissa stowed her bag and jacket in the bottom of her locker and slung the lanyard with her name tag over her head. She was only a few minutes late for her shift and hoped her supervisor wouldn't notice. Not that Tara would mind. She was Melissa's closest friend and allowed her the occasional lateness. Tara understood how difficult things were for Melissa and never put too much pressure on her for slight tardiness. Despite their friendship, Melissa still hated being late. The last thing she wanted was the other staff members thinking she got away with everything.

She left the staff changing room and headed for the reception desk to check in with Tara and find out her assignments for the day. Being in A&E, every day was different, each with its challenges. She loved the thrill of an emergency, but her main love of the job came from helping people. She loved nothing more than holding the hand of a patient and offering them comfort, especially those at the end of their life. She hoped, when the time came, that she, too, would have someone holding her hand, telling her it would be all right. Her mind wandered to Ellis. *From what I could gather, she doesn't have anyone in her life. How sad.* She didn't know whether Ellis's self-isolation was by choice or not, but she knew Ellis was trying to reach out to her. It had been so nice of her to give them a lift and offer to swap out her battery. *I'll have to pick up some flowers or something on the way home as a thank you.*

29

"Mel, glad you could make it." A grin stretched Tara's lips.

"Sorry. Car trouble."

"It's fine." Tara reached behind her and passed a stack of folders over. "You're on triage duty this morning. Donna is about to knock off shift, so you need to get in there quick."

"Okay." Melissa cradled the folders under one arm and made her way to the triage room off to the left of the reception desk. The door was closed, as Donna was in with a patient. Melissa waited a few minutes. After the patient exited and made his way to the waiting area, Melissa went in. "I'm sorry, Donna."

Donna pushed out her bottom lip, one eyebrow raised. "I was starting to think you'd never get here."

Melissa mentally rolled her eyes. She was literally five minutes late. *And since when do we nurses ever finish on time anyway?* She could count on one hand the number of times she left work on time. There was always more paperwork to finish or another emergency to attend to. That didn't excuse her behaviour. She really shouldn't be late, but Donna didn't have to be such a bitch about it. *I hope Ellis manages to fix the car. I can't have another day like this tomorrow.*

For the next few hours, Melissa worked steadily through the mounting number of patients. There were only two major emergencies that needed her help. The rest of the patients were easy to handle.

"Hey, Mel."

Melissa glanced up from the intake form she was updating. A tall, dark-haired doctor leaned against the doorframe. His blue eyes sparkled as he gazed at her, his smile polite. Doctor Winters had a crush on Melissa. It was no secret. Everyone could see it. When he found out she was divorced, he spent even more time trying to get to know her, even inviting her out a few times. Melissa always declined. She wasn't in the right place in her life for dating. He was handsome and nice enough, but she just didn't feel anything for him beyond friendship.

"Hey, Mark. How's it going?"

"All the better for seeing you."

She smiled at his flirty reply, but inside she groaned. He said the same thing every time she asked him that question. "Is Oncology not keeping you busy enough, so you've decided to scout some of our patients?"

Mark swept his hair back, his grin widening. Melissa did not doubt that move garnered plenty of interest from loads of women, and probably men too.

"I just thought I'd pop down and say hello while I had a spare minute. How's the new house?"

"It's really good. I think it'll be our forever home."

"I'll have to come over sometime and take a look."

I don't think so. "Sure, that'll be great."

Tara poked her head into the doorway, her grin matching Mark's. She had been wanting Melissa to go out with him for months now and never failed to bring it up. She knew Melissa wasn't interested, but that didn't stop her from trying to be their matchmaker. "Hey, Mel, I've got a kid here with a knock to the head. Can you see him now?"

"Sure." Melissa was surprised Tara hadn't teased her about Mark's presence but realised treatment of patients always came first. Tara was an excellent nurse, and Melissa never faulted her. No doubt there would be teasing later, when things settled down.

"I'd better get going," Mark said. "It's great to see you."

Melissa nodded, then rolled her eyes at Tara after he walked away. "Not a word."

Tara held her hands up in a defensive manner. "Wasn't going to say anything." Her smirk did not support that statement.

"Yeah, right. Give me the chart."

Melissa carried on working for the rest of her shift. By nine that night, she was dead on her feet. She was looking forward to a hot bath and sliding into bed. She would need to ring Craig first, to make sure Justin was okay. After that, the night was hers.

†

"Thanks for the lift, Tim," Melissa said, as her colleague rolled to a stop in front of her car.

"No probs. If you have trouble in the morning, just give me a bell. I'll swing by and get you."

"Thanks." Melissa smiled at him and then opened the door. She climbed out, carefully. She reached back in to collect the orchid that was in the footwell. Melissa had been unsure what to get Ellis. She'd gone down to the gift shop on her lunch break to find something, but aside from a few ratty-looking bunches of flowers, there wasn't anything that would be right. Somehow, she didn't think Ellis would appreciate an "It's a girl" teddy bear. The soft purple orchid had caught her eye. With the right care and attention, it should continue to bloom for a long time to come.

Melissa waved at Tim as he drove off, then looked over at Ellis's house. All the lights were off in the windows.

Maybe she's in bed. She fished her keys out of her pocket and unlocked her door, noticing the old battery next to the stoop. Her car key lay on the mat just inside the threshold. She picked it up and went through to the kitchen. She placed her bag and the orchid on the breakfast bar and opened her patio doors. Melissa took a few steps outside and peered over the fence. Ellis's face was illuminated by her computer monitor. Her head was lowered, and her bottom lip was pulled between straight, white teeth. Even from this distance, Melissa could see she looked tired. *She's probably been sat there all day.* Melissa went back inside and grabbed the orchid. She went down the garden and to the gate. She didn't stop to think whether her presence in Ellis's garden would be welcomed. A security light flashed on, momentarily blinding her. Melissa blinked and shielded her eyes, as she approached the conservatory. Ellis was now standing, arms folded across her chest, and frowning. *She looks pissed. No time to turn back now.* Melissa reached the conservatory door and waited for Ellis to open it.

"Hi." Melissa hoped her smile would crack Ellis's stiff veneer. "I couldn't see any lights on out front, so thought I'd come around the back." Ellis remained stoic, her features unreadable. Melissa held out the plant. "This is for you, to say thank you for helping me out today."

Ellis quirked an eyebrow above her glasses but dutifully took the orchid. "You didn't need to do that."

Melissa shrugged. "Yes, I did. You didn't have to help me. Thank you."

Ellis placed the plant down by her feet, her posture loosening. "It's okay. The car runs fine now. You shouldn't have any problems with it."

"You look tired." Ellis's eyes narrowed, and Melissa realised how that sounded. "Oh my God, that was rude of me. I just meant—"

"It's fine. You're right. I've been staring at the computer all day."

"Have you eaten?" Ellis's pale skin looked almost translucent through the glare of the security light. Dark smudges ringed her eyes, and she swayed ever so slightly. Melissa had no idea how she was even standing upright. *She doesn't take care of herself, that's for sure.*

"I had a banana after dropping you off this morning."

"That was twelve hours ago." Melissa shook her head. "You can't survive like that."

Ellis folded her arms again. "You sound like Lucy."

Melissa raised her brows in question.

"My therapist. She keeps nagging me to eat. The truth is I forget."

"Well, that changes now. I'm doing myself something, it's no bother to make double."

"I can't ask you to do that. I'll grab some toast or something."

"Ellis, just humour me, okay? I'm making cheese toasties. Come on over in ten minutes. No arguments,"

Ellis's chest rose, as she took a deep breath. "Okay. Thank you."

"You're welcome."

Melissa made a hasty retreat before Ellis could change her mind. She pulled the cheese out of the fridge and the bread from the cupboard. She made sure to add extra cheese to Ellis's, knowing she needed the calories.

A few minutes later, Ellis tapped on the glass patio door. Melissa looked up from the hob and gestured for her to enter. Ellis took a step inside but didn't venture any further. She stood ramrod straight, hands in her jeans pockets. She cut an imposing figure, despite her slim physique, dressed all in black and close to scowling.

Melissa swallowed hard, then smiled. "Hey, take a seat." She waved the spatula toward the breakfast bar. Ellis slowly approached and sat on one of the stools. "Would you like any sauce?"

Ellis shook her head.

"Okay." Melissa flipped the toasties one last time and plated them up. She slid Ellis's plate across the bar top toward her. "Enjoy."

"Thank you."

Silence filled the kitchen as they ate. Melissa was busting to get to know her better, but from the way Ellis avoided looking at her, she knew her questions would go unanswered.

Before long, the toasties were devoured, and the silence stretched on. Eventually, Ellis said, "That was nice, thank you. I best be going." She stood, carried her plate to the sink, and walked to the patio door. "Thank you for the flower." With that, she was gone.

Melissa watched her fade into the night. Ellis's security light flashed on for a few seconds, then went out. Melissa sighed and took her plate to the sink. After their talk in the car this morning, she'd thought maybe they could become friends. *Not after those painful few minutes. She looked so uncomfortable. Maybe I'll give her a wide berth for a while. She obviously doesn't like people.*

Melissa locked the doors and switched off the lights. It was gone ten, and she still needed to call Craig about Justin.

35

The bath she wanted would now be a quick shower. Her interaction with Ellis had drained her.

CHAPTER THREE

Ellis stared at the orchid sitting on the back corner of her desk, the sunlight illuminating the bloom to a point of frustration for her. The gift had distracted her for the last four days. She had never been one for flowers or potted plants, finding them too difficult to look after. She was surprised the orchid hadn't shrivelled up and died yet. *I'm sure I read somewhere that you're supposed to talk to plants to keep them healthy. If they're that sensitive to moods, that thing should have been dead the day she gave it to me.* Ellis still couldn't get that night out of her mind. She had been surprised that Melissa took the time to get her a thank-you gift, but she was mortified at the offer to cook for her. Ellis was almost positive no one had done that for her. She couldn't recall one single time. *Maybe Joanne?* Joanne had been her girlfriend in university for a short time, before Ellis chased her off with her lack of intimacy. Ellis just didn't have it in her to lay all her trust in someone. They made love, quite a lot, but Ellis was always distant. *And I haven't changed in the last twenty years.* She couldn't see that changing in the next twenty.

She gazed at the orchid again.

I wasn't exactly cordial to her. She went to the effort to get me that, and she made food for me, and all I did was stare at her calendar hanging on the wall. Ellis knew she needed to start making an effort. As much as she liked her privacy, Melissa was being nothing but friendly toward her. She didn't deserve to be given the cold shoulder.

A slamming door sounded from next door, followed by raised voices. Ellis glanced up from her paperwork and saw Justin bound through the gate and sit on the swing. He didn't try to move it. He lowered his head and put his hands in his lap. Ellis could still hear Melissa shouting at someone and a male's voice shouting back. She couldn't make out the words. Ellis stood from her chair and went outside. Justin didn't look up as she approached.

"Hey, Justin."

"Hi."

Ellis looked over her shoulder and into Melissa's kitchen. She couldn't see anyone, but the shouting continued. "What's going on?"

"Mum's having a go at my dad, because I missed school today."

"Why did you miss school?"

Justin lifted his head, his eyes wet with unshed tears. "I couldn't wake him up."

Ellis crouched beside the swing, using one hand to hold the chain to steady herself. Taking a guess, she asked, "Had he been drinking?"

Justin nodded.

Ellis never judged anyone. She believed you had the right to do whatever you wanted, and it was nobody's business. However, seeing the pain in Justin's gaze, his lower lip trembling, sent a wave of anger rolling through her. She didn't care his father liked to drink, but when it came to Justin's welfare, that just wasn't on.

"The school told Mum I wasn't in. She's mad at me." He lowered his head, sending a few tears tumbling down his long lashes.

"She's not mad at you, Justin. I promise you."

Another door slammed then, and a car engine revved loudly before fading into the distance. A moment later, Melissa came out and made her way over to the fence. Her cheeks were slightly pink, and a tight line replaced her usually carefree smile. Her chest rose rapidly, as she breathed heavily. Ellis could see she was trying to calm herself down but wasn't being remarkably successful.

"Justin, go inside please, and do your reading," Melissa said.

Justin hopped off the swing and stormed inside, rubbing his hand across his eyes. Ellis stood and folded her arms, eyeing Melissa carefully. She wanted to offer her comfort but had no idea where to begin. She settled with a smile and hoped came off as friendly.

Melissa took a deep breath. "I'm sorry about that."

"It's okay."

"No, it's not. I know you're working. The last thing you need is a slanging match going on next door." Melissa turned around and walked away, her shoulders slumped.

Ellis glanced at her computer sitting on the desk and thought of the mountain of work she still had left to do. Her gaze found the orchid. *Work can wait a few minutes; Melissa needs a friend now.* With her mind made up, she stepped through the gate and caught up with Melissa just before she reached the patio doors. "I'm a good listener."

Melissa raised an eyebrow. "You don't want to listen to my crap."

Ellis surprised herself when she reached out and lightly touched Melissa's shoulder. "I do."

Melissa stared at her for a few moments before nodding and stepping aside for Ellis to enter. "I can make you a tea or coffee if you like, but I'm having wine." Melissa went to the fridge, pulled out a bottle of white, then grabbed a glass from a cabinet.

"Wine would be nice." Ellis wasn't much of a drinker, especially at lunchtime. She liked the occasional glass, but as she usually worked late into the night, there never seemed any point.

Melissa poured a generous amount into each glass and passed one over to Ellis. They sat in the same position as they had the other night. This time though, Ellis was slightly more relaxed. She took a small sip of the wine and set the glass down.

"Justin thinks you're mad at him," Ellis said carefully, not wanting to upset Melissa any more than she already was.

"I know." Melissa tousled her hair and rubbed her forehead. "His father and I always try to keep our arguments away from him. Even through the divorce, we never fought in front of Justin. This time, I just lost it." She took a huge gulp of wine. "Craig promised me he never drank around Justin. I thought that was the truth, but that's changed now." Wounded eyes gazed across at Ellis. "What if something happened to Justin because Craig was too wasted to see to him? I should be able to trust him with our son."

Ellis didn't point out that Melissa was herself drinking with Justin in the house. She surmised, though, that Craig had consumed a lot more than Melissa's half glass of wine. And, as far as she could tell, Melissa hadn't failed to get Justin to school. "Yes, you should be able to trust him. I can't imagine the worry you go through as a parent." *It's not something I think I could cope with.*

"It can be terrifying. You're forever on edge. On the one hand, you never want to let them out of your sight. On the other, you know they need room to learn and grow. It's not easy balancing your judgement."

Ellis ran a finger over the condensation forming on the outside of her glass, trying to think of the right response. Her brain just wasn't up to the task. *I'm so useless. Stick me in a boardroom and I'm a whizz, but a few interactions with Melissa and I'm tongue-tied.* She knew, deep inside, that the trouble Stacy caused for her had seriously damaged her ability to open up. She had ever been great at relationships, but back before the incident, she could at least make polite conversation without feeling so inept. She took another sip of her wine to buy her some time. "I'm sure you're a wonderful mother and doing the best you can." Ellis mentally rolled her eyes at the platitude. Melissa pursed her lips and drew her brows down. Ellis tried not to squirm under her scrutiny.

"Why don't you like people?" Melissa asked without a hint of rancour.

"What?" Ellis blinked, caught off guard by the sudden change in subject. *She has no qualms about being so direct.*

"I can see you're trying to be friendly, but it's so obvious that talking to me is like pulling teeth for you."

Ellis looked away, embarrassed Melissa had caught on so quickly. She'd thought she was doing an okay job, but apparently, she sucked. She drew in a breath. "It's not that I hate people. I just find talking to strangers difficult. I can't trust them. It's easier to just keep myself to myself."

"Has it always been that way?"

Ellis shrugged. "Not really. I used to be an extrovert and had a good group of friends. I would still be careful about what I said to them, but we hung out and it was fun. I never had trouble at work either. I loved being in meetings and commanding people's attention."

"What happened to change all that?"

Ellis stood from the stool, panic bubbling up in her chest. She had already said too much. There was no way she would be getting into the story of Stacy and her life in foster care. "It's not important. I have to get back to work." She didn't give Melissa a chance to stop her, just bolted from the kitchen and out the patio doors. Twice in one week, she'd run away from Melissa. *If she didn't think I was a freak before, she sure does now.*

She reached her desk, her gaze finding the orchid. She took it into the lounge and closed the blinds over it. She needed to get on with her job. She didn't want the reminder of her uselessness staring at her while she worked.

CHAPTER FOUR

Saturday morning found Ellis taking a well-deserved break. She had worked past midnight all week and decided she could do with a few hours away from her desk. Not that she had any idea what she was going to do. She had no hobbies and detested exercise. As she chewed her toast, her eyes kept finding the computer. Her palms itched with the need to switch it on and check her emails.

"This is ridiculous." She tossed the last few bites of toast into the bin and grabbed her jacket. The only way to avoid working would be to be out of the house. She picked up her keys and made a conscious effort to leave her phone behind. Ellis stepped out into the sunshine, the brightness making her squint for a few seconds until her eyes adjusted. With no destination in mind, she started walking.

Ninety minutes later, Ellis made it home. The walk had done her good, clearing her mind and resetting her energy.

The fresh air felt good on her face, and she found herself smiling. Her plan for the rest of the morning was to sit in the garden and relax. The urge to work was still inside her, but she was determined to ignore it.

Ellis changed into a pair of shorts and an old T-shirt, then made her way into the garden. She dug out her ancient deck chair and unfolded it, facing the sun. After flicking off the cobwebs, she sat down and pulled the handles up to tilt the back down and lift her legs. She let out a breath and allowed the warmth of the sun to coat her skin. Being deathly pale, she knew she wouldn't be able to stay out for too long, but nothing was going to stop her from getting a good dose of Vitamin D. She wasn't sure how long she lay there for, eyes shut.

"Good morning, Ellis."

Ellis opened one eye and glanced over the fence. Melissa stood on the other side, her hair pulled back into a loose ponytail. She, too, wore a T-shirt, however Melissa's had a smattering of paint on hers. She also had a smudge on her left cheek. "Hey. I assume you're decorating?"

Melissa nodded. "Yeah, except I've run into a problem."

Ellis grasped the handles again and righted the chair. She stood and approached Melissa. "What's up?"

"I don't suppose you have a ladder. My dad was supposed to bring me his, but he's stuck shopping with Mum. I can't reach the top of the walls, and I want to get the living room finished before my shift later."

Ellis shook her head. "I only have kitchen steps."

"Damn. Same as me. They're not quite tall enough. That's the problem with being a short arse."

Ellis's gaze scanned Melissa's body. She was very petite, but Ellis didn't see anything wrong with that. To her, Melissa looked cute. "I think you're perfect." Ellis's eyes went wide as she realised what she'd said. She noted the slight tinting of Melissa's cheeks. "What I meant was—"

"It's okay. I know what you meant."

Ellis looked away, embarrassed. Stacy's image flashed through her mind, and she instantly went on alert. *Saying things like that can get you in trouble. Never forget that.*

"Are you okay?" Melissa asked.

"Yeah, I'm fine."

"You just went all weird on me."

"Sorry. I forget not all women like to be complimented by a lesbian."

"You're gay?"

Ellis straightened her shoulders, prepared to take whatever Melissa said next. She had dealt with homophobes before; she knew how to handle them. "Yes."

"Great."

Ellis looked for any sign that Melissa wasn't being sincere, but there was nothing but her usual carefree smile and kind eyes.

Melissa glanced up at her house. "I don't know what I'm going to do about finishing the painting."

"I can do it for you if you want."

"Really?"

Ellis nodded. "I'm taking a few hours off, so it wouldn't be any trouble."

"I don't want to interrupt your Saturday. You looked very relaxed before I disturbed you."

It was Ellis's turn to blush, not knowing how long Melissa had watched her. "I shouldn't stay outside too long anyway. It doesn't take me long to turn into a lobster."

"Well, if you're sure."

"Of course." Ellis made her way over to Melissa's property and followed her into the house. The living room was a carbon copy of Ellis's but flipped the opposite way. The furniture was pushed into the middle with a huge dust sheet covering it all. The walls were now a light, mushroom colour. Ellis looked up, seeing the dark green that had been the previous owner's colour scheme. Ellis agreed with Melissa's choice; it was a much better look. She picked up the paint scuttle and brush and went up the steps. "Justin isn't helping you, then?"

"No, he's at his dad's."

Ellis glanced down at Melissa, whose gaze was locked firmly on Ellis's thighs. She cleared her throat, and Melissa jerked her eyes up. *Was she checking me out? Don't be stupid, she was probably lost in thought.* "And you're okay with that?"

Melissa crossed her arms over her chest and shrugged a shoulder. "There's not much I can do. We share joint custody. I have warned him that if it happens again, I'll be contacting my solicitor to get the agreement revised. He knows I'm serious."

Ellis stepped down and moved the steps across a couple of feet. She dipped the brush into the paint and continued making her way along the ceiling. With something to concentrate on, she wasn't as anxious around Melissa and found it easier to talk to her. "I don't know how you manage to work full time, bring up a son, and run a household. You must be exhausted."

"It definitely has its challenges. Sometimes, I feel like I'm spread so thinly that one of these days I'll tear myself apart."

Ellis heard the sadness in Melissa's tone. At that moment, she wished she could do something to lighten Melissa's load. She stepped down again and faced her. "That sounds awful."

Melissa's eyes glistened over a half smile. "It's not all bad. I love my son and my job. Yes, it's a lot harder since the divorce and now being on my own. But I'd rather this than be stuck with a lying cheat who barely makes it as a passable human being, let alone a husband and father."

"He's that bad?"

"Damn, I shouldn't have said that. He's Justin's dad. It's not right for me to slag him off to a stranger."

Ellis reached out and lightly touched Melissa's arm. "He was more than that to you. If he's hurt you as much as I imagine he did, you have every right to be angry."

"I should be over it by now."

Ellis's mind, once again, went to Stacy. The pain from that betrayal was just as strong as it was back then. "I don't think you ever get over someone you trusted hurting you like that."

"Sounds like you're speaking from experience."

"Yeah." Ellis didn't elaborate. She moved the steps and resumed making her way around the wall.

"Can I get you a drink or anything?"

Ellis was glad for the change in subject, not wanting Melissa to question her further about her troubles. She looked down at her. "Coffee would be good, thank you."

47

Melissa nodded. "You're welcome." She took a few steps away but turned around. "It's none of my business, and tell me not to pry if you want, but have you eaten today?"

Ellis groaned and rolled her eyes, but her lips were smiling. "Are you sure you're not in cahoots with Lucy?" Without waiting for an answer, she continued, "I had some toast first thing."

Melissa narrowed her gaze and clicked her tongue as she studied Ellis. "I'm thinking you didn't have more than one piece. I'm going to whip us up something."

"You don't need to do that."

"Ellis, let me take care of you."

Ellis didn't get the chance to object, as Melissa marched into the kitchen. A warm feeling settled in Ellis's belly. It had been a long time since anyone had cared anything about her, and although she knew Melissa was just being neighbourly, it felt good.

†

Ellis dropped the brush into the paint scuttle and took a step back to look at her work. She was pleased it had turned out so well. There were a couple of patches where the bristles had touched the ceiling, but they could be easily covered with a drop of white paint.

Satisfied with a job well done, she found Melissa in the kitchen. Ellis's eyes grew wide. Melissa had her back to her, hips swaying back and forth, as she hummed a tune Ellis didn't know. She made a conscious effort to avert her gaze from the sensual display. Her eyes went wider still, when she saw the mountain of food on the breakfast bar. Melissa had plated up a choice of thinly cut meats, olives, crusty rolls, and cheeses. It was the most food Ellis had seen in ages. She felt full just looking at it. "When you said you'd whip something up, I thought you meant a sandwich or something."

Melissa whipped around, salad tongs gripped tightly in her hand. She glanced at the breakfast bar, heat rising to her cheeks. "I got a little carried away, didn't I?"

"Just a little." Ellis grinned and sat on her usual stool. "Are you trying to fatten me up?"

"Yes."

"Wow." Ellis reached for a roll and pulled the tray of meats closer. "I've never met someone as direct as you."

"Sorry." Melissa brought the bowl of salad and settled opposite Ellis. "I guess that's my nursing side coming through. I spend a lot of time trying to get patients to open up. Sometimes they find it hard to admit the truth about their health, or they outright lie. Being direct is the only way I find to catch them off guard and get the truth out of them. I'm sorry if I've offended you."

"Don't be." Ellis waved her off and began selecting bits and pieces to add to her plate. She wasn't sure how much she'd be able to get down, but she was determined to make a decent effort. Melissa had gone to a lot of trouble, and she didn't want to disappoint her. "It's nice to know someone being so honest. It saves me having to figure out whether you're being legit or not."

"Has that happened to you a lot?" Melissa started to make her own roll. "People being deceitful."

Ellis couldn't help but be fascinated by how much Melissa was adding to her roll. *How is she even going to get that in her mouth?* Melissa was very slender, but apparently, she had a big appetite. Ellis found Melissa endearing.

Without commenting on Melissa's roll, Ellis responded to the question. "A few times. I grew up in foster care." She took a breath and decided to be honest with Melissa. *If I have any hope of building friendships, I need to start trusting again.* "No family ever wanted to take me permanently, so I was bounced from one house to the next. Eventually, I got too old and was signed off to fend for myself. I've never felt comfortable laying my trust in people. Lucy is the only one who knows everything, and I pay her for her wisdom. And that's not even mentioning what happened at my last job— forget I said that." Ellis was all for making new friends, but her past with Stacy wasn't something she ever wanted to chat about. Admitting how she had let herself be fooled so easily was too traumatic.

"What happened?"

"It's not important. It just reaffirmed that people inherently can't be trusted. That's why it's so refreshing to have you tell me I look tired or too skinny. It doesn't feel like you have an ulterior motive." Ellis popped an olive into her mouth. The feta inside burst free as she bit down, leaving a delightful mix of flavours on her tongue. She popped another one in before she finished the first, deciding she'd grab a tub the next time she went shopping.

"If you ever want to talk about what happened back then, I'm here to listen, but I understand your need for privacy. I hate that you've grown up never finding the good in people."

Ellis gazed across at Melissa, thinking she might be someone who was nothing but good. Her eyes were kind and bright, her smile sincere. She thought of the orchid Melissa had gotten her and the spread before her. *Someone selfish would never do these things, would they?* "I'm sure there are good people out there, but it hasn't been my experience."

Melissa nodded. "And that's why you shut yourself away."

"You can't get hurt if no one knows you." Ellis shrugged and took a bite of her ham roll.

"But you also go through life alone."

"It's been that way all my life. I've never known any different. I'm not missing out. The one time I did open myself up, I got fucked over so hard that I'm still not over it." It hurt her heart just thinking about it.

"I hope you don't think I'd do that to you."

Ellis's pulse quickened as she stared into Melissa's eyes. The look Melissa gave her was so earnest, so desperate for Ellis to believe her. Tension rose in her body. It was too much, too soon. She did the only thing she could think of, she made a joke. "I don't think you'd have the time. You're too busy working and bringing up Justin."

"I would never do that to you, Ellis," Melissa said softly but with heat, ignoring Ellis's joke.

Ellis licked her lips. "I'm beginning to believe you."

Melissa cleared her throat and took a huge bite of her roll. After a few moments of chewing, she said, "Now we're friends, I feel comfortable in telling you that you need to open your blinds and water that orchid."

Ellis squinted. "How do you know I haven't watered it?"

"I have eyes, Ellis. Aside from the fact it's drooping badly, I'm in and out at all times of the day and night. No matter when I come home, your blinds are always shut."

"It's not that I keep them closed on purpose." Ellis frowned. *Do I?* "I just get caught up with work that I forget to open them."

"And the plant that's hidden behind them?"

Ellis was busted. She hadn't thought Melissa would be able to see it stuffed in the corner of the windowsill. There was no point lying to her. Melissa seemed to have a way of getting the truth from her. "Honestly?"

"Please."

"It made me uncomfortable, and it kept distracting me."

"How so?" Melissa's forehead creased as she pulled her brows together.

"I didn't know what you wanted from me."

Melissa shook her head and put her roll down, giving Ellis her full attention. "I was being nice because you sorted my car out and gave us a lift. There was no motive behind it."

"I know that now, but at the time…," Ellis shrugged, feeling stupid. "I was confused."

"People can be nice, Ellis."

"As I said, that hasn't been my experience."

"Well, that changes now." Melissa smiled widely, her gaze dancing. "I finish my shift first thing in the morning. Justin will be home at lunchtime. Come over for dinner, and we'll play some board games or something."

"I'm not sure." Although that sounded fun, Ellis wasn't sure she'd be able to go through with a second day of being social. Talking to Melissa was getting easier, but it still drained her. *Then again, Justin will be there. That might help distract me from divulging too much personal stuff.*

"What would Lucy say?"

"She'd tell me to get out of my own way and accept your invitation."

"Then do it. Besides, I need to thank you for helping with the painting. You did a much better job than I did. I've still got the bedrooms and bathroom to do." Melissa tapped her chin and pursed her lips. "Hmm, I'm thinking of getting you to help with that, too."

One corner of Ellis's mouth lifted in a half smile. "Free labour, huh?"

"No, just a friend helping out another friend."

Ellis shook her head. "Nope, not buying it. I'm sticking to the free labour reason." At that moment, Ellis heard her landline ringing through the open patio doors. "Damn, that's my phone. I must get going. I was only supposed to take a few hours off." She stood and looked down at her half-eaten food. Her tummy growled, surprising her. She couldn't remember the last time she had felt that. Melissa must have heard it too, as she stood and began adding a few more bits to Ellis's plate and passing it over to her. Ellis smiled her thanks.

"I'm sorry I kept you so long."

"It's okay, I had a nice time. I haven't thought about work once since I got here." She thought she'd be disconcerted by that, but she found it was pleasant not to have her mind filled with numbers and graphs all the time.

"Good." Melissa walked her to the patio door. "So, yes for tomorrow?"

"I'll let you know."

"Okay, I won't push you. We'll be getting pizza, it's our Sunday tradition."

Ellis raised the plate in a silent thank you and stepped through the door. "I'll see you later."

"Bye and thank you again for your help."

Ellis made her way through the fence line and into her house. She set the plate of food on her desk and pressed play on the answerphone. As the message played out, she went into the lounge and opened the blinds. She grabbed the orchid and took it to the kitchen for watering. Melissa was right, it looked awful. She wasn't sure how much water an orchid needed, so she settled for a little bit, not wanting to drown it. If it didn't perk up by evening, she would add some more. She set the plant on the corner of her desk. As she worked and made her way through the food, glancing at the orchid brought a smile to her lips. She was making a friend and it felt good.

CHAPTER FIVE

"Justin! That's not fair, I wasn't ready."

"There are no rules when it comes to water fights," Justin called out from his position by the barbeque.

Melissa ducked behind the patio door, as Justin tossed another water balloon in her direction. Luckily, she was quick enough to avoid the hit and watched it splatter against the glass.

The day was unusually hot for the middle of spring, and Melissa was struggling to cool down. Having a water fight with Justin seemed like the perfect idea. That was until he cheated and started the fight before she was ready.

Justin darted to the end of the garden, giving Melissa a chance to throw a balloon at him. She hit him in the back and laughed as her direct hit made him screech. She scooped up two more balloons and dashed to the patio table. She crouched behind one of the plastic chairs, keeping her eye on him. Justin had no cover but didn't seem to mind. He stalked toward her, zigzagging across the grass. Melissa fired a balloon that missed him by inches. Before she had a chance to switch her remaining balloon into her dominant hand, Justin was upon her. He slammed the balloon onto her head. She shrieked, as the cold water penetrated her thick hair and ran down her T-shirt. Before she could get him back, another of his balloons hit her square in the chest.

"Just you wait, mister." Melissa aimed and put all her strength into the throw. Justin ducked at the last second. The balloon sailed over the fence and splashed onto Ellis's window. Ellis jerked her head up. Even from twenty feet away, Melissa could see her creased forehead. "We're in trouble now," she whispered to Justin. She knew Ellis hated to be interrupted when she was working, which was all the time.

"Good luck," Justin said. He grinned and sprinted inside the house, momentarily slipping on the water that was just inside the threshold from his earlier throw.

"Chicken!" Melissa took a breath and focused back on Ellis, who was now standing outside by the fence, arms folded across her chest. "Good afternoon, Ellis." She smiled as big as she could, hoping to diffuse Ellis's anger. "Lovely day, isn't it?"

"You both look like you were having fun."

"It's too hot to stay inside."

"So, a water fight seemed like a good idea?"

Melissa nodded, sensing Ellis wasn't as mad as she pretended to be. There was a slight gleam in her eye, the corners of her mouth twitching ever so faintly. "Yes. It's the best way to cool down." She glanced over at the remaining balloons, sitting in a bucket by the house. "In fact..." She stepped over to the bucket and lifted out a red balloon. "You look a little hot yourself." She bounced the balloon in her hand.

"Don't you dare." Ellis backed up a step.

"Why not?" Melissa took a step closer.

"I'm warning you, Melissa."

"Come on, it's only a bit of water."

"I don't care. Don't you do it."

Melissa darted to the gate and rushed through. Ellis's eyes went wide and looked like the proverbial deer in the headlights. She didn't try to bolt as Melissa slowed her step but continued to approach. *She thinks I'm actually going to throw it at her.* Melissa was all for having fun, but she would never do anything to anyone unless they wanted it. She stopped a few feet away. Ellis's gaze was fixed on the balloon, her breath coming in and out in a rush. Melissa grinned. "Ready to get wet?"

Ellis squeezed her eyes shut and held her hands out in front of her, palms facing Melissa. "Please don't."

Melissa tossed the balloon up above herself and allowed it to crash onto her own head. She let out a small yelp as the water made contact with her skin.

Ellis opened her eyes and then lowered her hands. "You didn't throw it at me."

"Of course I didn't. It would hardly be fair."

"Thank you."

Melissa was about to reply, when she noticed Ellis's gaze drop to her chest. She followed the movement with her own eyes, shocked to see her nipples poking through the thin, wet fabric. Heat rose from her neck to her face. She looked back up at Ellis, whose gaze hadn't moved from her shirt. Melissa thought maybe she should cross her arms or something, but she didn't. It felt nice to have someone other than Mark take notice of her. The fact Ellis was a woman didn't matter. Every human on the planet liked to be complimented. Having Ellis stare at her was flattering. Ellis herself was incredibly attractive, tall and lean. The dark clothing she always wore lent an air of danger about her. *And her thighs are strong.* Melissa had noticed them when Ellis was up the steps, painting. Melissa had been taken aback by the thick muscle running from hip to knee. Considering Ellis sat at her desk all day, every day, she was in good condition.

"Are you still coming over for dinner later?" Melissa grinned at Ellis's flushed face. It wasn't fair to get her so flustered, but it wasn't Melissa's fault Ellis was ogling her.

"Huh?" Ellis blinked and looked up. She shook her head, almost like waking from a dream.

"Dinner? Tonight. We eat around six thirty. Justin has picked Trivial Pursuit as his game of choice."

"I, um, still have a lot of work to do."

Melissa looked at Ellis closely. A slight tremor ran through Ellis's body, and she wouldn't look Melissa directly in the eye. Melissa surmised her nipples standing to attention had embarrassed Ellis. *And all I did was stick my chest out farther, like a prize turkey. She must think I'm a right hussy.* She crossed her arms, feeling ridiculous. After nearly two months of living next door, she'd been making progress with their friendship. Now, she'd stuffed it up by preening in front of her.

"Ellis, I'm sorry—"

"I'll try, though."

"What?"

"I'll try to make it to dinner. I have a report to finish and a few calls to make. If you can refrain from distracting me for an hour or two, I'm sure I'll be done in time."

"That'll be awesome. Just come on in when you're done."

Ellis's gaze dropped quickly to Melissa's chest again, then away. "Can I assume the water fight will be over before I get there?"

Ellis was making it sound as if she referred to the threat of being doused in water, but Melissa knew what she really meant was would Melissa be wearing something decent and not a nearly see-through, wet T-shirt. "Yes, we're done for the day. I have a bit of housework to get on with now."

"Great. I'll maybe see you in a couple of hours, then."

"Yes. See you later."

Melissa retreated to her house and went up to the bathroom to dry off properly. Justin was on his bed, Xbox controller in hand. "Thanks for leaving me out there to face the firing squad."

Justin grinned over his shoulder at her. "Sorry, Mum, but I'm too young to die."

"Well, she said she'll be able to make it for Trivial Pursuit and pizza. She can kill you then." She laughed at his worried features and made her way into the bathroom. Ellis kept surprising her. Just when it seemed she was pulling away, Ellis would do a one-eighty on her. Not that Melissa minded. Melissa was finding herself intrigued by the shy, workaholic. She also noticed the orchid had been moved and was looking almost like new. It touched Melissa that Ellis had taken the time to nourish it and put it on her desk where she could see it all day. *We're going to be great friends.*

†

Melissa made her way into Justin's room. "Are you ready for bed?"

Justin nodded and let out a huge yawn. The day had been a long one for him. The one game of Trivial Pursuit had turned into three, and it was nearly two hours past his usual bedtime. Melissa knew it was going to be a nightmare to get him up for school in the morning, but it was worth it to see him having so much fun beating Ellis at every game. Ellis clearly didn't like being beaten by a ten-year-old, even though she tried to hide it. He was a smart kid, and it wouldn't have surprised Melissa if he memorised all the answers on the cards.

Melissa tucked him in, not that he needed it at his age, and kissed his forehead. "Goodnight, son."

"Goodnight, Mum. I had fun tonight."

"Me too. Hopefully, we can do it again soon."

"Ellis is pretty cool."

Melissa nodded. "Yeah, she is." *And cute when she sulks.* She grinned, remembering the look on Ellis's face when Justin won the third game in a row. *She's such a sore loser.* She kissed Justin again and made her way out of the room. She softly closed the door and headed back downstairs. Ellis was in the same position she had left her, sitting on the floor with her back against the couch. Melissa grabbed her wine and settled next to her, close, but not touching.

"Have you finished pouting yet?" Melissa asked.

"I'm not pouting. I just don't think it's fair to play a game when I have no chance of winning. He's clearly memorised the cards."

Melissa laughed at Ellis making the same assumption, covering her mouth quickly when Ellis glared at her. "You can't be serious. He's a kid."

"Not the point. Games should be fair for all players."

"I can't tell if you're winding me up or not." She hoped she was. Getting pissy that a child beat you wasn't a very good character trait. In Melissa's eyes, winning gave Justin confidence, and that was something she always wanted to instil. She would never want him to feel he wasn't good enough.

Ellis glanced at Melissa out of the corner of her eye. "I'm starting to feel you'll never give me sympathy."

"Huh?

"First, you threaten me with a water balloon. Now, when I'm hurting that a kid beat me, you're not even remotely feeling sorry for me."

"Ah, I get it, you're a big baby."

Ellis narrowed her eyes and took a deep breath. "I'm not a baby. I would just like a little sympathy"

Melissa grinned and reached out her hand. She patted Ellis's shoulder. "There, there. Never mind. There's always next time." She withdrew her arm. "Is that better?"

Ellis smiled and nodded. "Thank you. That's all I wanted."

"You're a goofball." Getting to know Ellis was a study in contradictions. Sometimes she was so serious, Melissa thought she would never break through. Other times, she was playful and mischievous. She was night and day all wrapped up in an imposing package. She was still stoic most of the time, however, the tough veneer was slowly chipping off.

Melissa sipped her wine, then stifled a yawn.

"You're tired." Ellis glanced at her watch.

Melissa checked the time on her phone. It wasn't even nine yet, and she was lagging. The prudent thing to do would be to send Ellis home and get an early night. She didn't want to do that though. She was having a nice time, and with Justin in bed, she wanted to spend some time getting to know Ellis better. "Night shifts. They always take it out of me. Luckily, I'm off until Tuesday." She picked up the nearly empty wine bottle. "Can I top you up?"

"Sure. Thanks."

Melissa refilled their glasses and placed the bottle on the table. She shifted onto her hip, tucking her legs behind her and resting her elbow on the couch cushion. "So, Ellis, tell me about yourself."

"There's not much to tell." Ellis sipped her wine, then placed the glass on the coffee table next to the empty bottle.

"I highly doubt that." Melissa thought for a moment. "How old are you?"

"Forty-one."

You look younger. No lines marred Ellis's pale face, except a small one between her eyebrows. She looked to be no more than thirty. "How long have you lived around here?"

"About five years now."

"Do you like it?"

Ellis shrugged "It's a home."

"Do you have any hobbies?"

"No, not really. Reading if I can, but I'm usually too busy working."

"All work and no play…"

Ellis smiled sardonically. "It isn't the work that makes me dull."

"Have you got any friends?"

"Not really, not anymore."

Melissa frowned. "You must do something for fun."

"Playing Trivial Pursuit with you guys was good."

"That can't be your only enjoyment." *There must be something you enjoy after forty years on the planet.* Melissa had lots of hobbies. Crafting, hiking, swimming. Even knitting. Despite being busy with work and raising Justin, she always found a little time each day, just for herself, to do something that relaxed her. Even if that was a long bubble bath. She couldn't believe Ellis had nothing. "What about growing up?"

"Not to my knowledge. I never had the chance to settle in anywhere. If I started to, it wasn't long before I was moved on again. I never had the chance to join any clubs or anything."

"Were you a troublemaker or something?"

"No. I just wasn't wanted." Ellis didn't sound sad about that fact, but her eyes gave her away. They dimmed ever so slightly.

"What about your birth family?"

"I was told my mum was fourteen when she got pregnant. She and her parents gave me up. I never looked into finding her. I wasn't wanted, so why bother?"

"There had to be more to it than that."

"I've no idea, and I'm too old to even care now."

Ellis stood, retrieved her wine, and sat on the couch. Melissa thought she wasn't being wholly honest about the hurt being given away had caused. She got up and joined Ellis on the sofa. "You must be very lonely."

"I wasn't always a hermit. I had friends, right up until a few years ago, but things changed. Now, I'm happy on my own."

The regretful tone of Ellis's voice stirred Melissa's heart. It was obvious Ellis had been through something very painful. Whatever it was still haunted her to this day and caused her to shy away from the world. "Will you ever tell me what happened back then?"

"Maybe. Not right now. It's too painful and humiliating."

"It can't be any worse than finding out your husband had been having affairs the whole time you were married."

"Tell me about it?"

Melissa leaned her head back onto the cushion and gazed up at the ceiling. All the hurt from the past few years bubbled up in her chest and she feared she'd throw up. She swallowed hard and turned her head to look at Ellis, finding nothing but caring reflected in her gaze. She knew she would be safe telling Ellis about the worst time in her life. Even her parents didn't know all of it.

"I met Craig when I was in nursing school. He worked at the local chippy. He was shy and sweet. He used to give me extra chips." She smiled at the memory. She thought he was a nerd at first, but he soon won her over. "We got to know each other and fell in love. We married a couple of years later and had Justin. Craig started his own bike garage, and I thought everything was going well. Money began to run tight. He would stay later, work weekends, and try to find more business. But the finances never changed. They just got worse. He wouldn't talk to me about any of it.

"I started to get suspicious, when friends would tell me they saw him places he shouldn't have been. I let it slide for a while; I wasn't his keeper. If he wanted a drink after work, that was fine." She looked back up to the ceiling. "I did the laundry one day and checked his pockets like I always did. I found a napkin with a woman's name on it, saying thank you for an amazing night. I confronted him and he admitted he'd slept with her. I was prepared to forgive him, but his friend came to see me one day and told me it hadn't been a one-off. Craig had been having affairs for years. He wasn't working late; he was out fucking other women." How many, she didn't know. But Danny hadn't been shy in telling her it had been going on from pretty much the start of their relationship. Melissa couldn't believe she had never noticed. She put it down to being happy and in love. She was working hard and had Justin. She just didn't see the infidelity. *How dumb was I?* She felt Ellis's hand touch her leg.

"I'm so sorry, Melissa."

Melissa looked at her again, tears threatening to fall. "It's a kick in the gut, when you're not attractive enough to keep your husband satisfied at home."

A flash of anger zipped across Ellis's face. "That's not true. You're a very pretty woman, Melissa. Any guy would be lucky to have you. You're fun and vibrant, like the sunshine on a winter's day."

A tear slipped free from Melissa's eye, but she didn't wipe it away. She thought she was done crying over him, but apparently not. "Really?"

"Yes. Sometimes, when I'm working and stressed out, I look up and see you playing in the garden with Justin. Your smile is so infectious, I find myself smiling along with you. You didn't do anything wrong, Melissa. He just isn't the right guy for you."

"Thank you." Melissa stared at Ellis, the pain in her heart lessening a little more. "I can't understand why no family ever wanted you. You're an extremely sweet woman, behind this angry crease." She reached up and smoothed her thumb over the bridge of Ellis's nose, just above her glasses.

"I'm thinking about getting Botox."

"Don't. I like it. It adds character. It lets me know what you're thinking."

Ellis leaned in a little closer, her gaze intense. "What am I thinking now?"

Melissa's pulse pounded through her body. Ellis's eyes penetrated through her. Her body heated. *That you want to kiss me.* Melissa hadn't seen that look often, even from Craig, but she wasn't dumb. She knew lust when she saw it. *Is Ellis interested in me? She can't be. She knows I'm straight. But her lips do look soft. What am I thinking?* Stunned by the direction her thoughts had gone, Melissa pulled back an inch and smiled. "About the stack of paperwork on your desk."

Ellis blinked a few times and moved away. She cleared her throat, her skin turning pink. "That's an easy guess." She gulped the remainder of her wine. "I'm always thinking about work."

"You shouldn't. It isn't good for the soul."

"And what is good for the soul?"

"Laughter, and friends," she added, wanting to make it clear that's what they were. *It was just a tiny lapse on your part, Melissa, due to the intense conversation. You don't like Ellis that way. You're straight.*

"I've been lacking both of those recently."

"Well, it's a good job I moved in then, isn't it?"

"Yeah."

Melissa stood and carried the glasses to the kitchen, needing to keep a safe distance between them. It was time to say goodnight and put those three seconds behind them. "Thank you again for helping with the painting. It looks good."

"You're welcome."

Melissa jumped, having not heard Ellis move behind her.

"Did your dad get around to bringing you a ladder?"

"No, not yet." She swilled out the glasses and placed them on the draining board. "I'll probably go get it tomorrow, so I can get my bedroom sorted before my shift on Tuesday."

"How about I just help you again?"

"Really?" Melissa turned around and raised her eyebrows.

"Sure. It felt good to do something other than hunch over a desk all day."

"But what about your work?"

"I'm self-employed. My hours are my own." Ellis shrugged a shoulder. "I'll probably do some when I get home now and work again tomorrow evening."

"I don't want to put you out. You'll be exhausted." Melissa was scrambling to find a way to stop Ellis from coming back over. She needed time to think about what had almost happened. She didn't want to ruin the friendship between them, but she needed time to get her head on straight. *No pun intended.*

"Melissa, I'm sure you've noticed, all I do is work. Sometimes, I even work through the night, when I can't sleep. Giving you a hand for a few hours won't be a problem."

There was no way out. "Are you sure?"

"Yes."

"You're an enigma."

"How so?"

"You give off this vibe of stay away, that you're dangerous. In reality, you're just a big softie."

Ellis turned her features to stone, her eyes blank.

"See now, that won't work with me. You've shown your true colours. You can't scare me off anymore."

Ellis smiled softly. "I'm not sure I even want to."

Melissa felt the blood rush to her ears. *This can't be happening. Why am I all hot just from her gaze? Must be the wine.*

"I'd better get going if I'm going to get any work done tonight."

Melissa gave her one more chance to change her mind. "Are you sure about helping?"

"Positive. What time do you want me?"

"Around ten? After I get Justin to school."

"I'll see you then. Good night, Melissa."

"Good night, Ellis. Thank you for coming over."

"Thank you for inviting me. I had a nice time." Ellis gazed at her for another moment before shaking her body loose. "Right, bye."

"See you later." Melissa leaned back against the sink, hand on her chest. *Those were the most sexual few moments I've had in a very long time, and they came from Ellis. A woman. This isn't right. I don't like her that way. I can't.*

Feet heavy, Melissa locked all the doors and turned off the lights. She was glad she wasn't working in the morning; she wouldn't be getting any sleep tonight. *Fuck, I'll be seeing Ellis again in twelve hours. I'm not sure I can cope with that so soon.*

CHAPTER SIX

"Melissa? I thought you were off today."

Melissa glanced up from the notes she was writing about a patient and smiled at Tara. "I was, but I traded my shift. I have an appointment tomorrow that I can't get out of." She was surprised at how easy the lie came. Tara was her best friend. They had no secrets between them, but how could she tell her she had swapped shifts to avoid seeing her new neighbour? Sleep last night had been elusive. When it was time to get Justin up for school, her head was just as confused as it had been the night before. She still couldn't reconcile those few seconds of wanting Ellis to kiss her. Never in her life had she even been curious about what it would be like to kiss a woman. It just never entered her head. She thought maybe that was because she was married and busy getting on with her life. All that had changed, now that

Ellis had said those sweet things to her and looked at her with those dark eyes. *What am I going to do?*

"Hello? Earth to Mel."

Melissa blinked. "Sorry?"

Tara squinted at her and leaned a little closer. "Are you okay?"

"Yeah, I'm fine. Just got a few things on my mind."

"Anything you want to talk about?"

Melissa waved her off. "No, just decorating ideas." *And the lies keep coming.* "The house should be ready soon. I'm going to throw a housewarming. It'll just be my folks, you, Jane, and a couple of others. Nothing big."

"Are you going to invite Mark?"

"Why would I?"

Tara rolled a chair over and sat. "Come on. He's dying to take you out. That'll give you a chance to get to know him better, outside of work."

But I don't fancy him. Not one bit. On the other hand, it might be a good distraction from thinking about Ellis all the time. "I'm not sure. It's my home. I don't want all sorts knowing where I live."

"It's just Mark."

Melissa looked away for a moment. If she was honest with herself, she hadn't given Mark a fair chance. She had been so consumed with getting over the divorce and moving house that she hadn't given him a second look. Melissa thought it over. She'd have to admit his dimples were cute. And his eyes were kind. *Could I really invite him? What harm would it do? There'd be other people there, so it's not like it would be a date.* "Okay. I'll ask if he wants to come. But only as friends."

Tara's face lit up. "Excellent."

"As I said, it's not for a few weeks yet. I still have to finish decorating, and I have Justin's birthday party to plan." She closed the folder and added it to the pile. Her shift was over, and it was time to go home. "I'm back in on Thursday, for the night shift."

"I'm on then, too. We can have a proper catch up on our break."

"Great." Although they were best friends, it was hard to find time to talk to each other. Their shifts clashed often, and Tara also had her own family to be with. They texted frequently, but it was hard to get into any real discussions about their lives. *And what would I tell her anyway? I think I have a crush on my female neighbour. Tara would shit a brick and demand to know everything.* "I'll see you Thursday."

Melissa drove home, her hands tight on the wheel. Her parents had Justin overnight, so she would be on her own. She planned to make a quick bite to eat and go to bed early, hoping to avoid Ellis. That morning, she'd knocked on Ellis's door, told her she had to work, and made a hasty dash for her car, with Justin in tow. She didn't even give Ellis a chance to respond. She hoped Ellis was busy with work and wouldn't notice her arrival home.

She rolled the car to a stop and looked over at Ellis's front window. The lights were on inside, and she swore she saw Ellis twitch the blinds. Heart in her throat, she opened the car door, grabbed her bag, and hurried up the pathway. Her fingers fumbled with her keys for a moment, before managing to get the door open. Safely inside, she leaned back against the closed door, her breath coming in gasps. She waited to see if Ellis would knock on the door. Melissa knew she was being silly. Ellis probably didn't even realise Melissa was avoiding her.

After a minute of trying to calm herself, she shed her jacket and hung it and her bag up in the cupboard. She made her usual toastie and sat at the breakfast bar to eat. The beam from Ellis's security light flashed on. "Shit, she's coming over." Melissa peered through the night, waiting for Ellis to come into view. Despite expecting her appearance, catching sight of Ellis made Melissa jump. She briefly thought about installing her own security light. Ellis tapped on the glass with one hand. In the other, she held a small, white, paper bag. Melissa stood and unlocked the door. She stepped back, allowing Ellis to slide the door open.

"Hey, Ellis." Melissa crossed her arms over her chest and stared at a point over Ellis's shoulder.

"Hi. How was work?"

"Busy, as usual."

Ellis held up the bag. "I went shopping earlier and picked these up for you and Justin. I remember him saying last night they were his favourites."

Melissa reached out and took the bag, the smell of the Yum Yums tickling her nose. She put the bag on the breakfast bar and refolded her arms. "Thank you. I'm sure you'll be Justin's favourite person from now on."

Ellis smiled, but it didn't reach her eyes. She stuffed her hands in her pocket. "Are you okay?"

"I'm fine, why?"

Ellis shrugged. "You seem a little off."

"I'm okay, just thinking about work." *More lies. You're on fire today, Mel.* Melissa prided herself on always being honest. Life was too short to be anything but. She had lied to both Tara and Ellis, and she wondered if this would be her new normal.

"Okay. I'll leave you to your evening." Ellis stepped back and slid the door shut. She gazed at Melissa for a moment through the glass, her brows pinched tight and making the line between them deepen. She bit the corner of her lip, then turned and walked away.

Melissa blew out a deep breath and fell heavily onto the stool. She rested her head in her hands. Ellis wasn't stupid. She would know Melissa had a problem with her. *Not that she'd done anything wrong. She's entitled to be attracted to whomever she wants. I'm the one with the problem. Then again, how arrogant could I be? She never said she likes me that way. It was probably my imagination that she wanted to kiss me, because I wanted to kiss* her. *Argh, I'm so confused. I won't be able to figure any of this out tonight.* Her best option would be to avoid Ellis as much as possible until she unscrambled her thoughts.

CHAPTER SEVEN

"She's avoiding me," Ellis murmured to herself as she stared, unseeing, at the computer screen. It had been over a week since she'd dropped the doughnuts off. Nine days, and she hadn't seen her once. Ellis knew when Melissa was home. The car would be out front, or Justin would be in the garden playing, but never Melissa. Ellis didn't know what she had done wrong. She thought over the evening she had spent with them. She couldn't recall anything that would have upset her. *Apart from pretending to be disappointed Justin beat my ass at Trivial Pursuit, there was nothing.* Their conversation had gotten intense at one point. Melissa had been unhappy over her ex's cheating. *Could it be because I complimented her? Perhaps she didn't like to hear that coming from a lesbian.* Her mind went to Stacy, thinking the same thing had happened with her. *Maybe that's why*

Stacy made the complaint about me. She must have thought I was coming on to her. Did Melissa think the same? She remembered staring into Melissa's soft blue eyes, wet with tears. It had been natural to say something nice to her, to try and ease some of Melissa's agony of feeling she wasn't enough for Craig. *Maybe she thought I wanted something more from her.* The thought hit her hard in the gut. The last thing she ever wanted to do was make Melissa feel uncomfortable. *When will I learn to keep my mouth shut? That's another friendship you've ruined.*

Ellis sighed and refocused on the screen, knowing the best way to forget about Melissa would be to immerse herself in work. The gate creaked. She looked up, seeing Justin go over to the swing. *At least he doesn't hate me.* She gave him a small wave and carried on working. A few minutes later, she heard Melissa call him in for dinner. It was the first time Ellis had heard her in days, and the sound of her voice brought a tiny flutter to her chest. With shocking clarity, the truth hit her. She had a crush on Melissa. She shot up from her desk, panicked. *Melissa must have noticed the way you've been looking at her. She must think you're a pervert. No wonder she's avoiding you. You've messed up again, you idiot.*

Ellis's body trembled with fear, worried the same thing was going to happen all over again. Any minute now, there would be a knock at the door, the police ready to question her about stalking the neighbour. It was all too much. She had to get out. She grabbed her keys from the sideboard and fled.

Her feet pounded the pavement, her lungs burning with the effort to keep up with her speed. She ran like her life depended on it. Maybe it did. Maybe there was something so wrong with her that no one wanted her, and people were afraid of her. Maybe Stacy had felt threatened and had every right to try and protect herself. Maybe that was why her bosses let her go, as she was a danger to the staff. *And maybe that's why I never found a home as a kid. I'm evil, a force for bad.*

Ellis ran until her legs threatened to give way. She slowed to a jog, her legs barely carrying her forward. She hadn't noticed before, but now she felt the tears streaming down her face. *I've fucked up. Again.* She looked around to find her bearings, glad the sun hung low in the sky, casting shadows around her. She didn't want to be seen. She made the long walk back home, her mind setting out the steps needed to sell the house and find another home she could curl up in, away from everyone. There was no way she would be able to live next door to Melissa, knowing what she had done.

She rounded the corner to her street and kept her head down as she passed Melissa's house. She opened the gate and stopped dead in her tracks. "Melissa?"

Melissa gasped and stood from the stoop. She rushed over to Ellis. "Ellis, thank God."

Ellis backed up a step. "What are you doing here?"

"Justin said he saw you jump up from your desk looking frightened, then run out of the house. I was worried something bad had happened."

"I'm fine." Even as she said the words, she could feel her body swaying. The run had depleted all her energy, and she was on the verge of collapsing. *Lack of eating today hasn't helped. I need to start looking after myself.*

Melissa's gaze roamed over Ellis. "No, you're not. What is it?"

"I don't want anything from you, Melissa, I swear," Ellis said in a rush. "I'm sorry I made you uncomfortable."

"What are you talking about?"

"You've been avoiding me, and I know it's because of my behaviour." Ellis reached out and held onto the gate to keep her upright.

"Your behaviour?" Melissa shook her head. "Ellis, you've done nothing wrong."

"But I look at you sometimes, like I like you."

Melissa's shoulders raised, as she drew in a deep breath. "We need to talk. Come inside."

Ellis didn't want to go anywhere with Melissa, but she didn't have a choice. Melissa took her hand and pulled her along to Melissa's house. Ellis looked around for Justin, but he wasn't there. She assumed he was either in bed or playing on his computer. Melissa guided Ellis onto the sofa, then went into the kitchen. She returned with a glass of orange juice.

"Here, drink this."

Ellis took the glass and gulped down most of it in one go, hoping the sugar would at least give her some energy to make it through this and get home so she could sleep. She placed the glass onto the coffee table and leaned back on the couch. Melissa sat opposite her on the table, next to her glass.

"Ellis, the other night had nothing to do with you. Of course, I've noticed you looking, but it didn't make me uncomfortable." She half smiled. "It's nice to know I'm still attractive."

You're more than attractive. You're divine. Ellis tightened her hands into fists and rested them on her knees. "Then why have you been avoiding me?"

Melissa glanced away for a moment, her forehead creasing as she frowned. "Because, Ellis, at that moment, sitting next to you on the sofa, I wanted you to kiss me."

"Oh." *That was unexpected. She doesn't look too pleased with that confession though.* Melissa's normally bright eyes were dim, and she wrung her hands together. It was easy to tell Melissa didn't like this conversation one bit. *But she's doing it because I freaked out and she wants to clear the air. Is there no end to her generosity?*

"Yes. And I panicked. I never wanted that before from a woman. I didn't know how to process that moment. It's taken a while, but I know it was just a fleeting thought. I was caught up in all the emotions of talking about Craig, and you were being so nice to me, that for a split second, I wanted to kiss you."

"But you don't want that now?"

"No. I'm sorry. You're a great friend." Melissa's gazed deeply at Ellis. "I like spending time with you, but there will never be anything more."

Ellis took a breath and smiled, letting Melissa know it was all right. She had never expected anything to happen between them, anyway. Ellis had a little crush, that was all. For all she knew, she was probably confusing her feelings. She hadn't had a friend in years. "That's okay, I kinda knew that. I'll stop with the leering."

"You don't leer, and there is nothing wrong with you looking."

"I don't want you to be uncomfortable or always thinking I'm after you." Ellis looked away. "I can't deal with that again."

"Again?"

"It doesn't matter." Ellis tried to stand, she didn't want to talk about Stacy, but Melissa's hand on her knee stopped her from rising.

"Is this to do with why you left your last job?"

Ellis stayed quiet for a moment. The thing with her past was so overwhelmingly horrifying, she never wanted it brought up again. She looked up at Melissa. *It would be nice to tell my side for once, not just to Lucy, who I pay to believe me. But what if Melissa doesn't believe me? Then you continue with your plans to move.*

"What happened, Ellis? Whatever it was, it's skewed your view of the world."

It didn't just skew it. It tipped it right on its head. Now or never. She gripped her knees and gazed directly into Melissa's eyes. "I was arrested for sexual harassment."

Melissa leaned back on the table, her eyes widening. "What?"

"The allegations were unfounded. I wasn't charged with anything, but it made working at the company difficult."

"It was someone you worked with?"

"Yes. She was my assistant. We were friends, or so I thought. She went to my bosses and told them I had been making advances at her, touching her inappropriately, and stalking her. They contacted the police."

"Oh, Ellis."

"It wasn't true. We'd hug goodbye after a night out. I'd occasionally be in the same shop as her. I'd ask her to meet up for coffee. These were all things you do with friends. I don't know why she made up those lies. I spent months trying to prove my innocence. I even had our phones tracked to prove I was in the shops before her some of the time. Her messages to me proved our relationship was equal, and I never said anything to give her the idea I was after her. We were just friends." Ellis glanced at her thighs, where she now drummed her fingers. "Now though, I look back and wonder if maybe, on some level, I did give her the wrong idea." She shrugged. "That maybe I came across as a threat."

"And that's what scared you tonight?" Melissa's voice came out in a whisper. "That you had done the same to me?"

Ellis nodded.

"And that's also why you've shut yourself away from everyone, so it can't happen again."

"Yes."

"Oh, Ellis." Sympathy laced Melissa's tone. "I'm so sorry you went through all that. You have to know you didn't do anything wrong, back then or now. You've never made me uncomfortable or done anything to cause me alarm. Yes, I've noticed the interest in your eyes sometimes, but that's no different to a guy. I know you would never do anything to hurt me."

"I didn't think I would either, but now, I'm questioning everything again, and I hate it. I just want things to be normal." Much to her dismay, Ellis broke down in tears. She hadn't cried this much since the allegations against her. She worried, now the tears had started, she would never be able to stop them. She covered her face with her hands, shoulders shaking.

"You're a good person, Ellis." Melissa moved from the table and sat next to her. "Come here." She lifted her arm, waiting for Ellis to move. She didn't. "It's okay, Ellis."

Ellis wiped her eyes and sniffed. Melissa looked inviting and safe. Ellis hadn't been comforted in years, and the desire to have someone, anyone, hug her built up in her chest. That it was Melissa who offered comfort was even more tempting. She leaned slowly toward Melissa. Melissa's arm dropped over her shoulders and pulled her in closer. Ellis rested her head on Melissa's chest and let out a long sigh. They stayed that way for a long while. Without meaning to, Ellis's eyes drifted shut. The emotions of the last two hours left her feeling drained and heavy. She didn't mean to, but she fell asleep, wrapped securely in Melissa's embrace.

CHAPTER EIGHT

Melissa opened her eyes and couldn't feel her arm. She was lying on her side on the sofa, Ellis next to her. Her head on top of Melissa's arm was making it numb. Ellis's back was against Melissa's front. How they both fitted side by side on the sofa was a miracle. She'd bought a sofa suited to her own shorter frame. How Ellis hadn't rolled off baffled her. The lounge was dark. Melissa had no idea what the time was. Her breasts rested against Ellis's shoulder blades, the pressure causing a thrill to run through Melissa's body. She needed to move. She had lied to Ellis earlier. The desire hadn't been a fleeting thought. Since that night, Melissa had been thinking of nothing but of how it would feel to touch Ellis's lips with her own. Their shared moment had awakened something within her that she didn't know how to shut down. *And lying like this isn't helping.* Despite their size difference, Ellis fitted quite well against her. Her hair smelled like mango, her body throwing off loads of heat. Melissa hadn't lain next to someone since Craig. Even back then, they never really spooned. Having Ellis this close was playing haywire with her brain.

She had been so scared when Justin came running in to tell her about Ellis racing off. From his description, something terrifying had happened to her. Worry overrode the need to avoid Ellis and propelled her from the house. She had been too late to stop Ellis. She'd given Justin his dinner and settled him in for the night, then waited outside Ellis's for her to return. She didn't care how long it took. She had to know if she was all right. She'd never imagined the horrors Ellis had been through. Ellis had alluded to things in the past, and Melissa knew it had to have been something really bad. She never thought, for a second, it would have been sexual harassment. *How can anyone think you would do that? You're the sweetest, most caring person I know.* They'd only been friends for a couple of months, but it was long enough for Melissa to know Ellis was a good person. *And now I'm all mixed up over you.* Ellis had been so devastated, thinking she had made Melissa uncomfortable; Melissa didn't know what to do. Her only choice was to address Ellis's attraction and shut it down. *Even though I feel it's reciprocated.* But how could she tell Ellis that when she hadn't figured it out herself yet. She couldn't give her false hope. For all Melissa knew, this was all just a momentary lapse brought on by high tension. *Though my hand is just itching to touch her waist and draw her closer to me.*

As carefully as she could, Melissa slowly moved out from behind Ellis. She needed distance. Ellis stirred but promptly fell back to sleep. Melissa escaped to the kitchen and checked the time on the cooker. It was coming up to three in the morning. She eyed the wine she had opened last night and sighed. Drinking wouldn't make her thoughts any clearer. She settled for milk instead. She opened the fridge and grabbed the milk bottle. She poured herself a large amount and took a long swig.

"Hi."

Melissa spun around, her hand going to her chest. Ellis stood before her, shrouded in darkness. Melissa set down the glass and wiped her mouth with the back of her hand. "You scared me."

"Sorry. What time is it?"

"About three."

"I have to go."

Ellis turned away, but Melissa reached out and grasped her wrist, her skin still warm to the touch. "Are you okay?"

Ellis shrugged. "I have no idea." She pulled her arm free and went to the front door. She let herself out and was gone.

Melissa closed her eyes, her body shivering. It was as if Ellis took all the heat from the room with her. Melissa rinsed the glass and made her way upstairs. She checked in on Justin, who was sound asleep, and readied herself for bed. She slipped between the covers and pulled one of her pillows against her body. She didn't even try to pretend it wasn't a replacement for Ellis.

†

Melissa hadn't seen or heard from Ellis in three days. She hadn't expected to. When Ellis had left in the early hours of the morning, despite the darkness in the kitchen, Melissa could see Ellis felt ashamed and embarrassed. Melissa wanted to talk to her, but what would she say? She herself was in turmoil. Her thoughts still weren't clear on her feelings for Ellis. All she did know was that she wanted to be her friend. *But is that an option now? We're both afraid of seeing each other. Unless we clear the air, we will forever be strangers.* That wasn't a prospect she relished. She liked Ellis. She found her charming and caring. Melissa couldn't believe anyone would think she would ever do anything to hurt someone. *I can't believe someone brought sexual harassment charges against her.* Melissa didn't know the full story, and only knew Ellis's side of things, but she couldn't fathom her doing what the police thought she had. *Then again, I never thought Craig would cheat on me. Perhaps I'm rubbish at reading people.*

"Here you go, Mum."

Melissa blinked away her ruminations and focused on Justin. He held out a small stack of invitations for his birthday party. "All done?"

"Yeah. There were a couple of mates I wanted to come but you said only ten. It was hard to choose."

Melissa took the stack and leafed through the names. She was surprised when one name caught her attention. She glanced up at Justin. "Ellis?"

He nodded and smiled. "She's cool. I also didn't think it would be nice if we were all over here having fun and she was stuck inside watching."

"That's very sweet of you, but are you sure you wouldn't prefer one of your friends?"

"No, I want Ellis."

"Okay." She placed the stack down on the breakfast bar but kept Ellis's invitation in her hand. Popping over with it would be the perfect excuse to see her. It would hopefully help break through the wall that had sprung up between them. She turned to Justin. "We need to leave in half an hour. Go get your bag packed. I'm just going to go give this to Ellis now." Her night shift was due to start in an hour and she needed to drop Justin off at her parents on the way. Justin nodded and wandered off. Melissa eyed the invitation again. *Just do it. She can hardly be mad at you for doing Justin's bidding.*

She slipped her trainers on and headed out into the garden. She glanced over the fence. Ellis wasn't in the conservatory. Melissa went through the gate and up to the door. She knocked and waited. Ellis appeared a few moments later, dressed in black jogging bottoms and a tight long-sleeved polo neck. Melissa dragged her gaze away from the flat planes of Ellis's stomach to her face. What she saw shocked her. Ellis was the palest Melissa had ever seen her. The circles around her eyes were darker and more pronounced. Melissa was sure she had lost weight. Her cheeks looked gaunt. "Oh my God. Are you okay?"

Ellis nodded but swayed on her feet.

Melissa grasped Ellis's hand and pulled her back into the house. She didn't stop to look around, despite this being the first time she had been in Ellis's home. She tugged her through to the lounge and pushed her onto the couch. Ellis fell back with no resistance. Melissa knelt in front of her and cupped her cheeks, noting they were hot to the touch. She checked her eyes and found them somewhat dazed. Melissa held her wrist and began counting beats. Ellis's pulse was thumping rapidly. Something was wrong. She didn't need to be a nurse to figure that out. "Ellis?"

"I'm fine."

Melissa shook her head. "You're not. When did you last eat or drink?"

Ellis shrugged. "I've been busy."

"That's not good enough, Ellis. You're going to kill yourself if you carry on like this."

"Sorry."

Melissa sighed. "You don't need to apologise. You do, however, need to come to the hospital with me. You need fluids and we need to check your electrolytes."

"I'll just have some toast."

"Ellis, you can barely stand up. You need proper treatment."

"I'm fine."

Melissa got to her feet, anger coursing through her. If Ellis thought, for one minute, she was going to leave her here like this, she needed a brain scan. "You're coming with me." She was that worried about Ellis that she would call her mum to collect Justin. She didn't want Ellis to have to wait longer than she needed for treatment. "I'm going next door to get my things and call my mum. I'll be back in five minutes."

"Melissa, honestly, I'll be okay." Even as she said the words, her head lolled to the side.

Melissa went back to her knees. She cupped her cheek again, but this time as someone who cared about Ellis and not as a nurse. She gazed into her eyes. "I don't know why you're fighting me on this. Please, Ellis. Please come with me."

"Why?"

"You're sick. You need help." She softened her voice. "Let me help you."

Ellis stared at her for a long moment before finally nodding. "Okay."

"Good." Melissa smiled and stood. "I'll be as quick as I can." Melissa rushed back home and called her mum, then explained to Justin he was to wait there until his grandmother came to get him.

"What's wrong with her?" he asked.

"She just has a bug that needs treating."

"If it's just a bug, then why do you look so scared?"

Melissa tried to relax her features, knowing her panic was worrying him more than he needed to be. It was hard. All she wanted to do was to get back to Ellis. "I promise, buddy, she's going to be fine, but she needs a few tests. It's just quicker if I take her."

"Okay."

Melissa grabbed her bag and keys and hastened back to Ellis's. Ellis was in the same position as before. Her eyes closed. *I wonder how long she's been like this.* Melissa feared it stemmed from their talk the other night. She berated herself for not coming over sooner.

"Ellis?" Ellis opened her eyes, but her gaze was unseeing. "We need to go." Melissa helped her stand and led her to the door. She scooped up Ellis's keys and headed out. Ellis was unsteady on her feet, and Melissa struggled to keep them both upright. Thankfully, her car wasn't far away. She managed to get them there without a disaster. Within seconds, Melissa was speeding toward the hospital.

Chapter Nine

"How is she doing?" Melissa asked Bernice, another nurse on shift.

"She's asleep. We've got the fluids on rapid, and we're still waiting for the blood tests to come back. Her heartbeat still isn't settling, and she's twitching a lot."

Melissa gazed over at Ellis in the far bay of the emergency ward. Tubes ran into her arm and hand. A pulse metre was clipped to her finger, and leads from the heart monitor disappeared under her gown. She looked so vulnerable, that Melissa nearly fainted from the sight. She was used to seeing Ellis being strong and authoritative, not this weakened version of herself. A question had been rattling around Melissa's mind for the past few weeks. She turned her attention back to Bernice. "Do you think she has an eating disorder?"

"You don't need me to answer that."

"No, I don't." Melissa had been a nurse long enough to spot the signs. If she didn't have one now, it wouldn't be long until she did. "I know work stresses her out, and she forgets to eat. I've never seen her like this, though."

Bernice squeezed Melissa's arm. "The results will be back soon. I'll find you when they get here."

"Thank you." Melissa smiled and made her way over to Ellis. Without thinking, she took Ellis's hand in her own, interlacing their fingers. She brushed back a loose strand of hair with the other.

Ellis stirred, her hand tensing in Melissa's. Her eyes fluttered open. "Hi." Her voice was raspy, but strong.

"Hey. How're you feeling?"

"Not great."

Melissa smiled softly. "I'm not surprised." She reached into her pocket and pulled Justin's invitation out. She passed it over. Ellis smiled when she saw what it was. "He picked you over his friends."

"He's a sweet kid. You've raised a good one there." Ellis held the paper to her chest, above her heart.

"Can I tell him you'll be coming?" Ellis eyed Melissa carefully, and Melissa knew she understood what the question really was. *Will you do what you must to get better?*

Ellis nodded.

"Good. We will both be delighted for your presence."

Ellis's eyes slipped closed. The heart monitor beeped wildly for a few seconds before settling back to a more normal rhythm, albeit slightly fast. "I think I need help, Melissa. I'm not coping so well right now."

"I know. I'm here for you, whatever you need."

"Thank you."

Ellis drifted off, and Melissa moved away. Her break was over, and she needed to get back to work. The good thing was, being a nurse in the emergency department meant she could keep an eye on Ellis. Whatever was going on with Ellis had been plaguing her for some time. Melissa figured it had started with the allegations against her. In the back of her mind, she couldn't help but think that she had made the situation worse. Ellis had lost a significant amount of weight in the few months Melissa had known her, and the last two weeks had stressed Ellis out even more. In the face of what Ellis was struggling with now, Melissa couldn't help but think that moving in next door had been a mistake. *She seemed to be doing all right until I came along. She might not have been a hundred percent, but at least she wasn't in the hospital on a drip. I need to help her, but maybe the best thing I can do is leave her alone.* Melissa glanced up from the patient she was seeing to. Ellis was watching her and smiled. Melissa smiled back. She couldn't leave her alone even if she wanted to. *I won't abandon you like everyone else has.*

✝

"Ellis?"

Ellis opened her eyes and looked up at Lucy. It took her a moment to remember where she was. "What are you doing here?"

"I'm your next of kin, remember?"

"Oh, yeah." Having no family, Lucy had suggested Ellis use her in case there was a problem. Ellis regretted that decision now. She hadn't wanted Lucy to find out she had failed and put herself into the hospital. She had planned to mention it over their next appointment, as if it wasn't a big deal. Having her here now scuppered that idea. "They didn't need to call you."

"I'm glad they did." Lucy pulled a plastic chair over and sat. "Have the doctors talked to you?"

"Yeah. My electrolytes were off due to lack of food." Ellis hadn't known that could happen from not eating for a couple of days. She got so consumed with work, and trying to shut down her thoughts, that hunger hadn't registered. This had never happened before, not even during the stress of dealing with the police and Stacy. It was a stark warning of where she was heading if she didn't sort herself out. The hospital psychiatrist had spoken to her, not long ago. It took all of Ellis's persuasion not to have him admit her for monitoring. They were all concerned she had an eating disorder. She didn't, that she was sure of.

"I'm sorry, Ellis. I've failed you."

"No, you haven't."

Lucy sighed, her eyes darkening. "I've been treating you for close to two years, and you're worse off now than when we started."

"It's not your responsibility to heal me. You've given me all the help I need. It's my fault if I didn't follow your advice." Ellis only blamed herself. She'd made the right noises, said the right things, but hadn't taken Lucy's help to heart. She thought she could do it all on her own. *How wrong was I? I need to take this seriously and get proper help dealing with my issues.*

"And why haven't you followed my advice?"

Ellis shrugged and gave the question some thought. Being alone with no friends and family had robbed her of any self-worth. She didn't trust anymore. Her only positives

93

were her client base and the work she did. It had taken a while to build up the business, and she couldn't be prouder of that aspect of her life. *It's a shame the rest of it sucks.* She looked at Lucy. "I guess I don't think I'm worth it."

"So, gradually killing yourself is your plan."

It wasn't like that. "It's not like I've sat there and thought about it. I just get so caught up working all hours; I forget to eat."

"We discussed setting an alarm."

"I forgot."

Lucy briefly closed her eyes, her frustration clear. "Ellis, they think you have an eating disorder. I'm inclined to agree with them."

"I don't, I swear. I have no problems eating when I do." She didn't fear food. She enjoyed most things, but when it came to working, everything else fell away. Including her health.

"So, what are you going to do?"

Something I never thought I would. "I thought, maybe, finish up the projects I'm doing now, then take the summer off to work on myself." She was close to completing the three projects she was working on. Now would usually be the time she would contact previous clients and scout for new business. The thought of not doing that turned her stomach. She had worked hard to build her success. She didn't want it to all go away if she took time off. Ellis didn't have a choice, though. Her body was screaming at her to fix herself. She needed intense therapy and she couldn't do that if she worked fifteen hours or more a day. "I don't want to die, Lucy. I just need a break."

"If you stop working, you'll have nothing to distract yourself. You'll have to deal with everything in your past."

Ellis looked away and caught sight of Melissa bending over a patient, checking his chest with her stethoscope. Things between them had been off the last few weeks. Telling her about her past had exhausted Ellis. She felt ashamed for letting things get so out of hand with Stacy. She didn't want that to happen with Melissa. Ellis had been embarrassed Melissa knew she had a crush on her, but Melissa had told her it was okay. Ellis didn't know if she was being honest, but she had no choice but to believe her. Ellis needed to get back on track. She wanted to be in Melissa's life, in whatever way that would be. *I've finally found a friend. I don't want to give that up.* She turned her attention back to Lucy. "I know, but it's time. I want my life back."

"Okay. I can make room for you in my schedule. We can do as many appointments as you need. I would like some of them to be in person. And I don't mean me coming to you."

"Okay. Thank you." Ellis wasn't thrilled she was being made to venture out to Lucy's office, but she understood it was part of her healing.

"You're welcome. I'll leave you to your rest." Lucy stood and squeezed Ellis's shoulder. "I'll check in with you tomorrow."

"All right."

Ellis watched her go, then closed her eyes. She had been in A&E for nearly seven hours. They had run all kinds of tests on her, including a heart and liver scan. Thankfully, everything came back normal, aside from the electrolytes. Ellis knew, with proper nutrition, this wouldn't happen again. *I can't believe how bad things have gotten. What would have happened had Melissa not come over? I need to thank her properly.*

"How are you feeling?"

Ellis's eyes popped open. Melissa stood before her, worry showing in her gaze. Ellis hated that she was the reason for that concern. "Much better. Thank you for helping me."

Melissa waved her off. "No thanks needed. Just don't do it again."

"I won't." Ellis took a breath. "I assume you know what's wrong?"

"Yes. Nothing that regular eating won't cure."

"You just missed Lucy. I'm going to take some time off work and sort myself out."

"It's none of my business, but can you afford to do that?"

"Yeah. The house is paid for, and my savings are in good shape. I don't do anything, remember?" She grinned.

Melissa smiled back. "Oh yes. A hermit is how you described yourself." Melissa grasped Ellis's forearm. "I was really worried about you."

"I'm sorry, Melissa. That's the last thing I wanted."

"Ellis…"

"What?" Ellis felt her heart speed up from the intense look Melissa was giving her.

Melissa sighed and withdrew her hand. "It doesn't matter. When are you being discharged?"

"In the next hour or so, I think."

"Okay. I'll speak to my supervisor and take you home."

"You don't need to do that. I can get a taxi."

"No. I'll take you."

"Thank you."

Forty minutes later, the doctor said she could go. Ellis rushed to dress, wanting to get out of there before they changed their minds and made her stay. She made her way to the emergency room reception and took a seat, so she could wait for Melissa. She stared off into the distance, drumming her fingers on her thighs, her mind going over what needed to be done on her projects.

†

Ellis entered the front door of her house. She strode across the living room and into the conservatory, where she woke her computer and connected to the internet.

"What are you doing?" Melissa asked from her place in the lounge.

Ellis glanced over her shoulder. Melissa stood with her hands on her hips. "Checking my email."

"Ellis, you've just walked through the door."

"I know, but—"

"Were you even serious about what you said in the hospital?"

Ellis rolled her eyes. "I can't just stop working at once. I have to close my projects down and let my clients know." Of course, it would be easier if she could just switch it all off, but that wasn't the way to keep a business. She needed to finish what she had promised and explain to her client base she would be out of commission for a few weeks. If she didn't, she'd probably have to start building a new client list, and that would take too long. She wasn't made of money. She needed to keep the clients she had.

"But you don't need to do that right this minute. You should be resting."

"I was lying down for hours. I feel fine."

"Do you know what? There is no helping you. You're going to work yourself into an early grave." Melissa turned around and stormed from the room.

"Melissa! Wait."

The front door slammed.

Ellis looked at her computer, the urge to crack on with work was strong. She slammed her fist onto the desk and went after Melissa. Melissa had gone out of her way to help Ellis. Ellis had made a promise to her and Lucy. Getting straight back into work was a stupid idea. Deep down, Ellis knew that, once she started, she'd be sat there for the rest of the day and would more than likely be back in the hospital by the evening.

She twisted Melissa's door handle, pleased to find it unlocked. "Melissa?" Ellis wandered through the lounge and spotted Melissa leaning against the breakfast bar in the kitchen, her head bowed. "Melissa?"

"Go home, Ellis."

"Are you crying?"

"Yes, I'm crying." Melissa turned to face Ellis, her cheeks red with a smattering of tears on them. "Do you have any idea what I went through when I saw you like that? I thought you were going to die."

"I was just unsteady on my feet."

"You're not taking this seriously, are you? You said all that crap about wanting to get better, that you needed help, as you're not coping, but as soon as you walked through the door, you're back in denial mode. I'm not going to watch you slowly kill yourself."

"I do want to get better, Melissa. I just don't know how to stop working. It's all I've known for the last five years."

"I know." Melissa angrily swiped her tears away with the back of her hand. "I don't mean to get mad at you. I just don't like seeing you like this. I feel like it's partially my fault."

Ellis frowned. "What are you talking about?"

"We haven't spoken since the night we talked. I feel like you've pushed yourself harder because of it."

"No, Melissa." Ellis rushed forward and took Melissa's hands in her own. "I'm the one who buried myself in work. Talking about Stacy and that period of time took me back to the past. I haven't dealt with it properly, and that's why I got lost in work. Lucy is going to help me with that."

"So, it wasn't because of us?"

Ellis didn't want to admit that it partly was. She had been so devastated when she thought Melissa might view her the same way Stacy did. Talking about her past had been the problem, but her attraction to Melissa was the catalyst. "Maybe a little. But it certainly wasn't your fault. All you did was explain your feelings. It was all the stuff with Stacy that drove me to distraction."

"That's good, because I don't want to ever do anything that hurts you."

Ellis shook her head. "You won't."

"So, we're friends?"

"We're friends. I promise, I'll slow down work as soon as I can and have some proper time off." It wouldn't be easy, but for Melissa, she'd try her hardest. It was nice someone cared enough about her to be this upset over it all, but Ellis would prefer Melissa didn't have to be worried at all. It tore her up knowing Melissa was this distressed because of her. Anything she could do to take that away, she would.

"Okay." Melissa took a deep breath and brushed the last of her tears away. "You can help me plan Justin's party. He wants a Fortnite theme."

"What fortnight?"

"Not a time period, it's a game he plays on Xbox."

"Oh." Ellis had never heard of it, not surprisingly. If she was going to be spending more time with Melissa and Justin, she would need to catch up on the things youngsters liked. "Um, I'd better do some research."

"Yeah, he wants all his friends to dress up as characters from the game."

Ellis's eyes went wide. "Surely you don't mean me?"

"You *are* on the guest list." Melissa smirked.

"Great." Ellis had assumed she'd be hanging out with Melissa and the other adults. She didn't think, for one second, she'd have to participate the same as his friends. She was, however, touched Justin saw her that way. "Will you help me?"

"Of course."

"Perfect, because I have no idea what I'm doing."

"I'll be by your side the whole way."

Gazing into Melissa's eyes, Ellis knew she meant more than just making a costume.

CHAPTER TEN

Ellis sighed and picked up the remote for the TV. She muted the channel and tossed the controller back down. *I have never seen such utter crap in all my life.* She had managed to finish up most of her work. This was the first day in God knows how many years Ellis hadn't worked at least part of the day. She'd kept herself occupied by pottering around, cleaning and sorting cupboards. Her house was the cleanest she had ever seen it. Now though, she was out of jobs to do. *And the TV sucks. No wonder I work all the time.* Ellis glanced over at her computer. *It's a good job Lucy convinced me to switch off the internet.* If she hadn't, Ellis knew full well she would be sat there working. She looked over at the notebook on the coffee table. Lucy had set her homework ready for their next appointment. Ellis was supposed to make a feelings chart, plotting down her thoughts about herself. That was worse than what was on the television. She didn't want to do that yet. She knew she was procrastinating, which was unlike her, but some things she would try to put off indefinitely.

Tapping on her conservatory window caught her attention. Melissa stood on the other side, holding a china dish. Ellis smiled, thanking the gods for the distraction. Melissa had been amazing. She popped around any chance she could, bringing food or magazines, sometimes just to check up on her. Ellis revelled in the attention. It was nice to have someone care about her and not want anything in return. Ellis wasn't keen on taking Melissa away from her other duties, but appreciated her, nonetheless. Melissa had enough on her plate without worrying about Ellis. That was part of the reason why Ellis was doing her best to avoid working. Seeing Melissa cry had torn Ellis up. She never thought anyone would care about her as much as Melissa appeared to.

Ellis stood and went to the door, her smile getting wider the closer she got. "Hey," she said as she stepped back, allowing Melissa to enter. Ellis took a sniff as she passed, figuring out that roast chicken was for dinner.

"Good evening, Ellis." Melissa's smile didn't quite reach her eyes. "I made extra." She placed the dish on the kitchen counter. "It's still warm if you want to eat it now."

"Thank you." Ellis eyed Melissa. Something was off with her. She wouldn't meet her gaze. She lightly touched Melissa's arm. "Are you okay?"

"I'm fine."

Ellis narrowed her eyes. "Really?"

Melissa blew out a heavy breath and leaned back against the counter. Her head lowered, the long strands of her hair falling over one shoulder. "I'm having some problems with Craig." Melissa looked up, brushing her hair back as she did so. "He was supposed to have Justin tonight, while I go to work, but he's just texted me and said he can't do it. I tried calling him, but he won't pick up." She shrugged a shoulder. "I assume he's out drinking."

"What about your parents?"

"They're away for the weekend. I'm going to have to call in sick again. I can't afford not to be working, but if Craig keeps doing this, I'm going to have to think about cutting my hours back. If I do that, I'll have to sell the house and move back with my folks. The school holidays are coming up soon, and I can't have Craig constantly flaking out on me."

"I'll watch him."

"What?"

"Justin. I'll watch him."

Melissa shook her head. "I can't ask you to do that."

"Melissa, I'm just sat here watching crap on TV. I can just as easily do that in your house."

Melissa looked up from lowered lashes. "You seriously wouldn't mind?"

Ellis nodded. "I'll be fine. He can teach me about that Fortnite thing, so I have some idea about what I should be wearing to his party."

"I won't be back until eight in the morning."

"We'll be fine. I've got your number if anything comes up."

"You're sure?"

Ellis half smiled. "Yes." It felt nice to do something for Melissa for a change after everything Melissa had done for her. Not that it should be tit for tat, but Ellis didn't want Melissa thinking she took her for granted.

Melissa beamed. She leaned up onto her tiptoes and kissed Ellis's cheek. "Thank you so much. You're a lifesaver. Justin will love having you over."

Ellis resisted the urge to reach up and trace her cheek where Melissa's lips touched. Her skin warmed, and she looked away. Ellis's crush was still in full effect, and she struggled to get past those feelings.

"I need to leave in about an hour. That should give you time to eat and grab what you need for the evening." Melissa took a few steps away but turned back around. "Thank you, Ellis. This means a lot. Oh, and when you're ready, you can just sleep in my bed if you want. The sheets were changed yesterday, so they're still pretty fresh."

Ellis's mind flashed an image of them wrapped up together in bed. She tried her hardest not to blush but failed miserably; her skin burned all over.

Melissa pulled her top lip between her teeth, and her brows pinched as she gazed at Ellis. "Ellis…"

"I'll see you in a bit." Ellis turned her back on Melissa and made a show of taking the foil off the dish, hoping Melissa would get the hint and leave. Whatever Melissa saw in her, Ellis didn't want to know. Melissa had made her feelings clear once before. *I don't need telling again. I need to get over this fruitless crush of mine, or I'll end up losing her for good.*

She heard the conservatory door close. Ellis's shoulders slumped, as she let out a huge breath. *That was close.* She grabbed a knife and fork from the drawer and carried the dish over to her small dining table. No way would she be sleeping in Melissa's bed. The couch would be fine.

†

104

†

"Come on, Ellis. Press *B*."

"I'm pressing it! Damn." Ellis rolled her eyes at her ineptness. Justin had been patient in teaching her how to play Fortnite, but after an hour and a half, she had only managed to land out of the plane three times. She was killed within seconds. She was never going to get the hang of it. She glanced at Justin, who was giggling beside her. "It's a good job your party is a costume party and not a gaming competition." Justin smirked. Ellis tilted her head and squinted at him. "Are we going to be playing this at the party?"

"Well, it's a Fortnite party. What would be the point unless you play the game?"

"Your mother left that part out." It was bad enough she needed to fashion a costume for the thing, but now she would be humiliating herself in front of a load of ten-year-olds.

"It's not for another couple of weeks. You could get better."

"I don't think that would be enough time. Are you sure you don't want a dinosaur theme or something?"

"Nope. Fortnite it is. Here, look at this." Justin pulled a drawing pad from his desk and flipped the pages until he found the one he wanted. He passed it over to Ellis. "This is what I'm going to be going as."

Ellis looked at the sketch. It was rudimentary in design—Justin was clearly not an artist—but it was easy to figure out the lasers, guns, and armour the character wore. "That's pretty impressive. How are you going to make it?"

"Dad said he can get some old bike parts and metal sheets and weld them together for the armour. I've got my old toy guns and stuff to glue on."

Ellis hoped Craig pulled through for Justin. From the conversations she'd had with Melissa, Craig wasn't very reliable. "That'll be awesome."

"What about you? Have you thought about your costume yet?"

Ellis shook her head. "Until two hours ago, I didn't exactly know what Fortnite was. Your mum said she would help me."

"You can be anything you want. The better you get at the game, the more skins you can buy. There's no limit."

Skins? That doesn't sound pleasant. "Can I go as an office worker?" She wouldn't need to do anything except throw on a smart trouser suit, and she had plenty of them stuffed in the back of her wardrobe.

Justin frowned. "If you want, but where's the fun in that?"

Ellis couldn't help but think he was right, and not just about the costume being boring. It had only been a few days since she cut down on her work. Although she was bored already, it was nice not to have the stress of filling out reports and dealing with numbers. "Don't worry, I'm sure your mum will sort me out with something cool."

"I've got a toy box full of stuff you can look through and use."

"Thanks, buddy. It's getting late. You should be in bed by now." As much as she was having fun with Justin, she didn't want to get into trouble with Melissa on her first night of child minding.

"Okay. If you want, you can take the Xbox downstairs with you and keep playing."

"You wouldn't mind?"

Justin shrugged. "As long as you don't break it."

Two hours later, Ellis switched off the Xbox, even more disgusted with herself than she was earlier. She could land on the island nearly every time now, but still couldn't get any kills or build anything. *I've never sucked so badly at anything in all my life.* She tossed the controller down onto the cushion beside her and yawned. It was nearing eleven. *Time for bed.*

She made her way upstairs to Melissa's room to find a blanket or something to use on the couch. Her stomach knotted as she pushed open the door to Melissa's private space for the first time. She flicked on the light and smiled. A familiar two-foot gap circled the top of the walls Melissa had painted. *Obviously, her dad hasn't dropped the ladder off yet.* Ellis's smile turned to a frown, remembering Melissa had cancelled their plans for decorating because she had been confused about wanting to kiss Ellis. *That whole thing was a shit show. I'm pleased we managed to talk things through, despite my lingering feelings for her.* Ellis would call them friends now, and not just acquaintances. She didn't want to do anything that would ruin that.

She glanced around the rest of the room. Traces of Melissa's personality were all around. Bangles, hairbands, and beaded necklaces cluttered her dresser. A bright-red tub chair was nestled in one corner, with a few of the colourful jumpers Melissa always wore, even though summer had arrived. Ellis looked at the bed, full of differently coloured scatter pillows. What looked like a hand-sewn throw lay spread out over the bottom half of the mattress. The whole room was eclectic, and it matched Melissa perfectly. Ellis's style was far more muted. Black, grey, and mushroom were her colours of choice. It was clear their styles matched their personalities.

Ellis went over to the bed and smoothed her hand over the soft cotton of the duvet cover. Despite the abundance of colour in the room, Ellis felt compelled to climb inside the nest of pillows and wrap herself up in the throw. *Melissa did say I was welcome to sleep in here.* Ellis debated for a few seconds, then decided to hell with it. *She's not back until morning. I can be up and have this all put back to normal before she even gets home. She never has to know I was in here.* She left the light on, knowing that would help her not to get into a deep sleep. Ellis could never settle unless it was pitch black.

With her choice made, Ellis slipped off her jeans and T-shirt and crawled under the duvet. Melissa's scent lingered on the pillows, and Ellis drew in a deep lungful of the floral aroma. She was asleep in seconds.

†

Ellis woke up to darkness, the smell of roses comforting her. She closed her eyes again and breathed the scent deeper into her lungs. She snuggled further into the pillow and sighed. *Wait. I went to sleep with the light on. And since when do pillows feel hairy against your skin?* She opened her eyes again and gave them a chance to adjust to the dark. What she saw had her heart in her throat.

"Melissa?"

Melissa was inches away, her long hair surrounding them both. Her eyes were open, gazing intently through the dark. "Hello, Ellis," she whispered.

"You're home early."

"Yes. The hospital was quiet, and it was my turn to volunteer to go home early."

"Why didn't you wake me?" Ellis felt a puff of air as Melissa breathed out.

"I don't know. I was going to, but then I *really* looked at you. You looked so peaceful, so comfortable. I switched the light off and crawled in next to you. I wanted to know what it would be like."

"What what would be like?" Ellis would have assumed Melissa would have slept on the couch if she didn't want to wake her. She certainly never expected to wake up and find Melissa snuggled next to her.

"Lying next to you." Melissa sifted and moved her hand. She placed her first two fingers against Ellis's lower lip, gently rubbing.

"Mel..."

Melissa removed her hand.

"Do you have any idea what you're doing to me?" Ellis's heart pounded, blood rushing to her ears. It would be so simple to close the gap between them and take Melissa in a fierce kiss. She knew that wouldn't be wise. She had no doubt Melissa was confused about a lot of things, and now wasn't the time to be pushing her.

"I'm sorry."

"It's not your fault, but we shouldn't be doing this. I should go." Entranced by the beautiful Melissa, Ellis didn't move.

"I just wanted to know what it would be like," she repeated. Melissa inched closer, her fingers traced Ellis's jaw and back to her lips. "They look so soft." Her gaze flicked up to Ellis's. "You are so strong, Ellis, so safe. I have to know."

Ellis was close to giving in. She could see how much Melissa wanted this, but she also knew she would regret it. Things always looked different in the dead of night. Come morning, Melissa would be mortified and would end their friendship. She wouldn't allow a few seconds of pleasure to ruin what they were building. "Mel, it's not a good idea. You don't like me that way. You've told me that already. This will just mess everything up. I'm going home now." With all the willpower she had, Ellis tossed the duvet aside and leapt out of bed.

Melissa sat up, her gaze wounded.

"I'm sorry, Melissa."

Melissa turned away and buried herself in the duvet. "Goodnight, Ellis."

Ellis desperately wanted to crawl back in beside her and talk about their feelings but knew she wouldn't be welcomed. Melissa was probably embarrassed, and trying to talk about it would only inflame the situation. The best thing to do would be to escape and come back another time. Melissa was going through something big, and would need someone to talk to. Ellis assumed Melissa had never had these kinds of feelings before and wouldn't know how to handle them. *Then again, what do I know? She could be bi. You can't just assume these things.* There would be no talking tonight. It was time to go home and sleep on it, but Ellis knew she wouldn't be getting much sleep. Melissa had been so close. Ellis's nerves were fried, and she would spend the rest of the night remembering the want in Melissa's eyes.

Finding Her Heart

Chapter Eleven

Ellis had had enough. Melissa had been avoiding her again for the last seven days. She could understand Melissa's need for space, but it wasn't fair on Ellis. She needed to know where she stood. It was clear Melissa had an interest in her. How deep that went, Ellis didn't know. It was time to find out. She was done being pushed around by everyone.

She went through the gate and strode up Melissa's garden to the patio door. Melissa stood at the cooker, stirring something in a pan on the hob. Ellis slid the door open. Melissa jerked her head around and let go of the wooden spoon when she spotted Ellis. "It's been a week, Melissa. Are you going to avoid me forever?"

"I was hoping to."

Ellis took a step forward, out of touching distance but close enough to catch Melissa's scent. "We need to talk about this."

"No, we don't."

"Yes, we do. This is twice now you've said you wanted to kiss me." Ellis raised her arms, exasperated. "What am I supposed to think?"

"I don't know, Ellis." Melissa looked to the floor and wrapped her arms around her waist. "I'm confused right now."

"Talk to me. Maybe I can help."

Melissa shook her head. "You can't. You're just making it worse."

"How? I'm just being me."

Melissa raised her voice. "Yes, and that's the problem."

Ellis quirked an eyebrow. "What are you talking about?"

"You, with all that tall, dark, and handsome vibe you got going on. It's distracting."

"I thought we were friends?"

"We are. But, Ellis, sometimes, when I look at you…I'm drawn to you in a way I never thought I could be, not with anyone."

"And that's a bad thing?"

"Yes! I'm not like you. I'm not *gay*."

"Why are you saying it like it's something to be ashamed of?"

"I'm not. I have no problem with people loving who they want. However, that's not me."

Ellis moved closer, into Melissa's personal space. "It must be a little bit you if you want to kiss me all the time."

Melissa gazed up into Ellis's eyes, her breathing erratic. "Stop it," she whispered.

"Why? It's true, isn't it?"

"Ellis."

"What would you do if I kissed you right now? If I pressed you up against this fridge and pressed my lips to yours?" Melissa's gaze dropped to Ellis's lips, her tongue moistening her own. Ellis was pushing her too far, but she couldn't stop. She could see the desperation in Melissa's eyes, the want. Melissa needed this as much as Ellis did. "Would it turn you on? It would, wouldn't it? Because you want me."

Melissa shook her head vigorously. "No, I don't."

Ellis dipped her head, her mouth inches from Melissa's. "You're lying."

"Please, Ellis."

"Please, what?"

Melissa's gaze once again dropped to Ellis's mouth. "Do it. Kiss me."

Ellis waited a fraction of a second before lunging forward and capturing Melissa's lips with her own. She pressed into her, cupping her cheek as she did so. Melissa's arms wound around Ellis's waist and clasped her tightly. Ellis traced Melissa's lips with her tongue, seeking entry. Melissa opened her mouth and allowed her in. Ellis moaned at the first brush of tongues. Melissa tasted like coffee and sunshine. Her stomach clenched, as Melissa deepened the kiss even more. Ellis was close to losing control. She hadn't kissed someone in over eight years. She was surprised at how much she'd missed it.

Melissa's hand moved around to Ellis's front and made its way to the underside of Ellis's breast. Ellis flinched at the contact. She was about to take things further, when Melissa's hand braced against her chest and shoved her away. Ellis opened her eyes. Melissa's lips were red and swollen, her eyes like saucers. She ran the back over her hand across her face and into her hair, straightening the blonde curls.

"You need to leave," Melissa said, angrily.

"Melissa—"

"Please, Ellis." Melissa held her hand up. "I can't do this." She shook her head. "I just can't. Not now."

"There's something here, Melissa, between us. I know you're scared. We can figure it out together."

"I don't want to. I don't *want* you." Melissa glanced away. "Besides, I have a date in a couple of days."

"What?"

"Yes. With a guy from work. A doctor. He's been asking me out for months."

And just like that, Ellis's heart slammed shut. *How can she do this to me? She's fucking me over like Stacy did. No, not like Stacy. Melissa is scared. She's running from this because she doesn't know what to do.* "I hope you find what you're looking for. I'll see you around." Ellis stormed from the house and back home. She had just experienced the most intense kiss ever. The immediate shut down was demoralising. She could tell how much Melissa wanted her; no one could fake a kiss like that. *She needs time to figure things out. I'll give her space. Maybe she'll come around.* Ellis wasn't entirely convinced, but at least now she had some hope. Before, she had worried about ruining their friendship, because Melissa would find Ellis's crush offputting. It was different now she knew Melissa had at least some feelings toward her. *I just need to wait.*

†

115

Waiting didn't come easily for Ellis. Two days had passed, and she hadn't heard a peep from Melissa. Her desire to go to her pulled strong, but she resisted. She wasn't going to push Melissa into something. It had to be Melissa's choice.

Ellis focused her attention on her computer. Lucy's face filled the screen. Today was her scheduled appointment. Being able to have the internet back on tempted her to work, but each time she plugged the phone line in, she promised herself it would only be for her therapy sessions. She had kept that promise, so far. "I'm telling you, Lucy, she's attracted to me."

"That may be so, but you can't force her to admit that. She's not ready to deal with her attraction to another woman. You need to let her be."

"I know, but Lucy, I know she wants this." The kiss they shared was still fresh in her mind. It tormented her while she slept and plagued her every waking moment. Ellis would never forget the feel of Melissa's lips against her own.

Lucy's fringe flew up, as she puffed out a large breath of air and shook her head. "Ellis, you're supposed to be sorting your life out, not chasing the neighbour."

"And I am. I already feel better about myself. I've kept a regular eating schedule and have put weight on." The dark circles around her eyes were gone, and she no longer needed a belt to keep her jeans up. In Ellis's opinion, she was back to full health. She knew it would take a while for Lucy to stop worrying, but Ellis knew she was okay. *Well, until I go back to work. I just have to hope that, when I do, I don't lose myself in the stress again.* "I've done all the assignments you've asked of me. I'm doing everything I can to heal."

"And how do you feel about your birth mother?"

116

"Wow, that's unexpected." Ellis leaned back in her chair. Most of the sessions had been about rebuilding Ellis's confidence and how she viewed the world and the people in it. They even talked a lot about the situation with Stacy, but Lucy hadn't brought her mother up before. The sudden change of topic threw Ellis.

"It's the one question we haven't addressed," Lucy said.

"That's because I don't know how to answer. It's been forty years. I shouldn't even be thinking about her." Deborah Davis never crossed Ellis's mind, not fully anyway. Occasionally, Ellis would think of her, but she soon moved her thoughts on to other things. *And that's where work always helped.* She couldn't think about her mother if her head was filled with statistics.

"It doesn't matter how long it's been. Feeling you were abandoned by your mother is never pleasant."

"I guess it's the same old thing, feelings of unworthiness. In my head, I've always been under the illusion no one would want me, because I'm unlovable." *And foster care hammered that point home.* A handful of friends was all Ellis ever had, and the occasional liaison with a lover. Stacy's accusations blew all that apart.

"And that makes you feel what?"

"Sad. Lonely." Ellis shrugged. "Angry."

"Angry?"

"Yes. I'm not a bad person, but she has put the thoughts in my head that I'm unlovable and that hurts. I'm angry she made me feel that way."

"Have you thought about trying to contact her?"

"No."

"Why not?"

"Because seeing her isn't going to change how I feel. Only I can change that. Even if she had a good reason for giving me up, it won't change the decades of feeling worthless. This is who I am now. It's only how I see myself from now on that matters."

"Good. You're doing really well, Ellis, and it's only been a few weeks."

"I've got nothing else to do except think about stuff." *And Melissa.* "My house has never been so spotless."

"And how do you feel about not working?"

"It was hard at first, but now I'm enjoying not being so stressed out all the time. I'm even thinking about a career move."

"Really?"

"Yeah." It was something she had been toying with the last few days. She loved her job, but working all those hours by herself wasn't healthy. She had a good client base and thought about maybe working for a company again or maybe something entirely different. She didn't know yet, but change was on her mind. "Working all those hours ruined me. I'd like a normal life, maybe with a wife and kids. I can't get that if I'm always working."

"I can see the change in you. Keep it up."

"I'll try." Movement next door caught her attention. She strained her neck to see, hoping it was Melissa. Even though Melissa had messed with her head, Ellis still wanted to catch sight of her. She missed her, despite the heartache. Spotting Justin dashed her hopes. That did mean Melissa was home, but Ellis hadn't taken to complete stalking, just yet, and would refrain from going over there or peering through her patio doors.

"You're looking over the fence again."

"Justin just came out."

"Are you still going to his birthday party?"

"I doubt it. Melissa won't talk to me, and I don't have a costume."

"Justin was the one who invited you. He wants you there. Give her a text and ask if you can still come, for Justin."

Ellis sighed. "She has a date tonight."

"So?"

"So, nothing." *So, she kissed me even though she's going out with someone else. Probably using me to get her kicks, like everyone else does.*

"Ellis."

Ellis sighed again. "I'm not sure I could go to his party knowing she had just been out with someone else."

"It would give you a chance to see her."

"I thought you wanted me to let it go?"

"I do. Maybe this is the way to do it."

Ellis removed her glasses and rubbed her eyes. "I highly doubt it, but I'll see how I feel."

"Good. I'll speak to you in a few days."

"Sure. Thanks, Lucy."

"You're welcome."

Ellis signed off and quickly unplugged the router from the wall. She leaned back in her chair and closed her eyes. The sessions with Lucy were getting easier. She found them helpful, especially when she did as Lucy asked, but they were still tiring. With nothing else to do, Ellis made her way upstairs and crawled into her cold bed for a nap.

The slamming of a car door woke her sometime later. She got out of bed and made her way to the window. A car she didn't recognise was parked behind Melissa's. She moved closer to the glass, trying to see who was at Melissa's door. She caught sight of the top of a man's head. His shoulders were broad and stuffed inside a tight-fitting dinner jacket. Whoever this guy was, he looked the opposite of Ellis. He worked out, while Ellis barely left the house. A wave of jealousy rushed through her body.

A moment later, Melissa came into view. Ellis's breath caught. Melissa wore a scarlet evening dress and matching heels. Her luscious, blonde curls were twisted up on top of her head, showing the curve of her neck. Ellis's mouth went dry. *I can't believe she is wasting that on him.* Ellis had no right to be jealous, but she couldn't help it. She should be taking Melissa out, not some random bloke from work. Just as her lust was getting out of hand, Melissa tossed her head back and glanced up at Ellis. Ellis jumped back from the window, hoping Melissa hadn't seen her. She carefully edged closer again. Melissa stood by the open passenger door. Mr. Beefcake leaned over and kissed her cheek. That was enough voyeurism for Ellis. She turned away and slinked back under her duvet, her heart turning to stone.

CHAPTER TWELVE

Mark is nice. Mark is charming. Mark is...dull.

Melissa swirled her wine glass and bobbed her foot under the table, as she listened to Mark talk about the engine size of his motorbike. He had been droning on for ages now, at least it felt that way to her. Melissa swore she was now an expert in horsepower and fuel consumption. He was pleasant enough, but he just didn't get her motor running. *Pun intended.* She smiled to herself, and her thoughts drifted. *So, what if he is enthusiastic about his stupid bike, at least he's good to look at.*

But you're not into just looks.

So? That doesn't mean I can't start.

Why don't you answer the real question of why he does nothing for you?

No.

Why not?

Because if I do that, then I'll have to admit something I don't want to.

Just say the name.

No.

It's just a name.

Yes, but saying the name brings her face to mind.

You're thinking about her anyway. You haven't stopped for weeks.

I can't.

I'll do it for you then. Ellis.

Please don't.

Ellis.

Stop!

Fine. Carry on with your boring date, when you know full well it is Ellis you want sitting across from you.

I do not.

Melissa had never been very good at lying to herself, but it was hard to admit that she had strong feelings for Ellis. They had begun to germinate from the moment she met her and amplified every day since then. When Melissa took Ellis to the hospital, she thought her heart would give out. She had never been so scared, not even when Justin broke his arm when he was four. Ellis was complicated in a way Melissa wanted to figure out. *God, when she kissed me.* Her body warmed, as she recalled the event in question. Ellis had pushed and pushed her into asking for it. With her standing so close, her eyes burning through Melissa, Melissa had no choice but to give in. And boy, it had been amazing.

Then why are you here with Mark?

It was a good question. He did absolutely nothing for her. Not like Ellis.

"That's if you want."

"Huh?" Melissa focused her attention on Mark, who was grinning at her, oblivious to the fact Melissa had been thinking of someone else.

"I asked if you wanted to go for a ride with me on the bike."

"Oh, sure. Sounds great." *What are you doing?*

Marks dimples deepened, as he smiled broadly. "That's awesome. Tara said the house is all up together now."

"Pretty much. I need to remodel the bathroom and do some final changes, but it's near enough done." Talking about the house reminded Melissa of her bedroom and the unfinished walls, which led her to remember Ellis sleeping in her bed. Melissa hadn't expected to find her there, hadn't expected to watch her sleep. She'd looked so inviting. Melissa still couldn't believe she had crawled in beside her. She lay there, hands clenched, trying desperately not to reach out. When Ellis opened her eyes, Melissa felt a wave of arousal she wasn't sure she had ever felt before, not even with Craig. It scared her.

All the pushing and pulling was selfish and mean. She wasn't being fair to Ellis. *Especially as she's trying to get better. You'll end up hurting her.*

You already have.

Melissa was ashamed of the way she'd been acting. She needed to apologise to Ellis, but she didn't know if she could be in the same room and not beg her for another kiss. *And a text is the coward's way out.*

"Are you okay?" Mark asked.

Melissa put her wine glass down, amazed to find it empty again. By her count, she'd had three glasses already. "I'm fine. Why?"

"You don't seem into this."

"I'm sorry, Mark."

Mark leaned back in his chair, his blue eyes dimming. "I don't understand. You were the one who asked me out."

Yes, but I did it because I told Ellis I already had a date. "I know." She shook her head. "I thought I was ready to start dating again, but I don't think I am." That wasn't a complete lie. She did feel gun shy about starting a relationship with someone new, but with someone like Ellis, she'd make the leap.

No, she wouldn't.

Ellis was too intense, too filled with raw passion. *And a woman.* She needed to figure things out in her head, first. "I'm sorry, Mark. You're a great guy, but I'm not ready."

"So, maybe in the future?"

Damn. That was the wrong thing to say. "Maybe."

His left dimple appeared as he half smiled. "That'll do, for now. Am I still invited to the housewarming?"

"Of course. I'm going to do a barbeque now summer is here."

"If you need a grill master, I'm happy to offer my services. I'm the king of barbeques."

"I can't ask you to do that."

"It would be my pleasure. My gift to you in your new home. That way you can mingle with the guests."

Melissa knew she should say no. Taking any kind of gift from Mark would be opening the door for him to get the wrong idea. However, what he said made sense. If he did the grilling, she could concentrate on entertaining. "I'll take you up on that. Thank you."

"You're welcome. Do you want to head back? Or maybe stay for dessert?"

Melissa smiled properly for the first time that evening. Thoughts of Ellis left her, as she decided to enjoy the company of a friend without the added pressure of it being a date. She had made her feelings clear to Mark. There was no reason they couldn't end the night on a high note.

That plan was shot to shit. Mark walked her to her door forty minutes later, and she turned to say good night. He caught her unawares and kissed her square on the mouth, his five o'clock shadow stinging her lips. It was a quick kiss, but it left no doubt in Melissa's mind that he still planned to court her. She pulled back and lowered her head.

"Damn. I'm sorry, Melissa. I had such a great evening with you. I got carried away."

"It's okay."

Mark cupped her elbow. "No, it's not. I shouldn't have done that. You made your feelings quite clear." He dipped his head to catch her gaze. "I'm sorry."

Melissa smiled. "It's okay, but, maybe next time, a little warning."

"You got it." He smiled his boyish grin and bounded down the path. "I'll see you at the barbeque." Within moments, he was gone.

Melissa let out a long breath and turned to go inside. She glanced at Ellis's window. The room's glow illuminated Ellis's form behind the blinds that were swaying ever so slightly. She knew Ellis had seen the whole scene with Mark. *And I keep on hurting her.* Melissa needed to get her feelings in check and talk to Ellis. If she didn't, things between them would only get worse.

†

Melissa checked her watch one more time and glanced through the patio doors. Ellis wasn't coming. She looked at Justin, sitting on the lounge floor with his friends all around him, waiting to play Fortnite together. They had all made a great effort with their costumes, but Justin's was the winner. Not that she was biased or anything. Craig had done an amazing job making it for him. *And he's someone else who had let Justin down.* Melissa could understand Ellis not showing up, but for Craig not to come to his own son's birthday party was deplorable. Melissa sighed and made her way through the kitchen and into the lounge. She knelt by Justin. "Come on, Justin. It's time."

Justin looked up, a frown marring his features. "But Ellis isn't here yet."

"I don't think she's coming, buddy."

"But she promised."

"I know." Melissa smiled sadly, hating that he was upset on his birthday. She couldn't even blame it on Ellis. Melissa had been the one to throw the proverbial spanner in the works. If she had just kept her attraction under wraps, Justin wouldn't be sitting here now, looking crestfallen. "Perhaps something came up."

"Can you go and see?"

"I can't leave the party."

"We can keep an eye on everyone if you want to pop over for a few minutes," Melissa's dad said from his place on the sofa, which had been pushed back to allow room for the boys to play.

"Can't you just play without her?" she asked Justin.

"No. Please, Mum."

"Fine." Melissa stood and smoothed her hands over her gypsy skirt, settling it back in place. She smiled gratefully at her dad, as she passed on her way to the front door. Her custom would be to enter Ellis's from the back garden. However, now there was tension between them, she didn't think that would be right.

She made her way to Ellis's front door and knocked. Ellis answered a few moments later, wearing an oversized T-shirt and shorts. Melissa forced her eyes to focus on Ellis's face and not the long expanse of her legs. "Hi, Ellis."

"Melissa. What are you doing here?"

Melissa licked her lips. "Justin wants to know where you are."

Ellis glanced away. "You'd better come in."

Ellis stepped aside and Melissa walked in, stopping in the lounge.

"I got this for him." Ellis went to the TV stand and picked up a small, wrapped gift. She held it out for Melissa.

Melissa took the package and lightly traced her fingers over the name tag. Ellis had done a good job wrapping whatever was inside, obviously taking the time to do it neatly. "Why don't you come over and give it to him?"

"That's not a good idea." Ellis shook her head. "I'm not in the mood."

"Ellis, this isn't for me. It's for him. He wants you there."

"I noticed your date went well."

Melissa's heart sank. She hoped she had imagined seeing Ellis's shadow behind the blinds. Knowing Ellis had witnessed Mark kiss her was humiliating, especially considering it had only been a couple of days before when Melissa had begged Ellis to kiss her. "You saw?"

"Yeah. He's a good-looking *guy*."

127

"I don't want to talk about Mark." Melissa's skin burned and her whole body tensed. She had come to ask Ellis to come to Justin's party, not rehash her date with a man she had no interest in.

"No, I don't suppose you do." Ellis took a few steps closer, coming close to being in Melissa's personal space. She looked fierce, her eyes blazing. "How many other people have you kissed this week? Or is it just the two of us?"

Melissa backed up. Her eyes stung with the urge to cry. "That's not fair, Ellis." She hadn't asked Mark to kiss her. Yeah, she shouldn't have asked him out in the first place, but she had to do something to put a stop to her desire for Ellis. *I didn't have to go out with him. I could have just told Ellis I was going. This is your fault, Melissa.*

"What's not fair is you messing with my head. I had enough of that with Stacy."

"I am nothing like her!" *How can she compare me to her? I'd never hurt Ellis in that way. But I did, didn't I?*

"It seems that way to me. Wanting a friendship, then shitting on me. The only difference is, she didn't crawl into bed with me and ask me to kiss me."

Melissa looked to the floor, her hands tightening around the gift. "Ellis."

"You should go." Ellis turned her back on her. "Tell Justin I'm sorry."

Melissa nodded, although Ellis couldn't see her, and made her way back home. She took a few calming breaths before opening the door and stepping inside. She found Justin still sat with his friends. He looked up at her, hope in his young gaze. "I'm sorry, buddy. She isn't feeling well. She got you this though." She passed the present over to him and watched him tear the paper off. Ellis's hard work went to waste.

"It's the new FIFA game. This is awesome." He held it up to his friends. "Hey guys, we can play this after."

Justin powered up the Xbox and logged into the game, thoughts of Ellis's absence seemingly forgotten. Melissa went to the kitchen and poured herself some water and took a large gulp.

"Are you okay, honey?"

Melissa glanced over her shoulder and smiled at her father. "Yes, Dad. I'm fine."

"Is there anything you want to talk about?"

She kissed his cheek, grateful for his support. "No, not right now."

"Okay. Well, I'm here if you need me." He patted her arm and then retreated into the lounge.

Melissa looked over the fence at Ellis's swing and watched it silently move with the breeze. She had messed everything up. All she had wanted was to be Ellis's friend, to help her find her way back from the darkness. Melissa never thought her offer of friendship would lead to these confusing feelings swirling inside her. She was attracted to Ellis, and that scared her more than anything she had ever faced before.

The swaying swing lost her attention, when Ellis came into view. She carried a large bag of compost over one shoulder, steadying it with her hands. She dumped it at the bottom of the garden, near the swing. Ellis turned around, her gaze finding Melissa. It would be usual for Melissa to wave hello, but Ellis looked away and kept her head down as she made her way back up the garden path. A lone tear rolled down Melissa's cheek. She didn't try to wipe it away. That tear belonged on her, stinging her skin with the reminder of all the hurt she had caused Ellis.

✝

Melissa held the bin liner open, close to the table, and scooped in the detritus from the birthday party. She should have made the effort to recycle the paper plates and cups, but she wasn't in the mood. The fake smile she'd plastered on for the last three hours had drained what little energy she had. She couldn't get Ellis's sad face out of her mind. Melissa had found herself drawn to the kitchen window a lot during the party, hoping to glimpse Ellis in her garden. When she did spot her, Ellis never looked her way. It would seem their friendship, and whatever else they had going on, was over for good.

"Do I have to help?" Justin said, as he placed a stack of cups into the rubbish bag. "It's my birthday."

"Of course not." Melissa ruffled his hair. "You can go play your new game if you want." A loud thumping on the front door caused them both to jump. The voice that bellowed after scared Melissa even more.

"Justin! Happy birthday, son."

Melissa squeezed her eyes shut at hearing Craig's voice. Justin clung to her side. She gazed down at him, hating the fright she saw in his face.

"I don't want to see him."

"It's okay." Melissa hugged him tightly. "Go on upstairs. Don't come down for any reason." She pushed him toward the stairs, as Craig banged again. She nudged Justin. "It's okay. Go."

"Justin!"

130

Melissa made sure Justin was out of sight, before fitting the chain on the door and opening it a few inches. Craig's beet-red face came into view, the stench of alcohol strong. There was no way he would be getting into the house in this state; she wouldn't allow it. "What are you doing here, Craig?"

"I've come to see my son on his birthday." Craig swayed as he leaned, one hand on the door frame.

"You're three hours late and drunk."

Craig's eyes narrowed. "I want to see my son." He took a step back and looked up toward Justin's bedroom window. "Justin!"

"Go home or I'll call the police."

He focused back on Melissa. "You can't stop me seeing my son."

"No, but I can." Ellis appeared behind Craig. Her stern face belied the rapid rising and falling of her chest.

Craig turned around. "Who the fuck are you?"

"I believe she asked you to leave," Ellis said, her hands balled into fists.

"And I believe you can fuck off." He whipped around again. "Justin, come on, buddy."

"Leave." Rage honed sharp edges to Ellis's voice.

"Make me."

"I called the police a few minutes ago. They will be here any second."

Craig turned and glared at Melissa, then thumped the door. "This isn't over. He's my son." He barged past Ellis, nearly knocking her over, and stormed off down the street.

Melissa took a shuddering breath, removed the chain, and opened the door wide. Her legs were weak. She had been terrified Craig would break his way in. Not knowing what he might have done had scared her senseless. She never thought she would be so pleased to see Ellis. She wanted to hug her, but she knew that wouldn't be welcomed. "Did you really call the police?"

Ellis took a step forward and shook her head. "No. I heard him yelling and just wanted to get here as quick as I could."

"Thank you."

"You're welcome." Ellis glanced away. "Did, ah, Justin have a nice party?"

"Yes. He loved the game you got him."

"Good."

"I'd better go check on him."

"Okay." Ellis turned away to leave.

"Ellis?"

"Yeah?"

"Can you come in for a few minutes?"

Ellis shook her head. "I don't think so."

"Please. I need to talk to you."

Ellis hesitated for a few seconds but then nodded. "Okay."

"I'll just be a moment." Melissa left Ellis in the lounge, while she headed up to Justin's room. She found him huddled on his bed, knees drawn to his chest. She sat on the bed next to him and laid her hand on his thigh. "Justin? Are you okay?"

"Why does he have to ruin everything?" Justin mumbled.

"I don't know."

"I don't want to stay with him anymore."

"It's not that simple. He's required by law to have visitation with you."

"Then let him see me here."

Melissa would never do anything to put Justin in harm's way, and she knew allowing Craig to have him overnight would do just that. Craig did have legal rights, but she would fight them as best she could to stop him from destroying her son. "I'll talk to him and try to figure something out." It wasn't a conversation she relished, but she needed to find out what was going on with him for Justin's sake. "Ellis is downstairs."

"I heard."

"Do you want to thank her for your present?"

"Can I do it later? I'm not in the mood."

"Okay."

"Tell her I'm sorry."

She patted his leg. "It's okay, she'll understand. Come down when you're ready, and we'll have some more cake."

"Thanks, Mum."

Melissa made her way back downstairs. Ellis was pacing the lounge, hands still tightened into fists. Mud stains were visible on her T-shirt and knees, from the gardening she had been doing.

Ellis stopped her pacing and looked at Melissa. "Is he okay?"

"No, but he will be."

"So, that was Craig?"

"Yep. In all his glory." Melissa slumped onto the couch and rubbed her forehead. Turning eleven was a big deal. Justin had been so excited about his party. His delight had now turned to tears. Melissa would never forgive Craig for doing that to him.

"Is he like that often?" Ellis perched herself on the edge of the coffee table.

"When we were married, he did like to have a drink, but I've never seen him like that before." She couldn't imagine what was going on with him. Aside from his numerous affairs, Craig had been the perfect husband. He'd been kind and caring. When he found out Melissa was pregnant, he had been overjoyed. *How much of that was a lie? Did I ever really know him at all?*

"What do you think is going on with him?"

"I don't know. He was able to do Justin's costume for him, and 99 percent of the time, he's fine. I'm not sure what's happened recently to make him this way. Justin was so frightened when Craig banged on the door."

"What are you going to do?"

Melissa shrugged. "Talk to him. If he won't sort himself out, I'll talk to my solicitor."

"Not that it's any of my business, but you said that before."

Melissa sighed. "It's complicated, Ellis." She had spent a lot of years loving Craig. He was Justin's father. She couldn't just cut him out of their lives, and he deserved a chance to make things right.

"Sorry."

"No, I'm sorry." Melissa caught Ellis's gaze. "About everything."

Ellis took a breath and briefly closed her eyes. "What are we doing here, Melissa, because, frankly, I'm not cut out for this."

"I don't know."

Ellis pulled her top lip between her teeth before letting it go with a tut. "Have you ever kissed a woman before?"

"No."

"Had a crush on one?"

Melissa shook her head. "No."

"But you do on me?"

"I think so." Melissa looked away. This wasn't a conversation she wanted right now, but they needed it if they were ever going to move on and repair the damage between them.

"But you're not sure?"

Melissa gazed at Ellis, her heart rate picking up. She had doubts about her sexuality, but she didn't doubt her feelings for Ellis. She couldn't put a label on it, but she knew she was very much attracted to her. "No, I am sure. Yes, I do have a crush on you. But I'm not ready to unpack that yet."

Ellis nodded and cleared her throat. "So, now what?"

"Can't we just stay friends? I know that's asking a lot, but I don't want to lose you out of my life, Ellis." She didn't know how to even begin to deal with the feelings, but she did know she wanted Ellis around as much as possible. *Surely, we can be friends. That's doable, right?*

"I'll try. I have a lot going on right now, anyway. We'd only complicate things further if we tried anything more."

"I'm sorry."

Ellis's eyes darkened. The intensity made Melissa's stomach clench. She squeezed her hands between her knees to stop them from reaching out and grabbing Ellis.

"Don't be. But the next time you ask me to kiss you, I won't stop."

"I know," Melissa whispered, her pulse hammering in her chest. She could hardly cope with the first kiss, let alone the thought of a second. *And more.*

"Does that scare you?"

"More than you know."

"I'm sorry you're going through this."

Melissa shook her head. "It's not your fault, Ellis." No one was to blame in any of this. They couldn't help who they were attracted to. It was just harder for Melissa, as she had never had feelings for a woman before. *If you were a man, I'd be kissing you right now.* Melissa stopped the thought. It wasn't just Ellis's personality she was drawn to. She liked her eyes, her smooth skin, and the softness of her lips. It was *Ellis* she wanted, not a male version of her, and that's what was making this whole thing difficult. Melissa had Justin to think about, and her parents. Telling them about her feelings for Ellis was impossible. *No, best stick to being friends. Eventually, this thing will go away.* Footsteps on the stairs interrupted their intense eye contact.

"Can I have cake now?" Justin asked. "Hi Ellis."

"Hi, Justin. Happy birthday. I'm sorry I couldn't make the party."

Justin sat next to Melissa, and she put her arm around him. "It's okay," he said. "I know it's because you suck at Fortnite."

Ellis grinned. "You figured me out."

"How are your footie skills?"

"I know what a ball is." She shrugged a shoulder. "Does that count?"

"You'll need some practice then, before my next birthday. Come on up and we can play the game."

Ellis glanced at Melissa. "Is that okay?"

"Of course," Melissa replied, happy that Justin had forgiven Ellis for not coming to the party. She doubted he'd be that forgiving of Craig.

"Let's go get my butt kicked then," Ellis said, as she rose from the coffee table.

Melissa stayed seated for a few moments, her mind whirling. She hadn't been able to have a relaxing thought for weeks. All she wanted was for things to go back to normal, before she had an awareness of Ellis. *You don't really want that, do you? No, I don't.* Whatever was going to happen was going to happen, whether she liked it or not. Ellis meant too much to her to shut her out of her life. Melissa would just have to deal with whatever came up, whenever it did. *There's no turning back now.*

†

Melissa opened the front door, and her mouth fell open. Mark stood on the other side. She hadn't seen him properly since their date. They had passed in the corridors at work, but never had time to talk. To see him stood there now, holding a gift-wrapped box, threw her. "What are you doing here, Mark?"

His dimples deepened, as he grinned widely at her. "I've got a birthday gift for Justin."

You don't even know him. This is weird. And his birthday was a week ago. "Um, Thank you."

He glanced over her shoulder into the house. "Can I come in and give it to him?"

"Um, okay." She stepped back and allowed him entry, the strong smell of his aftershave choking her. He had made the effort to see her, and it turned her stomach. She should have been pleased someone went through the trouble of buying a gift for her son, but she knew he was attempting to endear himself to her. This wasn't like Ellis's gift. Ellis had bought Justin the game because she liked him and not because of her feelings for Melissa. She didn't like his duplicity, but she didn't want to cause a scene. They still had to work together. "He's in the back garden with my friend." *Ellis isn't going to like this.* They had spent several evenings with each other over the past week, getting to know each other more and repairing their tenuous friendship. Having Mark show up would surely derail their progress.

Melissa led Mark through the lounge, kitchen, and into the garden. Ellis and Justin both looked up from their positions, seated on the grass, where they were playing Top Trumps. Melissa didn't miss the flash of annoyance that zipped across Ellis's face before being replaced with an ambivalent smile.

"Uh, Justin. This is Mark, a friend from work. He has a birthday gift for you. Mark, this is my son, Justin, and my neighbour, Ellis."

Mark glanced at Ellis and dismissed her. He crouched next to Justin and held out the gift. "Nice to meet you, Justin. Here you go. Happy birthday."

Justin looked wary, but he took the gift and tore off the paper, tossing it behind him. He beamed at the box he held. "It's a drone! Awesome."

"Maybe we can take it to the park and fly it some time." Mark ruffled Justin's hair.

"Can we go now?"

"No," Melissa said. "Ellis is here."

Ellis stood and brushed off her joggers. "That's okay. I have some stuff to do in the house. I'll catch you later." She smiled quickly at Melissa and made her escape.

"Ellis." Melissa sighed and folded her arms across her waist, hating that Ellis had fled. Not that she blamed her, but Melissa had been enjoying their afternoon in the sun, just the three of them. "Justin, go inside a minute. I need to talk to Mark."

Justin frowned but did as she asked, taking the drone with him.

"Am I in trouble?" Mark smirked.

"Mark, you can't just turn up here like this and bribe my son."

For the first time since his arrival, Mark's grin faded. "I wasn't bribing him."

"You've never even met him, and now you're buying him presents? Expensive ones at that. It's odd."

"I was just trying to be nice."

"No, you were trying to win him over, so I'd spend time with you."

He shrugged, his grin coming back full force. "Is that so wrong?"

"I told you two weeks ago; I'm not ready for anything."

"I'm just being friendly."

"Mark..."

"Honestly." He reached out and grasped her shoulder. "I'm sorry if I overstepped my place. That wasn't my intention."

"Okay, but please don't do it again."

"I won't."

"Can we go now, Mum?" Justin called from the kitchen.

"Looks like I don't have a choice." She would rather not go but didn't want to disappoint Justin. She could put up with an hour or two of Mark's company, providing he kept his hands to himself and stopped with all the flirting. She purposely kept her gaze from straying over to Ellis's house

139

on her way inside. Melissa wouldn't be able to take it if she saw Ellis watching them leave. *I'll need to talk to her later and explain that Mark doesn't mean anything to me.*

CHAPTER THIRTEEN

Melissa shouldered her way through the café's door and rushed to the counter, pleased to find it near empty at two in the afternoon. She only got a forty-five-minute break and didn't want to spend most of that time waiting in line. She glanced at the menu boards above the counter, already knowing that she wanted her favourite lunch. You just couldn't beat their spicy, meatball wraps and mochas. Melissa placed her order, paid, then scanned the café looking for a good place to sit. She spotted a familiar figure hunched over by the window. She was surprised she hadn't noticed Ellis on the way in. She grabbed the wooden table number for her order and made her way over. She lightly touched Ellis's shoulder, making her jump. "It's just me."

Ellis's smile was unguarded, her eyes lighting up. "Mel, what are you doing here?"

"I'm on break from work." Melissa climbed onto the stool and put her purse down next to the salt and pepper shakers. "I forgot to bring my lunch. The cafeteria food is awful, so this is where I come to grab something."

"Are you staying to eat?"

"Yes. I'm not due back for half an hour."

"Great."

"So, how have you been?" Melissa folded her arms across the tabletop and leaned in a little closer. "I feel like I haven't seen you for weeks."

Ellis hiked an eyebrow. "It's been, like, four days."

"Feels like longer." Although they texted every day, Melissa hadn't seen Ellis since Mark showed up with the drone. Ellis had texted that night, without mentioning Mark's visit, and that was fine with Melissa. Despite her original plans on the contrary, she didn't want to talk about him. Going to the park with Mark had been so awkward. Justin had enjoyed himself, learning how to fly the drone, but Melissa couldn't, knowing Mark had planned the whole thing so he could spend time with her. She had been polite, but she made sure she didn't give him any hint of a future for them. She'd even considered cancelling the barbeque, because she didn't want him there. As much as she wanted her friends to come over and see the house, she knew that would include Mark. She just couldn't deal with him at the moment. "What have you been up to?"

"Same old stuff. I finished building the planters and have got some bulbs in them. Not sure if they'll bloom. I'm rubbish at that sort of thing, and I'm sure it's too late in the year for them to shoot. If they don't flower, then I'll see what winter seeds I can plant."

"The orchid is still alive."

"By a tiny miracle." Ellis took a sip of her tea. "Lucy has me going out more often. She said I needed to start mixing with people again."

"And that's why you're here?"

"Yep."

A server brought Melissa's order over, and she inhaled the tantalising scent of the wrap. Her stomach rumbled. *I'm going to enjoy this.* Melissa wasn't usually much of a meat-eater, but for this, she'd make the exception. She looked up at Ellis and caught her gazing at the plate. "Do you want half?"

Ellis glanced up. "No, it's yours."

"I don't mind." Ellis had made great strides in her eating habits. Her skin looked fuller and had lost its waxy pallor, but Melissa still worried. If she could watch Ellis eat something, that would make her feel better. She grabbed a napkin from the holder and covered up half the wrap and tore it apart. She passed half over to Ellis. "Go on. I don't mind."

Ellis licked her lips and took the wrap. "Thank you." She took a bite and groaned. "God, that's good."

Melissa clenched her thighs at the pure, unadulterated pleasure on Ellis's face. She knew the wraps were good, but not *that* good. She cleared her throat and took a bite, but without the sensual moaning.

"How did Justin get on with the drone?"

So much for not talking about Mark. "I'm sorry about that. I had no idea Mark was coming over."

Ellis wiped the back of her hand across her mouth. "You're entitled to have visitors."

"I know, but I could tell you weren't happy about him being there."

"He's your friend, or whatever, you don't need to explain yourself to me."

"Yes, I do." Melissa put down her half-eaten wrap and dipped her head to get better eye contact with Ellis. She needed her to know there was absolutely nothing between her and Mark. "He's a work colleague, Ellis. He'd like to be more, but he knows I don't want that."

"Does he?" Ellis looked away. "From what I could see, he was practically drooling over you."

Melissa chuckled at Ellis's assessment.

Ellis huffed and folded her arms across her chest. "It's not funny."

"I know, but you're pretty cute when you're jealous."

"I'm not jealous."

"Really?" She shouldn't be teasing Ellis, but it was nice to know Ellis still harboured feelings for her. *Not that we're going to do anything about it.*

"Okay, maybe I am a little." Ellis uncrossed her arms and laughed. Her face turned serious when she looked across the café, her face blanching. "Oh, shit."

"What is it?"

"I need to go." Ellis grabbed her backpack and began to rise.

Melissa stopped her with a hand on her arm. "Why?"

"Stacy is here."

"Where?"

Ellis glanced over the café again. "Over by the till."

Melissa looked over to the counter and blinked. "That's Stacy?"

"Yeah, why?"

"Nothing. She's just so…gorgeous." Stacy was even taller than Ellis. Her hair was cut neatly around her ears, her fringe cutting across one eye. Even from this distance, Melissa could tell she had money. Her clothes fit her body perfectly. The tailored trousers showed off impossibly long legs. Stacy laughed with the clerk, throwing her head back and displaying her long neck. When Melissa had imagined what she looked like, it was nothing like the statuesque woman across the room from them. She could easily see why Ellis had been smitten with her.

"What does that have to do with anything?" Ellis said, grabbing Melissa's attention. "Look, Mel, I need to leave before she sees me." Just at that moment, Stacy turned and spotted them. "Too late."

Stacy's hand went to her mouth, and she made her way over. "Oh my God, Ellis!"

Ellis looked to the wooden floor, her shoulders slumping. "Hello, Stacy."

"How have you been?"

Melissa didn't like the way Ellis appeared to go in on herself. The imposing dark figure was replaced with someone small and scared. This was the Ellis Melissa had first met. She didn't like it. Not one bit. "You don't get to talk to her."

Stacy glanced at Melissa. "Excuse me?"

"You heard me. Leave, before I lamp you one." Melissa was never quick to anger. Her role as a nurse taught her compassion and patience. However, seeing Stacy have this effect on Ellis had her rage boiling.

Stacy smirked and turned her attention to Ellis. "Who's the pit bull?"

"Your worst nightmare if you don't leave now," Melissa ground out. She wasn't much of a fighter, but she would kick Stacy's ass if she didn't go.

"You sure can pick 'em, can't you?"

"Why did you do it?" Ellis asked. "Were we ever friends?"

Stacy took a breath, her gaze softening ever so slightly. "I didn't think it would go that far. I needed you out of the way, and it got out of hand."

"Out of the way of what? You had me arrested so you could take my job?"

"It wasn't like that. I made the complaint to the bosses, hoping they'd fire you. I never thought they'd go to the police."

"You could have told them the truth."

"But then I would have lost my job and been arrested myself."

"You bitch!" Melissa jumped off the stool and advanced on Stacy. It was one thing to make a complaint when you thought it had merit, but to do it just so you could steal a job was repulsive. Ellis's hands on her waist stopped her forward motion.

"Melissa, no. She isn't worth it."

Melissa turned around and glared at Ellis. "She ruined your life, Ellis. Dragged your name through the mud." She shook her head. "You lost everything because of her."

Ellis smiled. "It doesn't matter."

"It does."

"No, it doesn't. Not anymore." She lowered her head, her gaze soft but intense. "You know the truth, that's all that matters."

"How sweet." Stacy's voice bristled with sarcasm.

Ellis looked over Melissa's head. "You'd better go, before I release her and she rips your hair out."

Stacy flipped her hair and stormed out. Melissa scowled at the few patrons who were watching them and returned to her stool. Her heart was racing, her body filled with tension. She was all set to have her first ever fight. That it was over Ellis didn't surprise her. She'd do anything to protect her. That should have shocked Melissa, but it didn't. It was further proof of her growing attraction. It was time to deal with those feelings, as uncomfortable as they were.

"I can't believe I never noticed what she was like," Ellis said, a weary tone to her voice.

Melissa took Ellis's hand. "I'm so sorry, Ellis."

"It's okay. I'm fine. At least I know I never did anything wrong. I can start to rebuild my life properly, without that hanging over my head." Ellis grinned. "Thank you for sticking up for me."

"Always." Melissa squeezed Ellis's hand, then pulled away.

"I'm not sure you'd have much of a chance kicking her ass, considering your two-foot height disadvantage."

"Hey, I'm not that short."

"Okay." Ellis grinned wider.

"Brat." Melissa balled up a napkin and tossed it at her, pleased the drama with Stacy was over.

"I like you short." Ellis shrugged. "It's cute."

"That's good, because I still haven't painted the top of my bedroom wall. Feel free to finish it for me." That was the only thing left to complete in the house. She'd reached the other walls in the house by standing her steps on top of the lounge coffee table. It wasn't the smartest, or safest way to do it, but it got the job done. She wasn't sure why she hadn't completed the bedroom. *Maybe because I hoped to have Ellis in there again.*

"You still haven't got the ladder from your dad?"

"I keep forgetting, and besides, why use a ladder when I have my very own giraffe."

Ellis laughed. "Very true."

†

"Mel? What are you doing here?" Craig leaned against the doorframe. A week's worth of stubble marred his face beneath bloodshot eyes.

Melissa glowered at Craig. It was three in the afternoon, and it looked like he'd just gotten out of bed. "We need to talk about Justin."

"Is he okay?"

"No. You ruined his birthday."

Craig rubbed his chin, eyes narrowing. "I don't remember."

"You don't remember turning up at my door, banging and yelling? Scaring me and Justin?"

"No."

He stepped back from the door and retreated inside. Melissa followed. The smell was the first thing to hit her; stale cigarettes and dirty socks. Pizza boxes and chip wrappers littered the floor. She couldn't believe what she was seeing. Craig sat on the armchair, head in his hands.

"What's going on, Craig? What's happened to you?"

Eyes moist with unshed tears lifted toward her. "I don't know. Things just got out of hand, when you found out about the affairs… I'm so sorry, Mel. I never wanted to hurt you."

Melissa's heart went out to him, but she stopped herself from offering comfort. He had done this to himself. She would help him if he wanted it, but she wouldn't forgive

148

him for hurting their son. She couldn't believe she had ever allowed Justin to stay with Craig. Had she known the situation, she never would have let him set one foot inside.

"After the divorce," he continued, "things spiralled. I began to drink more, and I hated myself for what I did to you. And to Justin."

"You can't keep doing this, Craig. You need help. Justin doesn't want to see you. Is that what you want?"

Anger flashed across his face. "Of course not. But I don't know how to stop."

Not wanting to ruin her clothes by sitting on the furniture, Melissa crouched beside him. "We can get you help. If you want to get better, I'll be here for you. However, it's not fair to Justin to see you like this. You can come to the house, but you must be sober. I won't let you hurt him again."

Craig gazed at her the same way he used to when they were married. "You're a great woman, Melissa. Thank you."

He shot forward and kissed her awkwardly on the side of her mouth. She pushed him off, falling to the carpet as she did so. She climbed to her feet, her hands sticky from whatever had spilled on the carpet. She was appalled at his behaviour, stunned he thought kissing her was a good idea. "Don't you dare do that again."

Tears fell freely down his face. "I'm a fuck-up. If I were you, I'd keep Justin far away from me."

Melissa couldn't agree more, but she wouldn't let him wimp out on their son. She pointed her finger at him. "You *are* a fuck-up, but you need to sort your shit out. Call me when you want help. Until then, keep away from us." She didn't wait for him to reply. Melissa fled the apartment, wiping her mouth vigorously with the back of her hand as she did so. There was a time his kisses would have turned her into a puddle of molten arousal. Now, his kiss made her nauseous. She wished she could blame his actions on him being drunk, but, as far as she could tell, he was sober. There was nothing left of the man she'd married. She had wondered if she had made the right decision in getting divorced from him, wanting desperately not to have a failed marriage. Melissa had no more doubts. She and Craig were over for good. *And that's just as well, because now there's Ellis.* Melissa hadn't spent too much time trying to figure out what to do about her feelings. She was attracted to Ellis, that she knew. But she didn't know if she wanted to pursue those feelings. Getting into a same-sex relationship had never been on the cards for her. This deck before her had nothing but Ellis's face on every card. She was scared, and not just of being with a woman for the first time. She didn't want to get her heart broken again. Melissa trusted Ellis completely, but she was nowhere near ready to open herself up to misery if it all went wrong.

CHAPTER FOURTEEN

Ellis flinched, as another flash of lightning lit up the sky. The storm had been battering the area for an hour. A few scattered drops of rain had turned into a raging torrent. Storms in the summertime were rare, but the last few days had been particularly humid. The storm was almost a given. A roll of thunder sounded. The gap between the lightning and the rumble was closing in. Ellis focused back onto her computer.

"I must say, Ellis, you've come a long way in a few short weeks," Lucy said.

"Well, once work was out of the way, I didn't have much else to do." There were only so many times she could clean the bathroom. Having the time to think about things had worked wonders. She also found she was gaining interest in other things, like gardening. The day after watching a show about growing vegetables, she'd gone out and bought

151

the wood to make planters and set about sowing some seeds and planting flower bulbs. She wasn't optimistic about growing a good crop, but it gave her something to do. She hoped the heavy rain wouldn't ruin her first try at growing things. "It helped to see Stacy again. When I initially saw her, I thought it would set me back. Now that I know why she lied, I can put it behind me. I know I did nothing wrong." Ellis had spent so many nights replaying all their interactions, trying to figure out if she had done something untoward to make Stacy uncomfortable. Knowing that Stacy had made it all up to steal her job lifted the boulder from her chest. She wasn't happy about the grief it had caused her, but she was ready to let it all go. She had the rest of her life to get on with. "You have no idea how that makes me feel."

Lucy smiled. "I imagine it's very freeing."

"Yeah, it is. I was so worried I had done something without realising, that it scared me off people for years. It's such a relief, now it's over."

"Yes, now you can get on with your healing."

The lightning flashed again, the rumble not far behind. "Bloody thunderstorm. I can't believe it's like this in the middle of summer."

"It'll clear the air, get rid of some of this sweltering heat. How are things with Melissa?"

Ellis raised her brows, not expecting that question. They hadn't spoken about Melissa at all in their last few appointments. It threw her for a second. "It's okay."

"Just okay?"

"She told me she likes me." Ellis recalled the moment in her mind. She had been so angry with Melissa. Watching her go out on her date after they had kissed was like a stab in the heart. She knew Melissa had a lot to deal with. Having feelings for a woman had probably terrified her. But to go out with someone else, just because she couldn't deal with those feelings, hurt Ellis. That's why Ellis hadn't gone to Justin's party. She had been too frustrated and upset. When Craig showed up, Ellis didn't care about her own feelings anymore. She needed to get to Melissa before he did something to hurt her. Their conversation after had been tense but worth it. Melissa finally confessed her feelings out loud. Ellis should have been happy, but she knew Melissa had a long way to go before she ever acted on them. If she ever did.

"But?"

"But she isn't ready for anything to happen. It's a lot for her to deal with."

"Ellis, it sounds like she has a lot to figure out. Are you sure you want to get messed up in—" Lightning flashed above and the computer went off, along with the lights.

"Lucy? God damn power cut." Ellis stood and found her way into the kitchen. She rummaged through her junk cupboard and found a bag of tealights. She opened the drawer and grabbed the matches. She was about to start setting them out, when her mobile rang from the lounge. She retrieved it and saw Melissa's name flashing on the screen. "Hello?"

"Has your power gone out?" Melissa's voice sounded flustered.

"Yes."

"Mine too. Are you busy?"

"I was in the middle of an appointment with Lucy, but the computer went out."

"Oh."

Ellis put down the candles and gave her full attention to Melissa. "Are you okay?"

"Would you mind coming over? I hate to ask, but I loathe thunderstorms. So does Justin. Together we're in a right state."

"Um, okay, sure. I'll be there in second." She glanced at the bag of tealights. "Do you have candles?"

"No."

"I'll bring some. Anything else you need?"

"Just you."

Ellis smiled and hung up. She put the phone into her pocket and picked up the candles. She didn't stop to grab a coat. She rushed through the conservatory, into the garden, and then up to Melissa's patio doors. Melissa was waiting on the other side, Justin next to her. "Hey."

"Oh, my God. You're soaked." Melissa grabbed her hand and pulled her through the entryway. "I'm so sorry. Justin, get me a towel." Justin dashed off. Melissa patted down Ellis's bare arms, as if her hands were a towel. "I'm sorry, Ellis. You'll catch your death."

"It's just a little water. Don't worry." Ellis herself hadn't even noticed the rain. She was too desperate to get next door. Seeing Melissa's terrified face made her hasty decision to leave without a jacket worthwhile. All Ellis wanted to do was be there for her and make sure she was okay.

"Here you go, Ellis." Justin held a towel out toward her.

Melissa took it from him. "Thanks." She started to run the towel over Ellis's face and hair.

Ellis passed the candles to Justin.

"Go place them around the lounge and light them carefully." Melissa's gaze did not leave Ellis's face.

Although it was hard to see in the near pitch black of the kitchen, Ellis could still make out the intensity in her eyes. A low roll thrummed through her stomach. "You don't need to dry me, Mel," she said, her voice sounding raspy.

"I want to."

"Okay." Ellis didn't move, as Melissa continued to rub the towel all over her. She imagined Melissa doing this to her after they had showered together, both naked. It was a dream she'd thought would never be possible. Staring at Melissa now, Ellis thought the dream might have a chance at becoming a reality.

"Thank you for coming over," Melissa whispered.

"You're welcome."

Lightning flashed twice, the thunder a split second later. The storm was directly above them now. Melissa jumped at the sound.

"It's okay, we're fine."

"I've never liked thunderstorms."

"I love them."

Melissa's face slowly became illuminated from the dozens of candles Justin had lit in the lounge, their glow reaching them in the kitchen. "Good job you're here to protect us then."

"Always."

Melissa smiled and tossed the towel onto the counter. Justin reappeared and handed the matches back to Ellis.

"What do we do now?" he asked.

"How about we tell ghosts stories?" Ellis laughed at the mortified look Melissa gave her. Obviously, Melissa wasn't into horror.

Melissa shook her head. "How about no."

"We could play Trivial Pursuit?" Justin suggested.

"As long as I get to read the questions." Ellis wasn't in the mood to get her ass kicked. No matter what game they played, he always won.

Melissa chuckled. She took Ellis's hand and led her into the lounge, while Justin went to get the game. "You'll still lose."

"Probably." Ellis sat on the floor and pulled her shirt away from her chest. She was still damp but didn't care. She would soon dry off. Melissa sat next to her and put her hand on Ellis's knee. Ellis didn't acknowledge the move. It was clear the storm terrified Melissa, and she needed to have contact with Ellis for comfort. Soon, the game was under way.

†

Ellis gazed at the candles on the fireplace, watching the tiny flames swaying back and forth. Melissa was upstairs, saying goodnight to Justin. And for Justin, it *was* a good night. He'd beaten Ellis again, and she was miffed. She'd thought for sure there was no way he'd win this time. He was a smart kid, and Ellis liked him a lot. Lost in her musings, she didn't notice Melissa had rejoined her until she plonked herself down next to her.

"I swear he's cheating." Ellis pouted much like she had the first time they played a game.

Melissa rolled her eyes. "Stop grumbling. He's just really clever."

"Does he get that from you?"

"Hardly. I'm not sure it's from Craig either. Probably my dad. He's the smartest person I know."

"Have you spoken to Craig yet?"

"Yep."

"And?"

Melissa sighed. "He's a mess. I offered to help him get sober and he kissed me."

"You seem to have a lot of people kissing you these days." Ellis shut down the jealousy before it could grab hold of her. From the look on Melissa's face, she hadn't been happy about Craig's kiss. Ellis inched a little closer, her gaze dipping to Melissa's lips and hating that two other people had kissed her recently. She wanted to be the only one doing that. "Must be because you're so desirable."

"You're not mad?"

Ellis shrugged a shoulder. "I'm not happy if he made you uncomfortable or hurt you. But I also recognise he's in a dark place. He was probably reaching out for comfort."

"Is that what you were doing?"

Ellis shook her head. "No." Ellis once again glanced at Melissa's lips. She wanted to move closer and press into her, to feel Melissa writhing beneath her. "I kissed you because I had to know what you tasted like, how you would feel in my arms."

"Ellis…"

"You asked."

Melissa cupped Ellis's cheek and rubbed her thumb gently back and forth. "You're very hard to resist."

"But?"

"Resist, I must." Her hand fell away. "I'm not sure…"

"Stop." Ellis moved back to give Melissa her space. She wasn't going to push her into doing something she would regret. She wouldn't cross that boundary, because Melissa meant too much to her. "We don't need to talk about this. I know where I stand."

"I don't think you do." Melissa took Ellis's hand, her gaze strong. "Never before in my life, have I wanted to know somebody as much as I do you. You do things to me, Ellis, things I've never felt before. Things I never thought were possible. When I look into your eyes, I get lost. All I want to do is lie with you, with your arms around me, and feel loved by you."

Ellis licked her lips. "You're making this incredibly hard for me, Melissa."

"I know. I'm sorry."

"Don't be. You're worth the wait. I'll be here whenever you're ready."

"What if I never am? That isn't fair on you."

"Don't worry about that for now. Let's just enjoy being together, learning more about each other."

A clap of thunder boomed in the distance. Melissa recoiled at the sound.

"It's okay. Come here." Ellis held her arms open.

Melissa shook her head. "I don't think that's a good idea."

"I'll behave." Ellis grinned.

"I know, but I'm not sure I will."

Despite her words, Melissa moved into Ellis's outstretched arms. Ellis circled Melissa's shoulder and pulled her tight against her side. Melissa curled up, bringing her legs onto the sofa and settling her head on Ellis's chest. Ellis inhaled deeply, smelling Melissa's shampoo. It felt good to have her arms around her. She'd never thought that would be possible. Aside from believing Melissa would never be interested, Ellis had never expected to emerge from her self-imposed isolation a stronger and more confident person. She had Melissa to thank for that. Meeting her had started the thawing of her heart and paved the way for her to start living again.

They stayed huddled together for a long while, no words spoken. Ellis sensed Melissa had drifted off, but the feel of Melissa's fingers gently tracing over her thigh stopped that thought.

"It sounds like it's slowing down," Ellis murmured, as she listened to the rain tapering off.

"Yes."

"I should probably head home."

"Will you stay?" Melissa lifted her head and stared at Ellis. "I'm not offering anything. I would just really like it if you stayed with me tonight."

Ellis swallowed hard, knowing she should say no. The flickering candles gave the night a romantic feel. The dim light had lowered their walls, and Ellis knew that climbing into bed with Melissa would be a bad idea come morning. However, she couldn't say no. Her throat refused to make the sound. She nodded. "Okay."

Melissa smiled shyly and stood. She took Ellis's hand and led her upstairs.

†

Ellis stood awkwardly at the threshold to Melissa's bedroom, hands stuffed into her pockets, her gaze fixed to the far wall. Melissa divested the bed of the throw pillows and tossed them onto the floor. Ellis glanced at her. Melissa's hair obscured her face, so Ellis couldn't read what she was thinking. Her own chest hurt where her heart pounded incessantly. She felt she would pass out from the stress. Many a night she had thought about sharing a bed with Melissa, replaying the last time she had woken up to find Melissa inches from her face. She never dreamed it would happen again. Yet, here she was, about to lie down in Melissa's bed.

"I don't have anything that will fit you," Melissa said.

Ellis cleared her thoughts and focused on Melissa, who was standing at the foot of the bed, her fingers fiddling with each other. *Seems I'm not the only one who's nervous.* "That's okay. This is fine." She always slept naked at home, but somehow, she didn't think Melissa would like that suggestion.

"Okay. I'm just going to pop to the bathroom."

Ellis stepped to the side to allow her to pass, then turned her attention to the bed. She took a breath and walked forward. She pulled back the cover, sat on the edge of the mattress, and pulled off her socks. She swung her legs up and placed the duvet over her lower half. She kept her gaze locked on the doorway, waiting for Melissa.

A minute later, Melissa came into view. Her face looked freshly scrubbed, and she now wore sleep shorts and a singlet. "The bathroom is free."

"I'm fine." Ellis smiled and held her hand out. "Come on."

Melissa nodded and switched off the light. A moment later, she joined Ellis in bed. "Good night, Ellis."

"Good night." Ellis shifted down the mattress and rolled onto her side, facing Melissa. "Sleep well."

"Thank you for this."

"Whatever you need." In the dim light, Ellis saw Melissa's gaze drop to her lips. She knew what Melissa wanted, but Ellis held back. If Melissa wanted to kiss her, she would have to make the first move. Ellis wasn't going to do it this time. She needed Melissa to be one hundred percent certain. She wouldn't push her into it. Not that it was easy for Ellis. She was desperate to feel Melissa's lips again. "Are you okay?"

Melissa continued to stare, but her hand reached out and cupped Ellis's shoulder. "I don't know what I'm doing."

"We're sleeping." Ellis wanted to roll over but Melissa's grip stopped her from moving. "Mel..."

"You're an incredibly special person, Ellis. I never thought I'd have these kinds of feelings again."

Melissa shifted closer. Ellis caught the whiff of toothpaste and soap. She was about to reply, when Melissa surged forward and pressed her lips against Ellis's. Melissa rolled Ellis back and draped her body across her, their mouths staying in contact. Ellis held onto Melissa's waist, as their tongues continued to dance together. Melissa slipped her hands into Ellis's hair and held her head in place. As Melissa began to writhe, Ellis felt herself grow wet. She hadn't been with anyone in years, and her libido was screaming at her. If she wasn't careful, she'd climax before they even did anything.

Melissa lifted her mouth away. She sat up and straddled Ellis's pelvis. Her movements became frantic, her hips grinding in all directions. Her eyes were closed, her teeth biting down on her lower lip.

"Melissa." Ellis cupped her face, wanting to see her eyes. Melissa didn't acknowledge her. She continued to grind. "Mel, look at me." Ellis wanted to make sure Melissa was present with her and not just using her to quash her arousal. Ellis's excitement shut down the second Melissa opened her eyes and looked at Ellis. Melissa's movements stopped. Her hand went to her mouth, and she gazed around the room as if seeing it for the first time. Things had gotten out of hand, and this was obviously too much for Melissa to deal with. She scuttled to the side and off the bed, her breathing laboured. "Mel—"

"I'm sorry. It's too much. You need to go."

Ellis looked away, a sharp pain stinging in her chest. *This must be what heartbreak feels like.* She climbed from the bed and picked up her socks, her face burning hot. They had crossed the line. Melissa needed to decide what it was she wanted, because Ellis knew their platonic friendship was over. If Melissa didn't want a relationship with her, they would no longer be friends. It would be too much for Ellis. "I'm sorry, Melissa."

"Not your fault." Tears gathered in the corners of Melissa's eyes.

Ellis took a step toward her, wanting to hug her, or *something*, but Melissa turned her back on her. Ellis sighed. "See you around." With as much dignity as she could muster, Ellis walked away.

CHAPTER FIFTEEN

Ellis had been in a cleaning frenzy for the last three days. She hadn't heard from Melissa, and she was too embarrassed to seek her out. She wouldn't go harassing her, begging her for a relationship. She wasn't happy about waiting for Melissa to figure things out, but if they ever had a chance at making things work, Melissa would have to be the one to make the first move.

She finished wiping down the last windowpane in the lounge window and tossed the tea towel over her shoulder. It had taken her two hours, but all the windows in the house were now spotless. A familiar car pulled up outside Melissa's. Ellis's stomach sank, when Mark appeared from the driver's side. *I guess that settles that then.* He rushed around the front of the car and opened the passenger door. He held his hand out and helped Melissa from the car. Melissa kept her head down, as Mark led her to her front door. *Something isn't right.* Ellis squinted her eyes as she studied Melissa's gait. *She's got a limp and looks stiff.* Mark wrapped his arm around Melissa's waist, but to Ellis, it didn't appear to be the way a lover would. It was almost like he was supporting her, keeping her upright. Ellis's heart rate picked up. Now her initial jealousy had passed, she noticed Melissa had her nurse's tunic on. Melissa unlocked her door and shook her head at whatever Mark had just asked. She went inside and Mark retreated to his car. Within a moment, he was gone.

Ellis flung the tea towel down and began to pace, her mind whirling. Something bad had happened to Melissa. Her gut told her to go and check on her, but Melissa had sent Mark away. *She probably wants to be on her own. Then again, Melissa wasn't on the verge of coming on him three nights ago.* Melissa was Ellis's friend, despite their current situation. Ellis should be there for her. At the very least, she should check she was all right.

With the decision made, Ellis slipped on her trainers and rushed out the conservatory door. As she went up Melissa's garden path, she saw Melissa sat at the kitchen table, head in hands, and a glass of red wine in front of her. Ellis stared at her for a moment, then gently tapped on the glass. Melissa jumped and looked her way. Tears were on her cheeks, one of which looked swollen.

"Mel? What's happened." Ellis said, through the glass. Melissa stood and slowly made her way to the door. She unlatched it and slid the door open. Now Melissa was in front of Ellis, it was clear someone had slapped her. Ellis could see the imprint of fingers on her skin. "Are you okay?"

Melissa lowered her head and covered her mouth with her hand. Her shoulders shook as she wept. Ellis stepped forward and took her in her arms. She cradled her against her chest but made sure not to hold on too tightly, fearing there were other bruises on Melissa's body she couldn't see.

"I'm sorry," Melissa said in between gasps.

"It's okay. Come with me." Keeping her arm around Melissa, Ellis led her to the sofa. They settled together, Melissa with her head on Ellis's shoulder and Ellis wrapping her arms around her. Ellis kissed the top of Melissa's head. "Can you tell me what happened?"

"There was an accident at work."

Accident? Your face doesn't look like an accident. Someone hit you. Ellis tried to stay calm. "What kind of accident?"

"A young girl was brought into the emergency room. She'd slipped and fallen into the family pool. Her dad came with her in the ambulance. He wasn't allowed to go into the treatment room with her, as the doctors and nurses were trying to revive her. He was getting more irate by the second. My colleague tried to calm him down, but he rushed past her. It was my fault really. I was too distracted thinking about something else, and I didn't see him coming. He flew into me and knocked me over. I went to grab his arm to stop him from entering the room, but he swung and caught my face."

Ellis's jaw repeatedly clenched, as she tried to hold in her anger. *Some asshole thought it would be okay to attack you when you were trying to save his daughter?* She wanted to fly down to the hospital, find him, and beat ten bells of shit out of him.

"You've tensed up." Melissa shifted away from Ellis and gazed at her. "What's the matter?"

"He hit you." Ellis's jaw clenched once again. Her free hand balled into a fist. "How dare he do that to you?"

Melissa shook her head. "He didn't mean to. He was just desperate to see his little girl."

"That's not the point." Ellis turned steely eyes onto Melissa. "He hurt you."

"I'm fine, Ellis. A little shook up, and a bit sore, but I'm okay." Melissa cupped her jaw. "You don't need to worry."

"I always worry about you. I lo..." Ellis looked away and bit her lip. *I was going to tell her I love her. What's wrong with me? She doesn't need to hear that.* As true as it was, Ellis knew Melissa didn't feel the same, at least not yet. Telling her now would be dumb. Melissa raised her brows and blinked steadily a few times. Any idiot would know what Ellis nearly said. Ellis chided herself, waiting for Melissa to ask her to leave, again.

Melissa gave a small smile, put her head back on Ellis's shoulder, and her hand on her thigh. Ellis let out a breath and held her tighter. There was no doubt in Ellis's mind that Melissa knew how she felt about her. It should have scared her, but it didn't. Melissa hadn't recoiled from her. Ellis took that as a good sign.

They must have drifted off to sleep. The next thing Ellis knew, someone was knocking on the door. Melissa moved out of her arms and gingerly rose from the couch. Ellis stood also and stretched out her body, while Melissa went to the door.

"Oh, my God," the newcomer said. "Are you okay?"

A woman Ellis had never met before followed Melissa back into the lounge. She was roughly the same height as Ellis. Auburn hair flowed around the woman's shoulders. Her skin was creamy white and blemish free. In a word, she was stunning.

166

"I'm fine," Melissa said, quickly glancing at Ellis.

"Mark called and said you were attacked."

"Hardly an attack. Just an accident."

The woman finally noticed Ellis in the room. Her gaze narrowed, and she folded her arms across her chest. "Hello."

"Hi," Ellis said.

"Ellis, this is my best friend, Tara." Melissa looked back at Tara. "Ellis is my neighbour."

Neighbour? Well, that stung. I don't expect you to announce the things we've been doing, but you could at least call me your friend. "I just came to check up on Melissa. I'll get going now."

"You don't have to leave," Melissa said, her eyes pleading.

Ellis waved her off. "You're in good hands." She nodded a farewell to Tara and made her way to the patio doors.

"I don't want you to go."

Ellis turned around to find Melissa behind her. Ellis glanced over Melissa's shoulder at Tara, who was watching them with interest. "Your friend is here now; she'll look after you. I'm glad you're not hurt too badly." She briefly touched the back of Melissa's hand. "That would have killed me."

"Ellis."

Ellis flicked her head in the direction of Tara. "Go. She's waiting for you. Call me tomorrow, and let me know how you are." Without waiting for Melissa to respond, she slid the patio door open and stepped through. She was being a coward. There was no reason they all couldn't sit in the lounge and talk, but Ellis would have found it excruciating. All she wanted to do was take Melissa in her arms again. She knew that wasn't something Melissa would be able to explain to Tara. *No, best I leave and let Tara look after her. After all, I'm just the neighbour.* She knew she was being unfair to Melissa; she was still in shock, after all, but being introduced as if she was a nobody hurt more than she'd thought possible. Until Melissa was ready to admit the way she felt about Ellis, Ellis would always be on the sidelines.

†

"Well, that was strange."

Melissa blew out a breath and carefully sat in the armchair. Her side hurt more than she cared to admit, and her cheek still burned where the back of his hand had caught her. Huddling with Ellis had helped lessen the pain. Now Ellis was gone, all the discomfort came flooding back. She looked over at Tara, who gazed at her suspiciously. "What?"

"Your neighbour, she was acting weird. And I must say, you're not exactly being normal."

"I don't know what you mean. She was just concerned about me."

"Mel, you practically begged her to stay. What's going on?"

"I thought you came here to see how I was, not question me about my friends."

Tara hiked a brow, her lips pursing. "Now I know something is going on."

Melissa sighed and looked away. She didn't want to talk about Ellis. She had no idea what she would say. *I was on the verge of coming on her the other night. Her kisses turn my whole body to jelly. I want to touch her in places that I've only touched on myself.* None of those options were wise. She could barely explain to herself how she felt about

168

Ellis, how could she tell Tara? But it would be good to talk to someone. *There's no one I trust more than Tara.* Melissa closed her eyes for a moment, psyching herself up. There was no going back now. She opened her eyes and stared at Tara, hoping she wasn't about to make a mistake.

"Ellis and I have grown close since I moved in."

Tara gave her a long look. "How close?"

Melissa licked her lips. "Very." She stood and paced a small circle, her body filled with restless energy. She was about to come out to her best friend, even though she still wasn't sure who she was. All she did know was that she wanted to be with Ellis. She stopped and faced Tara. "We've kissed a couple of times. And she stayed with me the night of the storm, we nearly slept together."

Tara's jaw dropped open and her eyelids fluttered, as she absorbed Melissa's confession.

"Say something."

"I don't understand." Tara shook her head. "Are you telling me you're a lesbian?"

"I don't know."

"What do you mean you don't know?"

Melissa sat back in the armchair. "I don't *know*." She gazed at Tara, pleading with her to understand. "I've never been attracted to a woman before."

"But you are to Ellis?"

"Yes. Like crazy. She does things to me, Tara."

"I don't know what to say."

"You don't hate me, do you?"

"Of course not. I'm just shocked."

"Me too."

Tara stood and made her way to the armchair. She perched on the armrest and laid her arm along the back of Melissa's shoulders. "What are you going to do?"

Melissa shook her head. "I don't know."

"Do you want a relationship with her?"

"I don't know."

"Mel…"

"I know, I know. There are a lot of things to consider. I must think of Justin and my parents. And Craig and work. It's not as simple as it would be with a man."

"That's true, but, Melissa, at the end of the day, it's your happiness that matters. And, of course, Justin's. If she makes you happy, that's all you should be worried about."

Is it really that simple? Should I just do what makes me happy? Melissa wasn't so sure she'd be able to do that. She liked Ellis, a lot, and it was clear Ellis loved her, but was that enough to risk her family and career over? She didn't know. She recalled the night of the storm, kissing Ellis and grinding against her. She'd gotten so worked up. Ellis would have only had to touch her bare skin gently, and it would have set Melissa off. She had never been so primed and ready, not even in the early days of dating Craig. *Ellis is the only one to turn me on like that. I can still feel what she does to me. I don't want to let that go.* Melissa knew she had a long way to go before she was fully comfortable telling people about Ellis, but that didn't mean they couldn't date.

"You're daydreaming," Tara said.

"Sorry. You're right, I should take the chance." Melissa looked up at Tara and smiled. "Thank you for not freaking out."

"Oh, I am freaking out, but on the inside." Tara chuckled. "Now I know why you weren't interested in

170

Mark." She squeezed Melissa's shoulder. "I hope it works out for you."

"Thank you."

"Now, what happened at the hospital?"

Melissa spent the next few minutes detailing the incident, how Mark insisted he take her home, and the relief she felt when she saw Ellis standing at the door. She had been able to keep her emotions inside the whole time leading up to that point. Once she saw Ellis outside her door, the dam had broken and all she wanted to do at that moment was to have Ellis's arms around her. Ellis hadn't disappointed. *She never has.* Curling up with her on the sofa was everything Melissa needed at that point, and she wanted to do it again, and again, and again. She was falling in love with her, and she found she wasn't nearly as scared as she had been. *Now, I just need to tell Ellis.*

CHAPTER SIXTEEN

Melissa climbed into the passenger side of her dad's old Austin 1100. It was a pile of rust and falling apart, but it was the car he'd had when he met her mum. He spent hours tinkering with it and making sure it was roadworthy. So far, it hadn't completely disintegrated. Melissa understood his sentimentality. It was sweet that he wanted a reminder of the time they fell in love, but it should have been parked up years ago. Not that she was complaining. She needed to get her car from the hospital, and the Austin would do the job nicely, even if the ride was a little hair raising.

She slammed the door, praying the wing mirror wouldn't fall off, and reached for the seatbelt. The move caused her shoulder to throb, and she grimaced from the pain. "Thanks, Dad," she said, as she plugged in the belt.

"Are you sure you're okay?"

Melissa glanced up, noting the concern in his eyes. "Yes. I'm a little stiff, but I feel fine." She wouldn't tell him that her jaw ached when she chewed, or that her torso felt like it had gone ten rounds with Tyson. As the morning wore on, she'd loosened up some, but she knew it would be a few more days before she was back to normal. The guy hadn't hit her that hard, but it was enough to knock her off balance, slamming her back into the swing door and crumpling her to the floor. Being so petite hadn't helped either. A strong gust of wind could blow her over. She'd had no hope of staying on her feet when he ploughed her down.

"That place needs better security," Christopher said, as he pulled away from her house. "You lot work your butts off. You all deserve to be protected whilst working."

"I know, but it was an accident." Melissa bit her lip, as the car bumped over a large pothole. She was surprised the wheels stayed on.

"Hmm, I'm not so sure about that, but I'll take your word for it."

"Are you sure you don't mind having Justin the extra night?"

"Of course not. We love having him over. Your mother and I have missed him since you've moved."

"You see him three times a week. And more in the school holidays."

"Yes, but it's not the same." He glanced at her. "Have you heard from Craig at all?"

"Not yet." Melissa had a long chat with her mother about the way she'd found Craig and the state of his home. Patricia hadn't been impressed and took great delight in informing Melissa that she knew all along he was a waste of space. Melissa didn't agree. Sure, he'd cheated on her relentlessly, but he'd been a good father and provided for her and Justin. They'd had their share of happy times, and Melissa would never regret marrying him. She hoped with all her heart he would find the courage to sort himself out and be the father to Justin he used to be. "I texted him a couple of times, but he didn't reply. I assume he's still drinking."

"Justin talked about him last night. He said he still doesn't want to see him."

"Can't say I blame him. He looked terrified when Craig turned up on his birthday." Just thinking about that evening brought her out in chills. God only knew what he would have done if Ellis hadn't turned up.

"I know you're worried about taking up all our time babysitting, but honestly, we love having him. He's a great kid, always polite and very funny."

"I wish he was always that way with me."

"Children are like that with their parents. They like to push their boundaries. I remember when you snuck out of the house in the middle of the night to go play with the neighbour's cat."

"I was six." Melissa chuckled, remembering the incident in question. Fluffles the cat was huge. His fur was long and soft and the colour of slate. Melissa had been obsessed with him. She visited Mrs. Murphy, her neighbour, every chance she could get. Mrs. Murphy would tell stories, while Melissa stroked Fluffles and buried her face in his hair. It broke Melissa's heart when Mrs. Murphy passed away and Fluffles got rehomed. Melissa had begged her parents to adopt him, but they said no. She still hadn't forgiven them for that.

"It about gave your mother a heart attack when she found your bed empty."

"What can I say? Fluffles was cute."

"Cute enough for the telling off you got?"

Melissa grinned. "Maybe not *that* cute."

"Justin is a normal lad. You don't need to worry about him."

"I just want him to be happy."

"And he is."

They rode in silence for a few minutes, then the hospital came into view. Melissa directed him to the staff carpark and pointed out where her car was. He pulled up in front of it and cut the engine.

"Thanks for the lift."

"You're welcome. If you need more time to recover, we're okay to keep Justin."

"Thank you, but I'll be okay after today. I'll collect him from school tomorrow. Let him know I'll call him later." The swelling on her cheek had gone down, thanks to Tara's insistence on icing it, but a pale blue bruise was visible. She wanted to give it another day before Justin saw it, so he wouldn't worry too much. She would need to tell him what happened. He couldn't stay away until it was fully healed. Hopefully, by the next afternoon, with a little make-up, her cheek wouldn't look so bad.

"Will do. Take care, sweetheart."

"Thanks, Dad."

Melissa waved him off and got into her car. Twenty minutes later, she arrived home. She went to the kitchen and switched on the kettle for a cup of coffee. Her gaze wandered to the left and into Ellis's garden. Ellis was kneeling by the new planters, only her head and shoulders visible above the fence. Melissa's heart picked up speed, pumping so hard she could feel it in her chest. The pull was strong. Her coffee forgotten, Melissa entered her garden and stood by the fence. "Good morning, Ellis."

Ellis glanced over her shoulder and smiled. "Melissa, Hi." She stood and wiped her hands on her cargo trousers, leaving mud streaks, and made her way over to Melissa. "How are you feeling?"

"A little sore but okay."

"The bruise on your cheek looks bad."

Melissa waved her off. "It'll go in a couple of days. What are you up to?"

"Just replanting some of the bulbs that got washed out from the storm. I have a phone appointment with Lucy soon, so I'm wasting time until then."

"Good, great. Can I ask how it's going?"

Ellis smiled. "Of course. It's going well. I feel a lot better about myself and find I no longer want to bury myself in work all the time."

"That's good. I'm pleased for you." Melissa cleared her throat, looking away for a second. She hadn't planned on asking Ellis out this soon, but seeing her leaning on the fence, her gaze full of love and concern, confirmed to Melissa how desperate she was to kiss her again. She was done running from her feelings. She didn't need to understand them anymore. They were there, whether they made sense to her or not. *Tonight would be the perfect time to try having a date.* Justin wouldn't be there, and Melissa wouldn't need to explain to her parents why she wanted them to have him on a night she wasn't working. Her body wanted her to rest, but her need to see Ellis was stronger. "Listen, I was wondering if you wanted to come over for dinner tonight?"

Ellis quirked an eyebrow. "What, so Justin can beat my ass at Trivial Pursuit again?"

"He's staying with my parents tonight, so my face has a little more time to heal before he sees me." She took a breath. "It'll just be you and me."

Ellis's other brow joined its twin, and she stuffed her hands into her pockets. "Oh, um, okay."

"Really? You don't sound so sure." *Maybe I've got this wrong, and she isn't as interested as I thought.*

"No, I am. I just wasn't expecting it to be just us."

"Is that okay?"

"Of course." Ellis beamed. "It'll be nice. Do you need me to bring anything?"

"No, thank you, I'll get everything."

"Okay."

"Come by about six?"

"All right."

"Great." Melissa turned away but then stopped. She gazed intently at Ellis. "Ellis?"

"Yeah?"

"Just in case I wasn't really clear, this will be a date."

"A date?"

"Yes."

Ellis dipped her head, her gaze penetrating. "Are you sure that's what you want?"

"Positive."

"Okay. I'll see you at six."

"See you later." Melissa nearly sprinted back inside. Her belly contracted, as butterflies became eagles. She had never asked anyone out before. There'd only been Craig, and he did all the chasing. She couldn't believe the first time she did ask someone out, it was a woman. *Ellis.* Melissa knew it had to be this way. Ellis had made it clear that she would go along with whatever Melissa wanted. If they were to move toward having a romantic relationship, Melissa would have to take the first step. *And I did it. I asked her for dinner.* Despite her body's need to crawl into bed and rest, Melissa had too much to do to get ready. She would have to go shopping for groceries and set the table romantically. *And shave my legs, you know, just in case.* The birds in her stomach fluttered like mad, as anticipation of what the night might lead to set up residence in her whole being.

†

Melissa spun around and dropped the tongs she was holding, as she spotted Ellis standing at the patio doors. It wasn't just the shock of suddenly seeing Ellis stood there, but what Ellis was wearing. Her black jeans looked made for her, and the white shirt showed off her strong arms and shoulders. Melissa had never seen her wear her hair down, just brushing the collar of her shirt. She swallowed hard. If there was any doubt about her attraction to Ellis, it burned up in a flash at seeing her. Melissa scooped up the tongs, then slid the door open. She caught a whiff of Ellis's perfume, the scent making her insides flutter. "Hi."

Ellis's smile lit up her face, her eyes twinkling in the early evening sun. "You look amazing."

Melissa looked down at the yellow sundress she wore and her bare feet. She had planned to put on sandals before Ellis arrived, but Ellis was a few minutes early. Her legs were silky smooth, and her toenails were coated in a soft peach colour. "Thank you. Come on in." She stepped aside so Ellis could enter.

As Ellis stepped over the threshold, she dipped her head and kissed Melissa lightly on the cheek. "Thank you for the invite."

Melissa's cheek warmed from the contact. She wanted more, much more, but she stopped herself from reaching out. Instead, she said, "You're welcome." She slid the door shut and gestured toward the lounge. "Dinner will be about another half hour. Go take a seat, and I'll bring you in some wine."

Ellis didn't move, she just gazed at Melissa with a slight frown on her lips. "Are you okay?"

Melissa looked away for a moment, smoothing her hands over her hips as she did so. "I'm fine. Just a little nervous." That was an understatement. Her body had been buzzing with restless energy all day. She had already nicked her finger twice cutting up the carrots, and the constant tensing of her muscles hadn't helped in her healing from the episode at work. Preparing for tonight had taken her mind off the incident, and for that she was grateful. Now, however, her body was screaming out for Ellis's touch. She had no clue how to make a move. She stepped around Ellis and picked up the wine bottle. "I hope red is okay." She poured generous amounts into two glasses. "And I'm making lamb kebabs with salad." She turned around and held out a glass for Ellis to take. "How did you get on with the planting? The weather was good today, so that must have been nice."

"Mel, you're beginning to ramble."

"Am I?" She picked her glass up and took a large gulp. "I don't think so. I'm always chatty. Just ask my—" She didn't have time to finish her sentence. Ellis's mouth was on hers. She blindly put the glass onto the island behind her and wrapped her arms around Ellis's neck, pressing deeper into her. She didn't care that her shoulder hurt, she just wanted Ellis. Ellis's hands gripped Melissa's waist and backed her up against the island, which was good, because Melissa's knees went weak. She about had a heart attack when Ellis ran one hand up Melissa's side and settled it on her breast. Melissa groaned, feeling her nipple harden against Ellis's palm. She threw her head back, allowing Ellis to trail kisses down her neck.

"You drive me crazy, Mel." Ellis cupped Melissa's bruised cheek tenderly. "I want to make love with you."

Melissa closed her eyes and clenched her centre. She had no doubt just how ready she was for Ellis to take her. She looked up at Ellis. "I want that too, but I don't think now is the right time."

Ellis kissed her quickly on the corner of her mouth and stepped back out of touching distance. "You're right. I'm sorry."

Melissa shook her head. "You don't need to apologise for wanting me. I want you just as much. You have no idea." Melissa took a step forward and took Ellis's hands in her own. "This is all new to me, and not just being attracted to a woman. I've never wanted someone as much as I want you."

"Yeah?"

"Yes." To strengthen her statement, Melissa leaned up and kissed Ellis. The contact bolstered her confidence. She worried she wouldn't know what to do when the time came, but all her fears were unfounded. She knew exactly how she wanted to touch Ellis. She stepped away and turned off the oven. "Come with me." She held out her hand for Ellis to take and led her toward the stairs.

"I thought you said—"

"Forget what I said. I don't want to wait anymore." She let go of Ellis's hand, leaving her at the foot of the bed, and closed the blinds. The sun hadn't set yet, so there was plenty of light to see. She faced Ellis, her stomach twisting in knots. This would be the first time she would be naked in front of anyone since before her divorce. She wasn't shy about her body, but she wanted Ellis to find her attractive. Judging by the heat in Ellis's gaze, she didn't have to worry. "Make love to me."

"Are you sure? There is no going back after this."

Melissa didn't reply with words. She slipped the straps of her dress down her shoulders and allowed it to pool around her feet. Ellis's gaze scanned her semi-naked form, dressed only in matching white-lace underwear. She was a little self-conscious of the few stretch marks she had from carrying Justin, but she wouldn't let that stop her from being with Ellis. "Come to me."

Ellis licked her lips and took a few steps forward. "You look beautiful, Melissa."

"Thank you. Now, get undressed."

Ellis grinned and promptly unbuttoned her shirt. Melissa watched every movement with wide eyes, her anticipation building. When Ellis threw the shirt off behind her, Melissa swallowed hard at seeing Ellis's breasts, unencumbered by a bra. She had seen breasts before, at the gym or changing in work, but this was different. These belonged to Ellis. And although Melissa had never had the urge to touch another woman's breasts before, now, she couldn't wait to trace her tongue over Ellis's nipples.

"It's okay," Ellis said, as if reading Melissa's thoughts. "You can do whatever you like."

Melissa glanced up, breathing rapidly, and tentatively reached out. She cupped one breast. Her thumb flicked the nipple, and it hardened instantly. Fascinated, Melissa dipped her head and covered Ellis's other breast with her mouth. Ellis groaned and cupped the back of Melissa's head, holding her firmly against her. Melissa trailed her tongue over the hard prominence, thrilled at the sounds Ellis was making. *This is amazing. I need more.* Melissa lifted her head and unzipped Ellis's slacks. Ellis toe-ed off her shoes, and Melissa lowered the trousers, taking her underwear with them. Melissa caught Ellis's scent, her arousal apparent. She ran her hands up Ellis's thighs, stood, then pushed Ellis back onto the bed.

"I thought I wouldn't know what to do." Melissa climbed on the bed and settled over Ellis. "That I would be inept in every way."

"Mel..."

"It's okay. I know precisely what I want to do." She covered Ellis with her body. The contact of skin on skin nearly brought Melissa to an early climax. She kissed Ellis's jawline and worked her way to her lips. Her hand drifted down Ellis's torso and into the fine hairs guarding her most intimate parts. Her hand drifted lower, sinking into red-hot liquid. "Ellis." Melissa had never felt anything so glorious in her life. As her fingers traced Ellis's smooth folds, Ellis began to move against her.

"Go inside," Ellis begged, her chest turning red.

Melissa crushed her mouth against Ellis's lips at the same time as entering her. Ellis moaned loudly, her hips rising to meet Melissa's hand. Melissa kept pace with her, matching her thrust for thrust. She couldn't believe she was doing this and how amazing it felt. For weeks, she had chided herself on her inability to decide what she wanted. Had she'd known how exhilarating it would be to be with Ellis this way, she would have begged Ellis to do this back then. "You're close, I can feel it."

Ellis's hips moved faster, her hands gripping the duvet. Within moments, Melissa felt Ellis's walls clamp around her fingers, pulling her in further.

"I love you," Ellis cried out, as her orgasm ripped through her body.

Melissa kissed her fiercely, still pumping in and out, until Ellis's writhing settled to a stop. Ellis rolled them over and captured Melissa's lips again, holding her wrists against the bed.

"That was incredible," Ellis said, her breathing ragged. "You're incredible."

Melissa stared up at Ellis, her need building. She wanted to tell Ellis she loved her too, but the words wouldn't come. Instead, she said, "Make love to me." She thought Ellis would take her hard and fast, but she didn't. Ellis trailed gentle kisses all over her chest and stomach, avoiding her breasts for what seemed like hours, until, eventually, gently sucking her nipple between her lips. Melissa bucked her hips, wanting, needing more contact. Ellis moved away from her a few inches. "Stop teasing me," Melissa stammered.

Ellis smirked. "All good things come to those who wait."

"If you don't hurry up, I'll finish it myself."

In response, Ellis gripped her wrists tighter and shook her head. "Nope. I plan to explore every inch of you, memorising every mark, every freckle." Ellis licked her other nipple. "Only then will I give you what you need."

"Ellis, please!" It was too much. Her body burned for its release. "We can go slow later. I need you now."

"Okay, but only because I can see how desperate you are."

Melissa screwed her eyes shut, as Ellis's lips roamed lower. Melissa opened her legs wider, knowing where Ellis intended to be. At the first swipe of Ellis's tongue, Melissa nearly detonated into a million pieces. She concentrated hard on not climaxing too quickly. She wanted to enjoy this experience for as long as possible, but Ellis was making it hard. When Ellis clamped her lips around Melissa's clitoris and sucked hard, it was game over. Melissa whole stomach clenched, as her orgasm ripped through her. It was that intense that lights flashed behind her eyelids. She couldn't stand it. She pushed Ellis away and swung her legs over the side of the bed. She clutched the duvet and bent over, her lungs gasping for air.

"Are you okay?" Ellis's voice was panicked. "Melissa?"

Melissa slowed her breaths, counting them out in her head. After a few moments, her breathing had returned to a near-normal state. She fell back onto the bed, Ellis knelt next to her, her face contorted with worry. "I'm okay." Melissa took Ellis's hand. "That was just really intense. I thought I was going to have an asthma attack. I've never experienced anything so powerful before." If she didn't move for the next month, she might be able to walk again. "I can't believe how incredible that was."

"Yeah?"

Melissa tugged Ellis's hand, encouraging her to lie down, facing each other. Melissa traced her fingers over

184

Ellis's face. "You're so unbelievably beautiful. Thank you for making me feel so wonderful."

"Anytime."

Melissa grinned. "How about now?"

"As you wish."

†

Melissa sipped her coffee, then put the mug onto the windowsill. She looked through the blinds and up into the sky. She spotted a seagull and watched it fly around for a few moments, until it darted behind the houses opposite and out of view. Her body hurt in ways she couldn't imagine. The effects of the work incident still plagued her, and now she had pulled muscles to add to the mix. She couldn't recall any time in her life when she had done an all-nighter. Ellis had taught her things Melissa had never dreamed of doing with someone. She smiled to herself. It had been the best night of her life.

She glanced over her shoulder. Ellis was sprawled on her back, fast asleep. The duvet lay discarded on the floor, and only a thin sheet covered her. Melissa's gaze swept her body, remembering all the things they had done. *No going back now. I can't wait to do it again.* She turned back to the window and sighed. They wouldn't have time to go once more. In a couple of hours, Melissa would need to pick Justin up from school. Before then, she needed to shower and clear up the kitchen from the meal they never got around to having.

"Are you okay?"

Melissa spun around. Ellis now sat up against the headboard, holding the sheet up to cover her breasts. Her hair

185

looked wild, but her features were relaxed. Only her eyes lent support to the worry in her question. "I'm great. How are you?"

"Tired, sore. A little unsure."

Melissa crossed her arms and raised her brows. "About what?"

Ellis shrugged a shoulder. "I woke up and you weren't next to me. I panicked for a moment, until I spotted you. You look pensive."

"I'm fine. Just thinking."

"That maybe this was a mistake?"

Melissa shook her head vigorously and rushed to the bed. She settled next to Ellis and cupped her cheek. "Absolutely not. I was annoyed that we don't have time to make love. I have to get Justin soon. I have no regrets. Only that I can't have you right now."

Ellis's smile was radiant. She kissed Melissa's palm. "I was worried we had gone too far, that maybe you were going to pull away from me."

"I'm sorry you felt that way. But trust me, Ellis, I have absolutely no doubts in my mind about you. I want to pursue this. Our connection is too strong to ignore anymore." Melissa withdrew her hand and took a breath. "We do need to talk though."

Ellis's eyes darkened and her lips turned down at the corners. "Okay."

"As much as I want to see where this goes, I'm not ready to announce it to everyone yet. I don't want to upset anyone in case—"

"In case we don't work out?"

Melissa sighed, hating the reality of the situation. She didn't want to come out to her family if there was no need to.

She didn't want to have to think about those kinds of things, but she needed to think of Justin. It wasn't fair for him to come to terms with his mother being in a lesbian relationship when there was a chance Melissa and Ellis wouldn't be together in the long run. It wasn't a nice thing to contemplate, but it was the truth.

"I just need time, Ellis. I know you probably don't understand, but it's what I have to do."

"Melissa, I'm not asking you to shout it from the rooftops. It's only been one night. I get that this is a big change for you. You can take all the time in the world." Ellis ran her hand up Melissa's thigh and stopped just under the hem of her shorts. "Besides, I find it quite thrilling sneaking around." She kissed the side of Melissa's neck, below her ear. "Stealing kisses when no one is looking." Her hand inched higher. "Thinking of you sleeping in here, while you touch yourself, wishing I was with you to make you come."

"Ellis." Melissa threw her head back and straightened her legs, giving Ellis better access to her body. They didn't have time for this, but her body was primed and ready to explode. She gripped Ellis's other hand and pressed it against her breast over her shirt.

"I can't get enough of you." Ellis pushed her fingers inside and pumped hard. "You're so responsive." She leaned into Melissa, pushing her back onto the bed. "I bet I can make you come in less than a minute."

Ellis was right. Before long, Melissa had climaxed and now lay useless on the bed. Her breath came in gasps, her heart pounded painfully in her chest. Melissa looked up at Ellis, who sported a self-satisfying grin. "You think you're so clever, don't you?"

"I was just giving you a little taste of what's to come, as we begin our clandestine affair."

"Hardly clandestine." Melissa rolled her eyes. Turning serious, she said, "Are you sure this is okay? I don't want you to feel like I'm using you." *Like Stacy.* Although Ellis hadn't been intimate with Stacy, Stacy had still used Ellis. That was the one thing Melissa never wanted to do.

Ellis smiled gently and traced Melissa's lips with her finger. "You don't have it in you to be that cruel. I understand why you want to be cautious. I do too. Let's just enjoy each other when we can and see where this leads."

"Are you sure that's okay?"

"I love you, Melissa. I'll take whatever you can give."

Melissa kissed Ellis, careful not to work herself up too much. If they got carried away, she would be late getting Justin. She was glad of Ellis's words, of her understanding, but that didn't stop Melissa from feeling guilty that she needed to hide her feelings for Ellis. Ellis had been through so much and she deserved to be loved completely and freely, with no limitations. *I need to figure things out quickly, because I don't want to lose her due to my lack of courage.*

Melissa reached for Ellis, but Ellis rolled away and off the bed. Melissa allowed her gaze to wander over Ellis's body as she dressed, disappointed she wouldn't get the opportunity to touch her. She voiced her grievance. "What are you doing? I thought I'd get a turn at pleasing you."

Ellis looked up from tying her boots and smirked. "You please me just being near you." She stood and threaded her arms into her shirt. "And you said we don't have time."

Melissa huffed and climbed from the bed. She was being teased. Ellis knew damn well Melissa wouldn't be able to keep her hands to herself, and she was right. Melissa trailed her fingers over Ellis's shoulders and into her hairline. She made her way in front and batted Ellis's hands away from the buttons she was doing up. "I have a feeling you're trying to make me want you more so that when we're apart, I'll be desperate to have you." She slid her hands inside the shirt and squeezed Ellis's breasts. Ellis sucked in a breath, her eyes darkening. "The problem with that, Ellis, is that I don't like to be manipulated." She kissed Ellis's chin and moved one hand lower. She cupped her between her thighs and felt Ellis's heat. Melissa smiled. "You're burning for me, aren't you?"

Ellis nodded and tried to kiss Melissa. Melissa ducked out of the way. She squeezed her hard and stepped back. "And now I have to go clear up the kitchen. Have fun walking around horny all day." She darted from the room, laughing, as Ellis groaned loudly. Melissa made it to the lounge, before Ellis grabbed her from behind and spun her around.

"That's not fair. You've turned me on to the point of pain."

Melissa smirked, loving the fire in Ellis's gaze. "That's what you get for not letting me touch you."

"You can touch me now. It won't take long."

Ellis sounded so desperate, so close to losing control, that Melissa couldn't help but give in. She smoothed her hand down Ellis's side, to the waistband of her slacks. She lowered the zipper and slipped her hand inside. Ellis let out a woosh of air, as Melissa dipped inside. Ellis kissed her, as her hips circled Melissa's hand. In a flash, Melissa felt Ellis's walls clamp down. "Better?"

Ellis lowered her head onto Melissa's shoulder, her breathing erratic. "Much. Thank you."

"You don't need to thank me for pleasing you. It was my pleasure." Melissa pulled her hand free and glanced at the clock. It was nearing one thirty. She had an hour before she needed to collect Justin. "As much as I want to continue this, I need to start clearing up."

"I have an idea."

"What's that?"

"If I do the kitchen, while you shower, we can have some more playtime."

"You know what? That's the best idea I've heard in a long time."

Ellis took Melissa's hand and together they sprinted up the stairs. There wouldn't be time for much foreplay, but that was okay. The last nineteen hours had provided enough stimulation and had them at the ready.

CHAPTER SEVENTEEN

Ellis opened her email app on the computer for the first time in weeks. Her appointments with Lucy were going well, and with her flourishing relationship with Melissa, Ellis felt ready to think about going back to work. She was mindful of the fact that the reason she felt so positive now was due to the phenomenal night she'd spent with Melissa. The first blush of romance was always exciting, but she reminded herself that just because one part of her life was going great, didn't mean there were no lingering issues. She would talk to Lucy about this in their next appointment, but for now, there was no harm in dipping her toe back into work. She didn't expect to see seventy unread emails. *My clients know I'm on sabbatical. Why are they contacting me so much?* She scrolled down the list, noting the headings, and groaned. Her stomach tightened at the thought of replying to them. *Maybe I'm not as ready as I thought. Or maybe I've lost my passion for this.* A couple of months ago, Ellis would have relished diving in and cracking on with work. It had been the perfect panacea to her dim view of life. Now, nothing was appealing about spreadsheets and averages.

She closed the app and swirled her chair, putting her back to the computer. *Maybe I should seriously think about a career change.* A knock on the front door interrupted her thoughts. She grinned, knowing it would be Melissa. No one else ever came to her home. She had seen her less than twenty-four hours ago but missed her terribly. She had been loath to leave, but Melissa was already running late to pick up Justin. If it had been for any other reason, Ellis wouldn't have let her out of bed. They had texted last night but made no plans to meet up soon. Melissa would be busy with work and Justin. Having her at the door now brought a flush of excitement to Ellis. She pushed out of the chair, not caring it hit her desk, and hurried to the door. She pulled it wide. Her excitement blew up, replaced with shock.

"What are you doing here? And how did you find me, for that matter?"

Stacy stood before her, dressed casually in shorts and a flowing sleeveless blouse. Her skin was tanned golden. Her hair bobbed on the slight breeze. The sunglasses on her head kept the wisps from going into her eyes. She smiled uncertainly at Ellis. "I was wondering if we could talk."

Ellis folded her arms across her chest. "I have nothing to say to you. Goodbye." She uncrossed her arms and tried to close the door, but Stacy reached out and stopped it.

"Please? It won't take long."

Ellis drew in a deep breath, willing herself to slam the door in her face. However, there was something about Stacy's gaze that told her to at least hear her out. She sighed but nodded. She stepped from the door and allowed Stacy entrance. "You'd better make it quick."

Stacy stepped into the lounge and glanced around before settling her gaze on Ellis. "You look well."

"I don't want to hear that. What do you want?"

Stacy tilted her head and pursed her lips. "I wanted to apologise again for what I did and hoped maybe we could be friends again."

"Are you fucking kidding me?" Ellis stalked toward Stacy, her blood running cold at the mere suggestion she forgive her. "You destroyed my career, my reputation. Hell, even my life." She poked Stacy's shoulder. "Do you have any idea how god awful these past years have been? People staring at me, gossiping."

"I know, and I truly am sorry." Stacy furrowed her brow, her gaze pleading. She looked genuinely remorseful. "It was a ridiculously stupid thing to do, and I'll never forgive myself for it." She took Ellis's hand. "But, Ellis, I miss you."

"You've got to be joking." Ellis snatched her hand back. "I want nothing to do with you."

Stacy wouldn't be deterred. She stepped forward and kissed Ellis clumsily on the side of her mouth. Ellis was too shocked to move away.

"What's going on?" Melissa seethed from the conservatory.

Stacy was the first to recover. She turned around. "I remember you. You're the pit bull from the coffee shop."

"And you're the bitch that ruined Ellis's life."

"We've sorted all that out." Stacy waved her hand as if Melissa were insignificant. "Now, please, go away."

Melissa's gaze switched to Ellis, who was yet to speak. "Ellis?"

Ellis's brain finally began to function. Looking at Melissa, Ellis realised what she would be thinking. Her heart sank, hating Melissa had chosen that exact moment to walk in. Not that Ellis had anything to hide. She wasn't the one who had initiated the kiss; she had just been too dumbfounded to move away. When she was friends with Stacy, she didn't ever pick up any feelings of attraction. They were mates, nothing more, and not even that after Stacy betrayed her. She couldn't understand what game Stacy was playing, because it had to be a game. There was no way Stacy liked her in that way.

"Ellis?" Melissa repeated. "What is she doing here? Are you seeing each other?"

"No, never." Ellis hurried forward, desperate for Melissa to believe her. "She's leaving." Ellis glared over her shoulder at Stacy, who stood there looking smug. "Now."

Stacy's smile was sickly sweet. "No problem, babe." She reached into her back pocket and withdrew a business card. She placed it on the coffee table. "In case you've lost my number. I'm not finished with you yet."

Ellis turned back to Melissa, not watching Stacy leave. She didn't care about her. She cared about Melissa looking on the verge of tears. "You have to believe me. This isn't what it looks like."

"So, I didn't just see you two kissing?"

"No. Well, yes. But it wasn't like that."

"Then explain it to me, Ellis, because I thought we were together. I'm fairly sure I remember you in my bed for nearly twenty-four hours."

Ellis pinched the bridge of her nose, knowing she needed to gain control of the situation. If she didn't, there was a chance she'd lose Melissa before they'd begun. She took Melissa's hands; pleased Melissa didn't pull away. "She said she came to apologise. I told her I didn't care, that she had ruined everything for me. I was angry and shouting at her, and she just kissed me."

"Why would she do that unless she thought you felt the same?"

"Did you feel the same when Mark or Craig kissed you?"

A flash of fury zipped across Melissa's features, before she looked away, deflated. "No, I didn't."

"Then, can you understand how she caught me off guard?" Ellis raised her brows and hoped Melissa believed her. "I promise you, Mel, I have no interest in Stacy."

Melissa stared at Ellis for a long moment before finally nodding. She let out a breath. "I believe you."

"Thank you." Ellis beamed and gathered Melissa close. Melissa wrapped her arms around Ellis's waist and tucked her head under her chin. "I swear, I had no idea she was going to do that."

Melissa pulled back but kept within the circle of Ellis's arms. She looked up. "Do you think she's up to something?"

"My gut says yes. Up until we saw her at the café, I hadn't seen her since I got arrested. For her to turn up now, and kiss me no less, I would think she's got something planned."

Melissa shrugged a shoulder. "You never know, maybe seeing you the other week brought back old feelings and she does want you."

Ellis shook her head. "I can't see it. She never gave me any sign that she had any feelings for me. It was only a ploy to get me fired."

"Well, I wouldn't blame her if she did fancy you. You caught my attention the second I met you, I just didn't know how badly."

"Yeah?"

Melissa nodded and her cheeks tinted pink. "Yes. Every moment since then, I became drawn to you more deeply. You're special, Ellis. I don't want other people kissing you."

Ellis kissed Melissa's cheek, warmed by her words. "I don't want other people kissing me either. Or you, for that matter."

"Soooo, maybe we only see each other?"

"I think that's a great idea."

"Good."

Ellis grinned, then took Melissa's mouth in a searing kiss. Melissa held on, as Ellis backed her against the wall, their lips never losing contact. Ellis pressed harder into her, thrilled to have Melissa so close once again. Things became heated. Melissa ground down on Ellis's thigh and Ellis massaged Melissa's breast. All the while, their tongues battled for dominance. Ellis had been worried that Melissa wouldn't be ready for a sexual relationship with a woman. When Melissa had led Ellis upstairs and undressed, she hadn't looked timid. Ellis could see was she was nervous, but Melissa soon got over that. Spending the night with her had been everything Ellis had wanted. She thought maybe her attraction to Melissa might dwindle after satiating her lust for her, but her heart was true; she loved Melissa. She knew she always would. She hoped Melissa felt the same. Melissa

196

hadn't said the words, but Ellis could see it in her eyes and feel it in her touch.

"We need to stop," Melissa said, her breath coming in gasps. "I only came over to ask if you wanted to join us for dinner. Justin is on his own in there."

Ellis nodded but didn't step back. She smoothed her hand up Melissa's waist and into her hair. "That sounds great. I need a cold shower first."

Melissa chuckled. "Me too. I'm going to have to stock up on toiletries, because I have a feeling I'm going to be in a state of arousal all the time."

"You do know this is more than just sex for me, right?" Melissa frowned. "What?"

Ellis moved away and ran her hand through her hair. "Being with you intimately is phenomenal, but I'm just as happy sitting in a room with you sharing a meal or watching TV. I don't want you thinking sex is all I'm after."

Melissa took Ellis's hand and smiled. "Ellis, I know that. Not once did I think this was friends with benefits type of thing. I wouldn't be involved with you if I didn't think we had a proper future together. That's not who I am. I'm risking hurting my family to be with you. That's not a decision I've taken lightly."

"I don't want you to lose your family or friends over this. Are you sure this is worth it?"

"Are you asking if I think *you're* worth it?"

Ellis shrugged and looked away. This wasn't about her being needy. This was about Melissa potentially losing everything because she was in a same-sex relationship. In today's society, people were generally more acceptable to people's choices, but it was different when it was your friend or relative. Ellis didn't want Melissa to have to choose

197

between them. It would be easier to stop this now before they got too deep. *Well, too deep for Melissa. I'm already in love.* It would break her heart to have to end this, but she would if it meant Melissa didn't have to suffer.

"How could you even ask me that, Ellis?" Melissa took Ellis's face in her hands and rubbed her thumbs over her cheeks. Her gaze was soft and loving. "You mean the world to me. When I tell my parents and friends, if they can't see how much I care about you and don't support me, then it's their problem. I won't be dictated to about who I see. I'll be devastated, obviously, but I'm not giving you up because things might get hard." She kissed Ellis gently. "I just need time to figure out when and how to tell them."

"I don't expect you to announce it now. We already talked about that. I just don't want you to be hurt."

"That's sweet of you, but if I am, I'm sure you'll be there to comfort me."

"Always."

"Then stop worrying." Melissa stepped back. "I'm in this for the long haul, providing certain women keep their hands off you."

Ellis sighed at the reminder of Stacy. Her gaze found the business card on the coffee table. She had no interest in speaking to Stacy again, but she knew she would have to if she was going to find out what was going on. She looked back at Melissa. "I promise you, your lips will be the only ones to touch mine from now on."

"Good." Melissa grinned. "Right, I have to get home. Justin will be wondering where I am. Dinner will be at six."

"Great. I'll see you then." Before Melissa could escape, Ellis pulled her in for one more blistering kiss. She didn't know when she would next have the opportunity, so she wanted to take a moment to imprint the feel and taste into her soul.

CHAPTER EIGHTEEN

"I'm not sure I'm ready for this." Ellis bounced on the balls of her feet, as she watched Melissa baste the chicken. "I feel sick."

Melissa glanced up from her task. After putting the roasting tray back in the oven, she approached Ellis. "It's just my parents, Ellis. You don't have to get yourself so worked up."

Ellis and Melissa had been dating for two weeks. In that time, they had only spent one night together. Melissa had picked up extra shifts at work, and with also looking after Justin, there just wasn't time for them to be properly intimate. Ellis stole kisses when she could, and often joined them for dinner, but it wasn't the same as holding Melissa all night while they slept. Despite her promise to allow Melissa time to adjust to their new relationship, Ellis was finding it hard not to pressure her. If Ellis had her way, she'd be with

200

Melissa every night. In a way, though, she enjoyed the secrecy. It was quite thrilling to sneak in a make-out session before Justin came home and send naughty texts to one another. Still, the sooner they told everyone, the better. That's what today was about. Melissa had invited her parents over for a roast lunch to meet Ellis. She hadn't told them Ellis would be joining them, but she didn't think it would be a problem. Ellis knew she would be introduced as a friend and neighbour, and this would be the only time to make a good first impression. She already feared they didn't like her for letting Justin down on his birthday.

Her back had never been so sweaty, and her body was vibrating with nerves.

"That's easy for you to say. You won't have to do this for me." There was no one in Ellis's life to introduce Melissa to, except maybe Lucy, but Lucy wasn't a friend. Once their sessions were over, Ellis doubted she would ever hear from her again.

Melissa shook her head and briefly touched Ellis's forearm. "I could if you think about finding your mum."

"What?" Ellis snorted. "Not likely." She looked through to the lounge at Justin watching TV, paying them no attention. She took a chance, lowered her head, and kissed Melissa quickly on the lips.

Melissa stepped back, glancing at Justin as she did so. "You can't do that here."

Ellis rubbed her forehead. "Shit. I know. I'm sorry. I'm just...I dunno." She looked at the patio door, desperate to escape. She had never been with anyone long enough to meet their family. It petrified her that this was happening after only a couple of weeks. "I should go."

"Ellis, you need to calm down. If you keep buzzing around like this, they'll know something is up. And you're not going anywhere. I want them to meet you." Melissa made her way back to the worktop and began chopping up carrots. "I might not be able to introduce you as my girlfriend, but I still want them to get to know you."

Girlfriend? I like the sound of that. After a moment of silence, Ellis asked, "Is it too early for wine?"

Melissa looked up and smiled. "There's a bottle of white open in the fridge."

Ellis retrieved the bottle and a glass. "Do you want any?"

"I'm okay, thank you."

Ellis nodded and poured herself a large amount. Just as she took her first sip, the doorbell sounded through the house. She took another large gulp, hoping it would hit her bloodstream quickly and settle her down. She wanted to impress Melissa's parents. Bouncing off the walls with nervous energy wouldn't be the way to do it.

"I'll get it," Justin yelled from the lounge.

"You'll be okay," Melissa said. She briefly touched the back of Ellis's hand. "Mum can be a handful, but Dad is a sweetheart. It's just lunch."

Ellis smiled but knew it came off as a grimace. *It's just lunch.* Melissa had said she wouldn't let her parents' opinion of Ellis sway her thoughts on dating her, but that didn't mean Ellis wouldn't make an effort to impress them. *If I can get them to like me, they might be more receptive to the idea of Melissa being with me.* She squared her shoulders and faced the group coming her way. Justin led but darted out the patio doors and picked up his football. She wished she could join him.

"Mum, Dad. I'm glad you could make it." Melissa hugged her father and kissed her mother's cheek. "I'd like you to meet my friend."

Ellis stepped forward and reached her hand out.

"Ellis, this is my dad, Christopher, and my mum, Patricia."

"Nice to meet you both." Ellis shook their hands, not missing the puzzled look from Patricia. Patricia was the carbon copy of Melissa in height and looks. Her hair was cut short, though, and the ageing process was in full swing. Lines marred her shrewd gaze. Ellis could see signs of her use of Botox but it hadn't stopped all of the wrinkles. *Perhaps she's due a top up.* She still looked beautiful. Christopher matched Ellis in height. His hair was fully grey, but thick. He looked every inch the Hollywood silver fox. He smiled warmly at Ellis, his eyes twinkling. Ellis felt instantly at ease with him. "I live next door," she said unnecessarily.

"And you're staying for lunch?" Patricia asked.

Ellis felt her throat close at the incredulous tone of Patricia's voice. She glanced at Melissa. "Um, yes."

"Ellis is a dear friend." Melissa stepped between them. "I thought it would be nice for you to meet her."

"So, you're Ellis?" Christopher asked. "Justin talks about you all the time."

"Really?" Ellis wasn't sure whether that was a good thing or not.

"Yes. Usually about how you suck at Trivial Pursuit."

Ellis let out a belly laugh, glad Christopher had broken the tension. "He's right. I'm starting to wonder if he's got an encyclopaedia hid somewhere we don't know about."

Christopher's smile was engaging. "Don't take it too personally. I haven't beat him once, either."

"Melissa? May I have a word?" Patricia asked. She took Melissa's hand and pulled her to the far side of the lounge and out of hearing range.

Ellis watched from the corner of her eye, not liking that Patricia didn't want her there. She turned her attention back to Christopher. "Justin is a great kid. Melissa should be proud of him."

"You've spent a lot of time with him, haven't you? And Melissa."

Ellis didn't sense any ulterior motive with the question, so she answered honestly. "Yes. Usually playing ball in the garden or film nights, that sort of thing."

"And do you have a family of your own?"

Ellis shook her head. "No, it's just me. I work from home, so I'm always around. Melissa is always gracious enough to entertain me. I'm sure I get on her nerves."

Christopher chuckled. "I doubt that. Melissa is an incredibly open and honest person. She'd tell you if that was the case."

Ellis knew he was right. Melissa had been frank with her assessment of Ellis's eating habits and her feelings for her, even when she was confused about them. Ellis would never think of Melissa as untrustworthy. "Yes, she would." Ellis glanced over at Patricia and Melissa. Their heads were bowed together. Melissa didn't look too happy about whatever it was Patricia was telling her. Ellis turned her attention back to Christopher. "Melissa tells me you have an Austin. I love classic cars." She didn't, but she knew it would be a great way to bond with him. His eyes lit up, and he launched into all the specs of the car. Ellis nodded along with him. "I'd love to go for a ride in it sometime."

"Maybe after lunch, we can go for a little jaunt around the block."

Ellis was about to reply, when Melissa and Patricia rejoined them. Although Melissa smiled, Ellis could tell something was bothering her. She wanted to take her hand and lead her somewhere private and ask what was going on. She had a bad feeling it was to do with her. *Unless Patricia always looks like she's just stepped in dog shit.* Ellis couldn't remember ever having received such a hostile welcome.

"Lunch will be ready in twenty minutes." Melissa reached for the gravy granules. "Why don't you all go sit in the lounge and get to know each other, while I potter about in here."

Ellis's eyes went wide. She could probably hold her own if it were just Christopher, but with the daggers shooting from Patricia's eyes, Ellis couldn't think of anything worse. "Why don't I help?"

"No, it's okay. I've got it covered."

Melissa's parents retreated to the living room, and Ellis took the chance to quickly get Melissa on her own. "What's going on? What did she say to you?"

Melissa didn't look up from her task of stirring the gravy on the hob. "Nothing important. Go visit, get to know them."

Ellis glanced into the lounge, pleased they weren't looking, so touched Melissa's lower back. "Was it to do with me?"

Melissa looked up and sighed. She nodded. "Yes. But it's nothing bad, I promise."

"How does she know me?"

"Ellis, we'll talk about it later, once they're gone."

Ellis's hackles were up. "How can I go and sit with them, when I know she has a problem with me?"

"She doesn't. I set her straight."

"On what?"

"Everything okay?" Christopher asked.

Ellis straightened, turned around, and smiled at him. "Yes. I was just making sure there is nothing I can do to help."

"I was thinking maybe we could go for that jaunt now, before we eat."

"Um…" Ellis was all for going for a ride, but that was before she knew Patricia had something on her. More than likely, Christopher knew about it, too.

"You needn't look so worried, Ellis." Christopher's gaze showed nothing. He bounced his keys in his hands. "We won't be gone long."

Ellis looked at Melissa for help, but Melissa went back to stirring the gravy. *What the hell is going on?* "Sure." Feeling like a lamb to the slaughter, Ellis followed Christopher to his car. She folded herself into the passenger side, her knees hitting the dashboard. She adjusted the seat back, but it was still a tight fit. She clipped the belt across her lap and looked straight ahead, as Christopher pulled away from the curb. She kept her mouth shut and waited for him to speak.

It didn't take him long.

"Melissa means the world to me," he said. "She's our only child, and Patricia can be somewhat controlling. She doesn't mean to be, she just doesn't want Melissa or Justin getting hurt."

Ellis cleared her throat. "That's understandable."

"The other problem with my wife is, she likes to gossip." Christopher chuckled, then pulled in and parked up outside the local shop. He turned to Ellis. "You seem like a nice woman, Ellis. And I'm sure you are. Melissa wouldn't be friends with you if she thought you were not who you said you were."

Ellis licked her lips, fearing he was alluding to the business with Stacy. Her heart hammered in her chest. She felt she was in a gangster movie, and the mob boss was warning her off. She kept quiet. Ellis would defend herself only when she knew exactly what was going on.

"I wanted to talk to you about investing."

Ellis blinked and shook her head. "Excuse me?"

"Investing. Patricia being Patricia did some snooping when Justin kept talking about you, and after what you did when Craig turned up drunk on Justin's birthday. Thank you for that, by the way. I'm glad you were there to help Melissa."

Ellis's head whirled, trying to understand what was going on. She thought she was being brought out to be warned away from Melissa and Justin, but it turned out that wasn't what this was at all. "You're welcome." She rubbed her forehead. "I'm sorry, I don't understand what's going on."

"Patricia and I have our retirement funds tied up in ISAs and premium bonds. We'll never get around to spending most of it. We live a modest life. We were thinking of trying to do some good with it. Charities or something. Patricia found out you're an actuary consultant. We were hoping you could give us some advice on what to do. We'd pay you, of course."

"You want me to set up a plan for you?"

"Yes. Hang on, I'll be back in a second." Christopher got out of the car and went into the shop.

Ellis leaned her head back against the headrest, her mind playing catch up. *So, they don't know about Stacy? I can't believe this. I thought for sure they knew all about it.*

A few minutes later, Christopher got back into the car holding two bottles of wine. He passed them over to Ellis. "I forgot to stop on the way over." He turned the car on and pulled away. "So, as I was saying. We'd appreciate it if you could give us some advice or point us in the right direction. Patricia looked at your profile on LinkedIn and was really impressed. She asked Melissa, earlier, to talk to you about it, but apparently, you're not working right now."

"Um." Ellis was a little put out Melissa had told Patricia that. She didn't want them thinking she was a bum. *He just complimented you. He doesn't think that.* She then began to worry Melissa might have told Patricia the reason she wasn't working. *This is all so complicated. It was much easier when I lived in my own bubble. But then again, you didn't have Melissa.* Ellis would suffer all the anxiety in the world if it meant she could cuddle with Melissa at the end of the day. "I've taken a few weeks off to recharge."

"Nothing wrong with that." He winked and refocused on the road. "So, I don't want to put you on the spot, but I thought I'd mention it while we took a drive. Melissa wasn't receptive to the idea. That's why I got you on your own." He reached into his jacket pocket and pulled out a business card. "My number is on there." He passed it over to Ellis. "I haven't worked for four years now, but I couldn't throw these away. It makes me feel important to hand one over when meeting people. I miss being in business."

Ellis looked at the embossed card. "You were an auctioneer?"

"Yeah, for twenty years. That's where a lot of our money came from. Over the years, I was able to learn a few things and started buying and selling art."

"That's awesome."

"My only trouble now is keeping away from it all. Patricia is worried I'll buy the wrong thing and we'll lose everything."

Ellis shifted on the seat and put the card in her back pocket. "I wasn't planning on going back to work for a couple more weeks, but I'd love to meet up with you and discuss your investment ideas."

"Are you sure? You said you were recharging your batteries. Melissa will kill me if I interrupt that."

Ellis waved him off. "It's no trouble. I've already run out of things to do around the house. It'll be nice to do something different."

"Great. Call me whenever, and we'll set something up."

Just at that moment, they arrived back home. Ellis extricated herself from the car and stretched her body out. She couldn't understand why anyone would drive such a rust bucket. Melissa had told her the car's romantic history, but still, it was a pile of junk. *Must be to do with his love of antiques.* She leaned back in and grabbed the wine bottles, then followed Christopher back into the house.

Justin and Patricia were already sitting at the table. Serving dishes, piled high with food, covered the surface. Ellis's eyes went wide. She had never seen so much food before, especially as it was just the five of them eating. She looked over at Melissa standing in the kitchen, trying to wrestle the chicken onto a platter. Ellis put the bottles down on the island and went over to help.

Melissa smiled gratefully, when Ellis took the tongs from her. "You've been gone a while. Everything okay?"

Ellis nodded and plonked the bird down. "Fine. He wanted to get some wine and have a chat."

Melissa glanced over at her parents, who were loading their plates with veggies. "What did he want?"

"You know what he wanted." She put the tongs in the dish washer and faced Melissa. Keeping her voice low, she asked, "Why don't you want me to help them?"

"Let's discuss it later." Melissa picked up the platter and carried it over to the table.

Ellis sighed but dutifully followed. She took the seat next to Justin and reached for the potatoes. She didn't know why, but she suspected they were about to have their first fight. If Melissa had a problem with Ellis helping Christopher and Patricia, then obviously she wouldn't do it. *But she'd better have a bloody good reason, and not just because we're dating.*

She tucked into the roast, enjoying the light banter between Justin and his grandad. Patricia, on the other hand, was discussing furniture arrangements with Melissa. Judging by Melissa's constant eye rolls, the suggestions weren't appreciated. Christopher was correct in saying Patricia liked to be controlling. Ellis kept her head down and focused on eating and sipping the merlot Christopher had bought. She never thought meeting someone's parents could be so stressful. From her fear they knew about Stacy to the tension radiating off Melissa, Ellis couldn't wait for lunch to be over.

An hour later, they stood at the door and waved them off. Melissa closed the door and leaned into Ellis. Ellis put one arm around her waist, conscious of Justin still at the table finishing off his ice cream.

"Thank God that's over," Melissa said, sounding tired.

Ellis knew how she felt. Her cheeks burned from the effort it took to keep smiling. She wasn't a natural smiler, so to keep it up for that long was exhausting. Not that Christopher and Patricia weren't nice, it was just a struggle being on her best behaviour and watching what she said, lest she said something too intimate about Melissa. "It wasn't that bad. I like them."

Melissa pulled back and raised a sceptical eyebrow. "Were you in the same room as me? It was like pulling teeth." She stepped back and walked to the kitchen. Ellis followed. "Justin, when you've finished, can you get on with your homework, ready to hand in tomorrow."

"Sure."

Ellis helped clear up the kitchen and took out the rubbish. Soon, it was just the two of them. "So," Ellis said, leaning back against the breakfast bar, arms folded across her chest. "Can we talk about why you don't want me helping your father?"

Melissa threw the dishcloth onto the draining board and mirrored Ellis's position against the countertop. "I was thinking of you."

"How do you mean? I like your dad. He's very charming."

Melissa briefly smiled. "He is, but that's not what I meant."

Melissa stayed silent, and it only took Ellis a moment to realise what was going on. "This is because of how I was before I took a break from work, isn't it?"

"I don't want you to become ill again."

Ellis took a breath, thrilled Melissa cared so much about her, but also pissed she thought she knew what was best for her. Ellis knew her limits. She wouldn't go back to the way things were. And as of now, she wasn't even interested in going back to work. Helping Christopher would give her the chance to see if her old job was something she still had a passion for. "Mel, that won't happen. I'm in control now."

"You don't know that, Ellis. You might be fine for a while, but eventually, you'll get sucked back in and won't even realise it until it's too late and I'm rushing you to the hospital again."

The tears forming in Melissa's eyes shocked Ellis. She stepped forward and gathered her close. "I can promise you that won't happen again."

"How?"

"Because I have you." She cupped Melissa's cheek and gazed at her. "Before, I was on my own. I couldn't see how deep and lost I had become. Now, I have you. I know you'll be by my side to pull me back if things start to slip. I promise, Melissa, I won't lose myself again."

Melissa gave a tremulous smile. "You'd better not. I've only just gotten you. I don't want to lose you."

"You won't." Ellis dipped her head and touched her lips gently to Melissa's. "I want to make love to you. It's been too long."

"I know. I'm working the night shift tomorrow. If I drop Justin off early, I can come see you."

"Won't you want to get some rest before you start work?"

"I can deal with being tired at work, I can't deal with being horny."

Ellis laughed. "Okay then. Tomorrow it is."

"You don't need to leave yet, do you?"

"No, I can stay. After Justin finishes his homework, maybe we can watch a film or something."

"Trivial Pursuit?"

Ellis mock glared at her. "Not a chance."

CHAPTER NINETEEN

Melissa loaded the last batch of raw burgers onto a platter and headed outside to the barbecue, where Joey, Tara's brother, stood manning the grill. She placed the platter onto the table next to him. "That should keep you going for a while."

Joey smiled, his eyes so like Tara's. "Thanks. I can't believe how much everyone is eating."

"I know. At this rate, I'll have to head to the shop to get more." She glanced around the garden at the groups of friends who had all come to celebrate her new home. Although she had been there for a few months, she'd wanted the house to be finished before inviting everyone around. She couldn't have picked a better day. The sun was shining, not a cloud in the sky, and most of the colleagues she had invited had managed to come. Some switched shifts just for the occasion. Melissa's heart warmed, knowing she had so many

214

in her life that cared for her. It was only supposed to be a small gathering but she found herself inviting more and more people. The one person missing was Ellis. Melissa scanned the crowd again, trying to find her. She spotted her sitting by herself near the shed, head down, not engaging with anyone. Melissa had made a point of introducing Ellis to everyone, so she wouldn't feel left out. Apparently, that hadn't worked. She knew Ellis was generally a quiet person, especially after the last few years of solitude, but Melissa had hoped she would have made the effort to get to know her friends. She planned on being with Ellis for a long time. Ellis needed to at least try to join in. Melissa turned back to Joey. "Give me a holler if you need anything else, and thanks again for being the grill master."

Joey saluted her with two fingers. "My pleasure."

Melissa smiled her thanks and made a beeline for Ellis. She didn't get far. A hand on her bicep impeded her progress. She turned around and was face to face with Mark. She couldn't hide her surprise, because she was fairly sure she hadn't invited him. "Mark! You made it."

Mark grinned. "I nearly didn't. Tim said you were doing this today. I was shocked, as I was sure I had offered to do the cooking for you."

Melissa rubbed her forehead. The last thing she wanted to do was create drama, so she feigned innocence. "I'm so sorry. Things have been hectic, and I must have forgotten to mention it."

Mark raised an eyebrow, his grin still in place. "I was thinking maybe you didn't want me here."

"Of course not." *If you thought that, why did you come?*

215

"Mel, I'm not stupid. You've been distant since our date. I haven't seen you since I brought you home after that thing at work."

"I'm sorry, Mark. My head is a mess. I didn't mean to be rude."

Mark moved closer, inches from Melissa. He briefly touched the back of her hand. "It's okay. I know I came on strong. I'm willing to wait for as long as it takes."

This is getting out of hand. He still thinks he has a chance with me. Melissa glanced over her shoulder at Ellis, whose gaze was fixed on them, lips pulled down into a frown. She needed to put Mark straight. "Listen, Mark. You're a great guy, but I'm not interested. I'm sorry."

"I know you aren't right now but give it time."

How arrogant can one man be? "No, Mark. I won't change my mind." She stepped back from his imposing figure. "You're welcome to stay, but friends are all we will ever be."

For the first time since their exchange, Mark's grin faded. "Oh." His cheeks flushed. "Well, that's a kick in the teeth. I like you, Mel."

"I know, and I'm sorry. But it's not going to happen."

"Is there someone else?"

"No, there's no one." As soon as the words left her mouth, Melissa felt Ellis's presence behind her. She closed her eyes momentarily and turned around to face her. "Hi." *She looks heartbroken. But what can I do? I'm not about to announce we're together right this minute.*

Ellis bit her lip, her gaze moving from Mark and back to Melissa. "I thought I'd take some food up to Justin and his mate."

"You don't need to do that, Ellis. I will."

216

"It's fine." Ellis glanced once again at Mark, then strode away toward Joey.

Melissa blew out a breath, frustrated she couldn't talk to Ellis properly. She focused her attention back on Mark, who was watching her curiously. "You're welcome to stay, but I need to mingle." She didn't give him a chance to reply. She turned on her heel and spotted Ellis entering the house. She chased after her. Ideally, she should wait until after the party, but she didn't want Ellis to be upset for the next few hours. She followed her up the stairs and waited on the landing, while Ellis took the plates, laden with hotdogs and crisps, into Justin's room. A moment later, Ellis appeared in front of her. She looked away from Melissa. Melissa grabbed her wrist and pulled her into her bedroom.

"Ellis, talk to me."

"About what?"

"I know you heard what I said."

Ellis shook her head. "It doesn't matter."

"Yes, it does."

Ellis looked to the heavens for a moment before refocusing on Melissa. "I know you didn't mean it."

"But it hurt you just the same."

"Of course it did. But I get it. Until you're ready to come out to everyone, we can't be normal around each other. However, I can't pretend it's nice watching guys like Mark fawn all over you. It doesn't matter how much I know you're not interested in them. They won't stop until they know you're unavailable."

"I can't do it, Ellis. Not yet." They had only been dating a few weeks. It was too soon to tell everyone. Tears gathered in Melissa's eyes. She couldn't help but think Ellis would call time on them. *Not that I would blame her. I'm treating her like a stranger, not someone I'm in love with.* Melissa stared up at Ellis, her heart beating fast. *Oh, my God. I'm in love with her.*

"Are you okay?" Ellis asked.

"Yes." Melissa took a step back and sat on the edge of the bed. Her body trembled.

"What is it?" Ellis knelt in front of her and rested her hand on Melissa's knee.

Their attraction was undeniable, and they were extremely compatible in bed, but this was the first time Melissa understood how deep her feelings ran. "I'm in love with you."

Ellis beamed, her smile pure and true. "That's the first time you've said that."

"I know. That's why I'm shaking."

Ellis placed her other hand on Melissa's opposite thigh. "I love you, Mel. It's okay."

Melissa cupped Ellis's cheek, her skin warm to the touch. "I do love you, Ellis. More than I could ever imagine. I just need more time." A lone tear slipped from Melissa's eye.

Ellis rose and settled next to Melissa. She pulled her into a one-armed hug. "Not once have I asked you to tell people. I know you're not ready. It just pissed me off that Mark was all over you." She tilted Melissa's chin up and turned her face toward her. "If you're never ready, I'll try my best to be okay with that. I just want to be with you. I'll take whatever I can get."

"But that's not fair to you."

"I would rather stay hidden away than see you hurting over this."

"Oh, Ellis. I'm sorry."

Ellis kissed Melissa's forehead. "It's okay. I am going to go home though."

"No."

"Yes. This is a celebration for you. You should be enjoying yourself with your friends, not worrying over me."

"Ellis…"

"It's okay." She kissed Melissa's forehead again. "Call me later before you go to bed."

Melissa nodded and watched her leave, hating that they couldn't be themselves in front of her friends. *It can't go on like this. It'll end up tearing us apart.*

Melissa didn't know how long she remained in her room, thinking about what to do next. She knew the first person to talk to would be Justin, then her parents. They would be the biggest hurdle to jump. She'd also needed to tell Craig. She hadn't spoken to him since the day she went to his house and he kissed her. At some point, she would need to contact him, and not just about her relationship with Ellis. It wasn't fair to Justin for his father to be absent from his life. Melissa was so lost in her thoughts, the knock at her door made her jump. The door opened, and Tara poked her head around the corner.

"Hey," Tara said. "What are you doing up here? People are wondering where you've gone."

Melissa buried her head in her hands, desperately trying to keep her tears in. Tara sat next to her and hugged her much the same way Ellis had.

"What's going on, honey?"

Melissa lifted her head and gazed at Tara. Tara already knew she had feelings for Ellis. Maybe telling her about everything that had happened in the last few weeks would help lighten the load and make the prospect of telling the others less daunting. She took a breath, and said, "It's Ellis."

"What about her?"

It's now or never. "I took your advice and went with my feelings."

"Explain what that means."

"We're together. Lovers."

Tara grinned. "That's awesome! What's it like?"

Melissa pursed her lips. "Are you asking what it was like to be with her, *sexually*?"

"Of course."

Melissa stood from the bed, her cheeks burning hot. "I am not answering that."

"Oh, come on, Mel. Tell me."

"This is ridiculous. I'm going through hell right now, and you want to talk about sex."

Tara's grin faded, her features serious. She rose and grasped Melissa's hands. "I was joking around. What's wrong?"

"Ellis left, because Mark was chatting me up. She's upset that we can't be together as a proper couple. She's hurt, because I haven't got the guts to come out to my family."

"Mel, you're not gutless. This is a big thing you're doing. It's not easy to tell the people you love something this massive." Tara half smiled, her gaze soft and full of affection. "Don't forget, you've told me, and I haven't run for the hills. You're my friend and I love you. I'll stand by you, whatever happens."

Melissa let out a long breath, her heart feeling full of the support Tara gave her. "Thank you. That means so much to me." She flopped back onto the bed. "I'm just worried how everyone will take it. Especially Justin." The bed dipped, as Tara, once again, sat next to her.

"Is that the only reason?"

Melissa looked away from Tara's penetrating gaze. She always had a way of knowing when there was more Melissa wasn't saying. "I guess I'm also worried, if things don't work out with Ellis, I would have upset everyone for nothing."

"It's not for nothing. Even if you do break up, isn't living your truth now the right thing to do? For you and Ellis. And how long is long enough for you to know Ellis is the one? Will you keep her a secret for a year? Five? Ten?" Tara took Melissa's hand. "That's not fair on either of you. There are no guarantees, Mel. You just have to live your life and take things as they come."

Melissa sighed. "I know, you're right." She let out a groan. "I am such a chicken shit."

"Don't be silly. You're the bravest person I know."

"Come on, let's get back to the barbecue." Melissa rose and pulled Tara with her. She gave her a tight hug. "Thank you for having my back."

"Always."

Melissa still wasn't convinced this was the best time to tell everyone, but she at least felt better about the situation. She would call Ellis later, make sure she was okay, and promise her she would be telling Justin and her folks sooner rather than later. *I just hope they don't hate me. If my parents want to reject me, I'll learn to live with it. If Justin rejects me, I don't know what I'll do.*

†

A few days later, Melissa stood in the kitchen, wiping down the worktops after dinner. Justin was sprawled on the sofa, watching TV. It had been four days since the barbecue, and Melissa was no closer to finding the courage to tell Justin the true nature of her relationship with Ellis. Ellis had been wonderful. She still insisted not telling anyone about them was fine. However, Melissa could see a glimmer of rejection in her eyes every time they talked about it. Melissa tossed the cloth into the sink and dried her hands. She hadn't seen Ellis all day. Melissa had been on the day shift and only arrived home an hour ago. She didn't want to go a day without at least talking to her, face to face. She caught Justin's attention. "Hey, buddy, I'm just going to pop next door for a few minutes to see Ellis."

Justin didn't look away from the television. "Okay."

"I won't be long."

Melissa headed out the patio doors and through the gate. She could see Ellis sitting at her desk. Melissa's stomach clenched for a second. She couldn't shake the fear of Ellis falling back into old habits, but she resolved to allow Ellis the courtesy to know her limits. She would keep a watch out for her and wouldn't think twice about broaching the subject if she thought Ellis was becoming ill. She didn't knock on the door; she walked straight in.

Ellis glanced up, smiled, and removed her glasses. "Hey. What are you doing here?"

"I haven't seen you all day." Melissa took Ellis's hand and pulled her up. "I miss you."

"Really? Well, we can't have that, can we?"

Ellis wrapped her arms around Melissa and lowered her head to Melissa's waiting lips. Just like always, the first touch of Ellis's mouth on hers sent shivers coursing through her. She never knew kissing someone could bring so many different sensations. Ellis always seemed to know how hard or soft to press into her, how to go from sensual to raw passion in a flash. Melissa never wanted her to stop.

"I never get tired of your kisses."

Ellis kissed the tip of Melissa's nose. "It's a shame we can't do more."

"We could try?" Melissa cupped Ellis's breast and groaned at the hardened nipple. She'd give anything to be with Ellis right now.

"Don't tempt me." Ellis glanced away, then her eyes went wide. She stepped back swiftly. "Shit."

"What?"

Ellis nodded her head in the direction of the garden. "Justin."

"Justin?" Melissa swirled on her heels and saw Justin by the swing. He balled his hands into fists, and pulled his bottom lip between his teeth. He glared at them for a moment, then ran off through the gate. "Justin, wait," Melissa shouted but it was too late. He was already gone. Tears formed in Melissa's eyes. She was devastated Justin had caught them. "Oh, God. I can't believe he saw us. I have to go."

"Melissa."

She felt Ellis's hand on her shoulder and shrugged it off. "I can't do this right now." She fled through the garden and back into her house. She bolted up the stairs to Justin's room. His door was closed. "Justin?" She knocked. "Are you in there?" There was no reply. She turned the handle and flung the door wide. Empty. *He's gone. He's run away.* Her whole world was crumbling around her. She didn't expect Justin to jump for joy, but she never imagined he would run away. Her heart hammered in her chest, as she rushed back to Ellis's. Ellis was pacing in the garden, hands linked behind her neck. "Ellis, he's gone. He's not in the house."

Ellis took hold of Melissa's shoulders. "Okay, calm down. We'll find him. Would he go to your parents?"

"I don't know." Melissa squeezed her eyes shut for a moment, trying to stem her rising panic. He was only eleven years old. Not old enough to be wandering the streets on his own, filled with anger. In that state, he wouldn't be thinking clearly. Melissa had visions of him being hit by a lorry or worse, kidnapped. She was catastrophizing but couldn't help it. She opened her eyes and stared at Ellis. "Maybe."

"We can take a drive around, see if we spot him."

Melissa shook her head. "Actually, could you stay here in case he comes back?"

"Sure."

"Thanks." She briefly smiled. "I'll call you if I find him."

Melissa drove the route she would normally take to her parents' place. She hadn't been gone ten minutes when her mobile rang. She rummaged in her pocket, pulled her phone free, and turned on the phone's speaker. "Hello?"

"He's back," Ellis's calm voice sailed through the line.

Those two words released the vice-like grip of terror on her heart. She would be lost if anything happened to Justin. "Oh, thank God."

"He's on the swing. Do you want me to talk to him?"

"I'm not far away. Keep an eye on him, and I'll talk to him when I get there."

"Okay."

Melissa pulled up outside her house but didn't go in. Instead, she went through Ellis's front door. "Ellis?"

"Here." Ellis appeared from the kitchen.

"Has he said anything?"

Ellis shook her head. "No. He's just been sitting there." She pointed toward the swing.

"Okay." Melissa was relieved to see him in one piece. His head was bowed, his hands holding tight to the chains holding the seat in place. She feared what he would say to her. *That's if he even talks to me.* She took a deep breath and steeled herself for the hardest conversation of her life.

Ellis must have sensed Melissa's reticence. "Do you want me to come out with you?"

"I think it's best if you stay here." Melissa stepped through the conservatory door and approached her son. "Justin?" He didn't acknowledge her presence. "Are you all right?"

After what seemed like an eternity, he finally looked up. "Why were you kissing Ellis?"

Melissa crouched in front of him. "Because I care about her. A lot."

He frowned. "Like you did with Dad?"

"Yes."

"So, you like girls?"

"I like *Ellis.*" She hadn't given her sexuality much thought over the last few weeks, and she was in no hurry to label herself. She loved Ellis; that was all she needed to know.

"And Ellis likes you."

"Yes, very much. How do you feel about that?"

Justin shrugged. "I dunno. It's weird." He looked at the ground. "How long have you been, you know?"

"Not long. A few weeks." Melissa sighed and touched his knee. "Justin, I need you to be okay with this. I like Ellis, and I want to see where it goes. Is there any way you can get on board with what is happening between us?"

"I like Ellis, she's cool." He looked up, tears in his eyes. "I want you to be happy, but I can't get my head around this."

"I understand." *That's it then. It's over. I won't hurt my son.*

Justin rushed on. "I'm not saying I won't ever be cool with it. I just need some time."

"Okay." *I don't think you'll ever be fine with this.* "I'm sorry you found out this way. We never meant to hurt you."

"Don't worry about it, I'm getting used to dealing with crap all the time."

He stood forcibly from the swing, ran the back of his hand across his eyes, and made his way inside. Melissa sat in the vacated swing, her heart cracking into pieces. She couldn't go on seeing Ellis. It wasn't fair to Justin. His life had already been turned upside down with the divorce, moving twice, and his dad's drinking. She couldn't add to his issues. She heard the conservatory door open. She looked up as Ellis approached.

"Is he all right?" Ellis asked.

Melissa shook her head. "Ellis, he's been through so much. I never thought I would be another person to hurt him."

"Mel, you haven't hurt him. He just needs time to adjust."

"I'm not sure I can do that to him."

"So, what? We call it quits?"

"I always said if Justin wasn't okay with this, I couldn't carry on seeing you." She stood from the swing and lightly kissed Ellis's cheek. "I'm sorry, but I need to repair things with Justin. I'll call you." She stepped around Ellis and headed back into her own home. She could hear Justin's Xbox so knew he was upstairs and hadn't run off again. She made her way to the sofa, lay down, and wept. For the first time in a long while, Melissa had finally thought she would get the happy ending she desperately wanted. Being with Ellis was everything she'd ever dreamed of. Ellis was always courteous, kind, and funny. She made Melissa feel wanted and desirable. It may have taken Melissa a while to get her head around the fact she was attracted to a woman, but she had never been happier. *And now it's all gone. I'm alone once again.* She half expected to see Ellis charging in and demanding they work through this, but the door never opened. Ellis never came. *We're over, and she knows it.*

CHAPTER TWENTY

Ellis took her usual seat in Lucy's office and placed her cup of coffee next to her on the windowsill. She closed her eyes and took a few deep breaths. She found it helped clear her mind before the session started. A few moments later, the door opened. She opened her eyes and smiled at Lucy. "Hey."

"Good morning, Ellis." Lucy moved behind her desk and sat on her pink office chair. She shuffled a few files and put them to one side. She focused on Ellis. "You look well. You can't see it on the computer screen, but in person, you look a lot healthier."

"Thanks." Ellis felt her cheeks heated with the unexpected compliment. "I think I've put on about a stone, and I'm in a regular sleeping pattern now." Physically she felt the fittest she had in a long while.

"That's great. The last time we spoke, you raised some concerns about your work. Any improvements on that?"

"I'm still not sure what I want to do. The few times I've opened my email, it nearly gave me a panic attack."

"What do you think that means?"

"I've lost my passion for it." Ellis sighed. "Taking a break was the best thing I ever did. I realised I was spinning my wheels and not getting anywhere. I'm worried I might fall back into that trap."

"Is it the worry of reverting to your old ways, or no longer liking the work?"

"I don't know. Maybe both. Melissa's dad asked me to look into investments for him and research the market. When he brought up the idea, I was excited. It's still within my skill set but not the same as I was doing before. I thought maybe that could be a career move." She hadn't been able to start the research for him, though. It had only been a few days after he asked Ellis for help that Melissa called time on their relationship. Ellis didn't think it proper to call him now. The last thing she wanted was Melissa getting upset. "I thought about my list of clients that depend on me. I told them I would be coming back. It's not fair to leave them in the lurch like that." If she'd known back then how she would feel now, she would have recommended that they find a new actuary. Having made them wait weeks for her to come back, it wouldn't be ethical to just give up.

"When do you need to decide?"

"I've got a couple of weeks left until the date I set to sort myself out."

Lucy leaned forward in her chair and rested her arms along the edge of the desk. "I have a suggestion. Why don't you pick one of your clients and work on one project over

229

the next two weeks, get a feel for it again? If it doesn't feel right to you, you can let them all know you're no longer available. You never know, dipping your toe back into it might get your passion back."

"Yeah, I guess." Ellis looked away, her leg bouncing as she did so.

"Is there something else bothering you?"

Ellis looked back at Lucy and let out a long breath. "Melissa broke up with me." She hadn't seen or heard from her in two weeks. It was the longest two weeks of her life. So many times, Ellis nearly went next door and demanded they talk about things. She never did. Melissa had made her feelings quite clear. Ellis wasn't entirely sure Justin was the only reason Melissa had broken things off. She feared Melissa couldn't handle being in a same-sex relationship. Her rational mind told her Melissa was protecting Justin, but the little voice inside her head told her she couldn't deal with it all. *She told you she loved you and wanted to be with you. Stop second-guessing everything.* Her thoughts were driving her crazy. Things were so much easier before Melissa moved next door. Ellis wouldn't go back, though, even if it were simpler. She would never want to know a time when she didn't know Melissa, despite the distance between them now. Ellis hoped it was only temporary. She was prepared to wait for as long as it took for Melissa to change her mind.

"What happened?"

"Justin caught us kissing and freaked out. She said she doesn't want to be with me, because it's upsetting for him."

Lucy nodded. "You can't blame her for looking out for her son."

"I know, and that's why I've stayed away. Justin means everything to her. She'd die rather than hurt him. But it sucks for me. I was finally feeling happy for the first time since the whole mess with Stacy. Now, I'm on my own again, and I don't even have work to distract myself." Ellis didn't even bother getting up until ten, some mornings. She had never been one to stay in bed, but with nothing to occupy her time, she didn't see the point of getting up early. She was trying not to get into a bad habit, knowing it could worsen and probably lead to depression. She had lived five years in the dark, she didn't want to go back.

"I know it's tough, but you're doing amazingly well. Be who you are, and do the things you want. Don't rely on anyone else to make you happy. You'll only be miserable if you do."

"I get that, I do, but I thought she was the one."

"Give her time. If she loves you, like you told me she does, she won't be able to keep away."

"She's very stubborn."

"So are you."

Ellis grinned. "True. Thanks, Lucy."

"I think you're ready to go back to fortnightly sessions."

"Really?"

"Sure. As I said, you've done amazingly. You've sorted your head out, regained your health, and have a more positive outlook on things. I know you're struggling with your career choices and Melissa, but there isn't anything I can help you with day to day that you don't already know."

"You're right. I'm processing my feelings now instead of keeping them boxed away. I no longer feel trapped." She was in a funk over Melissa, but knew in time, those dark feelings would lighten. She just hoped it wouldn't take too long. *I'll wait for her, but I can't keep being so damn miserable about it.* It was time to get on with her life and pray Melissa would come to her senses. "Thank you for everything."

"This isn't goodbye, Ellis, just a reduction of appointments." Lucy smirked. "You're not quite ready to do this alone."

Ellis rolled her eyes, but smiled. "Thanks."

After she said her goodbyes to Lucy, Ellis drove a few miles out of town to a café she hadn't been to in years. The small chain had been one of her favourites to go to with Stacy after work. She pulled the heavy door open and scanned the dim seating area. She spotted the person she was looking for. She strode over and slid into the booth. The leather-covered seat crackled as she settled into place.

"Hello, Stacy."

"Ellis! You made it." Stacy's face lit up, her smile showing perfect white teeth. "I wasn't sure you would."

"I wasn't going to come, but I want this over and done with."

Stacy had texted a couple of days ago, asking to meet. Ellis hadn't replied right away. Stacy was the last person Ellis wanted to see. Her curiosity got the better of her. With nothing planned after her session with Lucy, she thought she'd take a chance on seeing her and finding out what it was she wanted.

"Don't be like that." Stacy reached across the table, but Ellis moved back and placed her hands on her own thighs under the table. Stacy frowned and withdrew her arms. "Can I get you a drink?"

"No. What I want is for you to tell me what game you're playing, so I can then tell you to leave me alone." She knew if she didn't shut this down properly, Stacy would keep on messaging and ringing until Ellis gave in. She didn't want or need the hassle of constantly waiting for Stacy to show up.

"I'm not playing a game. I've missed you. I want us to work things out."

Ellis raised her brows. "You set me up and got me fired. I never want to see you, much less be with you." *Is she freaking kidding me? I'd rather stick a fork in my eye.*

"Ellis, please." Stacy tilted her head to the side and pursed her lips. "I made a mistake."

"A mistake that ruined my life and cost me my career."

"I said I was sorry. Why won't you forgive me? We could be good together."

Ellis leaned forward and spoke through gritted teeth, trying to keep her voice low so the other patrons wouldn't hear her. "You're not listening. I don't like you. You're lucky I don't have you arrested for making false allegations."

"You wouldn't."

"Try me."

Stacy stared at her for a moment before her shoulders sagged. "Okay, fine. I truly am sorry, Ellis, for everything. We were good friends, and I ruined it."

"You were never my friend. It was all about the job for you."

"That's not true. I fell for you. I really did."

"But you screwed me over anyway."

"It was a dumb thing to do. I fucked up."

Tears gathered in Stacy's eyes, then fell down her cheeks. Despite her attempt at looking remorseful, Ellis didn't believe, for a second, that Stacy was sorry. "Are those tears for me, or yourself?" Stacy looked away, and Ellis finally had enough. She didn't need to listen to Stacy's pleas for forgiveness. Ellis would never be able to do that, but she would let her off the hook if it meant Stacy would leave her alone. "Look, it's okay. I've moved on. I'm over the whole mess. However, I'm not interested in being friends with you, or anything else."

Stacy ran her hand through her hair and sighed. She gazed at a point over Ellis's shoulder. "They want you back."

"What?"

"The company. I heard Philip and John talking. They said business had gone down since they fired you and were thinking about making big changes."

"You mean they want to sack you?"

"Yes."

"Oh, my God. I've figured it out." Ellis let out a deep throaty laugh, as she realised what Stacy's motive was for showing up again. "You thought if you could get me back on side and prepared to rejoin the company, they'd keep you on." Stacy's gaze shifted away for a moment, but it was long enough for Ellis to know she was right. *I can't believe she thought she could trick me into going back there. She is seriously messed up in the head.* "The look in your eyes tells me that's true."

"Is that so bad?"

"So, all that crap about being sorry and liking me was all a lie?" Ellis shook her head and slid out from the booth. She towered over Stacy and pointed at her. "You're a nasty piece of work. Fuck you, and fuck the company. You can all rot for all I care." Ellis wouldn't care if Philip and John crawled to her on their knees begging for her to come back, she would never set foot back in that place. And certainly not if Stacy was working there. *The world has gone nuts.* This whole mess was further proof that her desire to go back to being a consultant had vanished. There was a time she would have done anything to work in the biggest actuary company in England, but now she could think of nothing worse. It turned her stomach. "If you come near me again, I'll have *you* arrested for harassment. Goodbye, Stacy." Ellis wanted to storm from the café, but she kept her normal pace. She didn't want Stacy thinking she had upset her. *She'd better get the message and leave me the hell alone, or I'll make good on my threat.*

Finally, that chapter of her life was over. She could forget all about Stacy and concentrate on figuring out what she wanted to do with the rest of her life.

CHAPTER TWENTY-ONE

Ellis allowed the heat of the sun to coat her face, as she tilted her head back and closed her eyes. She was stretched out on her sun lounger, a notepad resting on her knees and pen in hand. She had decided on her future career. The meeting with Stacy a week ago had solidified her need to find something else. She'd traced an old colleague from years ago, who was doing well in the investment market. After emailing back and forth a few times, they had set up a meeting for next week, to discuss Ellis working for him. Her research skills had won him over. He said he was excited to bring her on board. She was excited too, but now she had the arduous task of contacting her clients and informing them she would no longer be able to handle their businesses. She didn't relish telling them. Over the last five years, Ellis had built an impressive portfolio, and her loyalty to her clients was second to none. The thought of upsetting or angering them turned her stomach. Still, she needed to do it. It was time for a change.

"Hi, Ellis."

Ellis opened her eyes and looked over the fence. Justin stood on the other side. He kept his head low but still made eye contact. She sat up and tossed her pad onto the stones. "Justin, hi."

"What are you doing?"

"Just drafting some emails."

"Cool."

"How are you?" This was the first time she had spoken to him in nearly three weeks. She had caught glimpses of him playing in the garden, but she had not once gone out to talk to him. Ellis had kept her promise and stayed away from them. Although she had seen Justin, she hadn't seen Melissa once in all that time. It killed Ellis not being able to see or talk to her, but until Melissa was ready to try, there was nothing Ellis could do. "How are you enjoying the last of the school holidays?"

"It's okay, boring."

"Yeah, I can imagine." A lot of kids couldn't wait for the school holidays, but the novelty soon wore off after weeks at home.

"Mum is asleep. She does that a lot now."

"Yeah?" Ellis's stomach clenched, hating that Melissa seemed to be struggling. Ellis would have thought it would have been herself who struggled the most with the breakup. Despite the few days of getting up late, she had done a good job of keeping busy. It crushed her to think Melissa wasn't doing okay.

"Uh-huh. She's sad."

"I'm sorry, Justin." Ellis stood and approached her side of the fence. "She'll be all right, though."

Justin shook his head. "I don't think she will." He looked up at her and shrugged. "She misses you. I do, too."

"I miss you guys, as well."

"She won't talk to me about it, but is the reason you're not seeing each other because of me?"

Ellis thought about lying, but decided it was best to be honest. The truth would find a way out in the end. "She doesn't want you to be upset."

He squinted and frowned. "But I'm upset anyway, because she's upset."

"Things will get better, I promise." Ellis reached over the fence and grasped his shoulder.

"I don't think they will." Justin glanced away and blew out a puff of air. "The thought of you and her is still weird for me, but I get you can't help who you like. I'm not mad she loves you. It'll just take some getting used to it. I'm sure the longer you're around each other, the easier it will be for me."

Ellis lowered her head and captured his gaze with her own. Her pulse fluttered faster at the thought of what he was implying. "What are you saying, Justin?"

"I don't want to be the reason she's crying at night. I want her to be happy. If that's with you, then I'm okay with it." He took a deep breath and smiled. "You should go see her."

Ellis shook her head. "I don't think that's a good idea."

"I'm telling you, Ellis, go see her. She's in her room."

Ellis glanced up to the house. "Are you sure about this?"

"Yeah. Like I said, you're pretty cool." He grinned widely at her. "She could do worse."

Ellis laughed and let the heartache of the last three weeks fade away. *I just hope she's willing to give us another try.* "Thanks, buddy. This means a lot." She made her way through the gate and into their garden. This would be the last time she would put herself before Melissa and ask for her heart. If Melissa turned her away, she wouldn't try again, despite her earlier claims she would wait forever. There were only so many times she could get her love trampled on before she gave up. She didn't like making a fool of herself.

"I'll wait out here," Justin said, his cheeks flushing.

Ellis nodded to her own house. "You can go in and watch TV or something. You know where everything is."

"Okay."

"Thanks again." She watched until he made it inside the conservatory, then she turned her attention to Melissa's house. She took a steadying breath and proceeded inside and up the stairs. Melissa's bedroom door was open. Ellis looked in and saw her curled up on top of the duvet. Old tissues were balled up on the nightstand, and once again, Ellis's heart broke for her. She perched on the edge of the mattress and gently touched Melissa's shoulder. "Melissa? Melissa, honey, wake up."

Melissa's eyes flickered open and focused on Ellis. She frowned. "Ellis, what are you doing here?" She pushed herself upright. "Is everything all right?"

"Everything is perfect." Ellis cupped Melissa's cheek and smiled softly. "I love you."

Melissa blinked for a moment, before tears trickled down her face. "I love you, too."

"Come here." Ellis gathered her in her arms and stroked her back, while kissing the top of her head. Melissa's tears soon soaked through Ellis's thin T-shirt.

"You can't be here." Melissa lifted her head. "What if Justin sees you?"

"He knows I'm here. He's next door watching the TV." She kissed Melissa's forehead. "He told me to come to you, to get you back."

Melissa raised a sceptical eyebrow and brushed the remaining tears away with the back of her hand. "Really?"

"Yes. He doesn't want you to be upset anymore."

"I've missed you so much, Ellis. I've been so broken without you."

"Me too. It's time to put us back together."

"Are you sure he said it's okay?"

"Yes." Ellis cupped Melissa's cheek again. "Now, kiss me." At the first touch of Melissa's lips against her own, everything slotted back into place, her whole world righted itself. The kiss felt different this time, like a promise to never be apart again. Ellis hoped that was true, because she didn't think she could survive ever being without Melissa. She pulled back an inch and gazed into Melissa's eyes. "I'm never letting you go again. These past few weeks have been hell."

"I'm sorry I did that to you."

"It's okay, I understand why you did it. I never want you to have to choose between me and Justin."

"She won't have to," Justin said from his position by the door. "I'm sorry, Mum."

"It's okay, sweetheart."

"No, it's not." He took a few steps forward. "You should be able to be with whoever you want. I want you to be happy."

"I want you to be happy, too."

Justin glanced down to where Ellis held Melissa's hands in her own. His lips turned down for a moment before breaking out in a grin. "Well, I say Ellis stays."

"Yeah?" Melissa asked, her gaze full of hope.

"Yeah. You two to do whatever." Justin waved his hand at them. "I'm gonna play on the Xbox." He closed the door behind him.

"I am sorry, Ellis."

Ellis kissed her quickly and hugged her close. "It's forgotten." Now they had Justin's blessing, Ellis hoped they wouldn't have any more problems, but she knew that was unlikely. They still needed to tell Melissa's parents. Deep down, she knew Melissa wouldn't send her away if they disagreed with their partnership. Justin had been the most important factor. Now he was on board, no one else's opinion mattered. *This is it now. Me and Melissa forever.* Ellis broke out into a huge smile, her life finally complete.

CHAPTER TWENTY-TWO

Melissa heard footsteps behind her. She recognised the brush of Ellis's feet against the carpet. She took one last look through the lounge window, then turned around. Ellis stood before her, dressed in cargo shorts and a polo T-shirt. Melissa's gaze scanned her from head to toe, loving the long expanses of tanned skin on show. Ellis was usually whiter than white, but she'd been spending lots of time outside during her break from work. Her skin now had a healthy glow. Melissa's mind flashed to two nights ago. Justin had stayed at a friend's house, so Melissa and Ellis had all night to spend together. It was the first time they'd been alone since they made up earlier in the week. No sleep was had that night. Their lovemaking had been raw and passionate, but some tears were shed by them both. The love of her life stood before her, and she couldn't believe she had ever sent her away. She was grateful Ellis hadn't given up on her.

Melissa never would have had the strength to go to her. She had Justin to thank for pushing them back together.

Ellis raised her eyebrow and smirked, as if reading Melissa's thoughts. She didn't comment though. "Are you sure you don't want me to stay?"

"That's sweet of you, but I'll be fine." Melissa was waiting for her parents to arrive. She decided she needed to tell them about Ellis as soon as she could. She didn't want to spend her life hiding. She loved Ellis, and it was time everyone knew. She kissed Ellis quickly on the lips. "Besides, I don't want Justin here if things kick off."

Ellis pulled her into a loose embrace. "Do you think they will?"

"I don't know. They've always been supportive, but this is different." Ellis looked away, but Melissa tilted her head back with gentle fingers on her chin. "Don't worry, they won't scare me off. It's you and me, always."

"I love you." Ellis lowered her head and touched their foreheads together. "We'll be gone about two hours, but call me if you need us to come back early." Ellis was taking Justin out for a game of mini-golf, certain she would lose.

"I will. Have fun."

"Justin?" Ellis stepped back and grabbed her wallet off the coffee table. "Come on, let's go."

Justin bounded down the stairs and waved as he headed to the door. "Bye, Mum."

"Bye, sweetheart." Melissa turned back to the window and watched them drive off. Things between Ellis and Justin were great. Ellis had been worried he would be distant with her, but Justin proved how mature he was in all this. His relationship with Ellis was as strong as ever. It probably helped that Ellis sucked at anything he got her to play with him. Melissa liked to think Ellis was going easy on him, but she knew Ellis truly was awful at sports and video games.

She was still by the window, when she heard the unmistakable sound of her dad's Austin. A moment later, the car pulled to a stop outside the house. Melissa's breath caught in her throat. She coughed. Her pulse hammered like a thousand elephants were herding through her bloodstream. She had never been so nervous. If she made it through this without being sick, it would be a miracle. She opened the door and allowed them in. They both kissed her on the cheek as they passed. "Thanks for coming. Take a seat." Patricia and Christopher sat side by side on the sofa, both wearing the same look of worry.

"Are you okay?" her dad asked. "You look a little frazzled."

"I'm fine, just nervous." Melissa sat on the edge of the coffee table, wanting to see them both directly. She gripped her hands together. "I'll make tea in a minute, but first, I need to tell you something."

Christopher smiled lovingly at Melissa and took Patricia's hand in his own. "It's okay, love. We've been expecting this."

Melissa sat straighter, her eyes going wide. *How could they possibly know? Justin said he wouldn't tell them. There is no way they found out.* They didn't look angry, so that was a good sign. "You have?"

"Yes, since all that trouble with Craig. We figured he wouldn't be paying his child support anymore and finding someone to watch Justin when we're not around is probably a nightmare. Especially through the holidays. We have no problems with you moving back home."

So, they don't know. They think I want to sell my house. Great. "This is my home. Everything is okay. Craig, despite his faults, has never missed a payment, and childcare isn't an issue. I haven't had to miss a shift in weeks. I'm not moving back in with you."

"Then what is going on?" Patricia asked.

Melissa took a huge gulp of air, and said, "I'm seeing somebody."

"Oh, that's wonderful." Patricia's eyes lit up. "What's he like?"

"That's the thing. It isn't a he. It's a she."

"I don't understand. You're dating a woman?"

"Yes. You've met her."

Christopher nodded. "Ellis."

"Yes, Dad."

"I can't believe this." Patricia dropped Christopher's hand and leapt off the sofa. "So, you're a lesbian now?"

"You don't have to sound so disgusted, Mum. I don't know what I am. I just know I'm in love with her."

Christopher stood and put one arm around Patricia's waist, Patricia buried her head in his chest. "You best put the kettle on," he said to Melissa.

Melissa stared at her mother, thinking she was being overly dramatic. It wasn't like Melissa had admitted to killing someone. *Go easy on her. It's a lot to take in.* "Okay." She stood and went to the kitchen and tried to block out the whispering between her parents. She filled the kettle but didn't switch it on. Melissa wrapped her arms around her waist and stared out over to Ellis's swing next door. She regretted not asking Ellis to stay. For all her bravado in wanting to tell her parents herself, she wished Ellis were there, holding her. She had never seen such disappointment from her mother before. As much as it hurt knowing she had hurt her parents, she wouldn't change her mind about being with Ellis. Nothing they could say would make her do that. If they chose to never speak to her again, so be it.

"Are you okay?"

Melissa glanced over her shoulder at her father and shook her head. "No." She dropped her arms and turned to face him. "I need to know how you guys feel about this."

Christopher took a few steps forward and grasped her hands. "Are you happy?"

"Very much so. Justin loves her, too." Her eyes moistened. "She means everything to me, Dad."

"All a parent ever wants for their child is for them to be happy." He smiled and patted her cheek. "If Ellis is the person who makes you feel that way, then I'm okay with it. I like her, and it's obvious how much Justin idolises her by how much he talks about her." He dipped his head, and his gaze locked onto Melissa's. "You don't have to worry, sweetheart. Nothing you could do could disappoint me."

Melissa smiled and hugged him, pleased she had his support. "Thanks, Dad. What about Mum?"

"She'll be okay. She just needs to let it sink in." He pulled back and glanced over her shoulder. "Now, where's the tea?"

Melissa grabbed three cups and set about boiling the kettle, while Christopher got the milk. In no time, the tea was made. She placed the cups onto a tray and carried it into the lounge. Her mother was staring out the window, her back to them, much the same way Melissa had been standing a short while ago. She put the tray onto the coffee table and glanced at her father. He nodded but didn't say anything. "Mum?"

"I'm not sure I'm okay with this." Patricia turned around, her lips set in a grim line.

"You don't have to be, but you have to respect my choices. Ellis isn't going anywhere."

Patricia looked back and forth between Melissa and Christopher, then sighed. "Are you sure this is what you want?"

"Yes."

"And Justin is okay with it?"

"He wasn't at first, but he understands we love each other. He's good with it."

Patricia nodded and sat on the sofa. She picked up a cup and took a few sips, silence surrounding them. Eventually, she said, "I can't pretend to understand all this, but you're my daughter and I love you." She put the cup down and stood. "If this is what you truly want, then I'll do my best to accept it and Ellis into the family."

"Thank you, Mum. That means a lot." Melissa tentatively embraced her mother, pleased when Patricia hugged her back. She didn't have a ringing endorsement from her, but the fact Patricia was willing to try was enough. Everything was falling into place, and Melissa couldn't be happier. *I can't wait for Ellis to get back. Maybe I can talk her into staying overnight.* They'd only had one night together since they'd made up and Melissa was desperate to fall asleep in Ellis's arms and wake up with her. This was the start of their life together and nothing was going to get in their way now.

†

"Mel?"

Melissa looked up from the chart she was filling in and saw Tara next to her, sporting a worried look. She closed the file and gave Tara her full attention. "Hey, Tara. What's up?"

"Craig is here."

"What?"

"He's got a laceration on his forehead from falling over."

Melissa let out a heavy breath. She hadn't heard a word from Craig in weeks. She could only surmise he still had a problem with alcohol. "Drunk?"

"He hasn't said it, but I can smell it on him."

"Okay." She placed the file into the correct cabinet and slammed the drawer closed. "I'll go see him." She found which bay he was in and made her way there. The curtain was partially drawn, only Craig's legs visible. She stepped through the gap and sucked in a breath. Craig sat upright, eyes closed. The wound on his head gaped open but wasn't bleeding. Bone was visible between the two flaps of skin. His eye socket was badly swollen, and deep bruising surrounded it already. *Whatever he did, he went down hard.* "Craig?"

Craig opened his good eye and sighed. "I told them not to tell you."

"I work in A&E. I would have found out anyway." Melissa stepped to the side of the bed and laid her hand on his forearm. "What happened?"

"I tripped over the coffee table and went headfirst into the wall."

"How much did you have?"

He sighed again, then licked his lips. "I don't know." He looked down at his lap. "There isn't much left in the bottle."

"Do you think now is the right time to get help?"

Craig didn't answer for a few moments. He continued to stare at his thighs, his index finger tapping the bed. Eventually, he looked up at Melissa. "I'm scared."

"I know it'll be hard, but I'll be there for you as much as you need me to be." Melissa ran her hand through his hair, then rested it on his shoulder. They may not be together anymore, but she hated seeing him like this. She had felt bad about stopping him from seeing Justin. Seeing him all bruised and battered, she knew it was the right thing to do. Justin didn't need to see his father like this.

"I suppose you mean as a friend, right?"

Melissa lifted one side of her mouth in a half smile. "Yes. I'm sorry, but there is no going back for us." She glanced away. "Also, I'm seeing someone."

"That doesn't surprise me." Craig nodded. "You're awesome. I'm just sorry I didn't appreciate you while we were together." He took her hand in his. "I've stuffed up so much."

"You can find your way back. You just need to be determined."

Craig pursed his lips and stayed silent for a moment. "What's he like? This new bloke?"

Melissa always knew she would need to tell him about Ellis at some point, she just didn't think it would be so soon. Not that she minded. Telling Justin and her parents was the hardest part. Letting Craig know didn't fill her with the same sense of dread. If he didn't like it, that was his problem. "I'm with a woman."

Craig's one good brow raised. "Really?"

"Yes."

249

"Wow." He smirked. "I never figured you for the lady-loving type."

"Me neither, but Ellis is wonderful. I can't imagine my life without her now."

"Does Justin know?"

"Yes, and he's okay with it."

He shook his head. "Then I guess we really are over." He squeezed her hand gently. "I'm happy for you, Melissa. You deserve the best."

"Thank you."

"Does Justin hate me?"

Melissa could lie to him, but she knew being honest might help Craig realise he needed to change. If he couldn't do it for himself, then maybe he'd do it for his son. "To be honest, he rarely talks about you. He's still hurting."

"I can't blame him for that. I want to make it up to him."

"You can start by sorting yourself out."

"And you promise you'll help me?"

"Yes."

"Okay. Is there someone here I can talk to?"

"I can contact Drug and Alcohol Services and get someone down to talk to you."

"Thanks."

"You're welcome." She bent at the waist and kissed the top of his head. "I'll be back in a bit." She stepped toward the curtain, but Craig's voice stopped her.

"Mel?"

"Yeah?"

"You'll never know how sorry I am for everything I've put you through."

She took a breath and smiled. "It's okay. Let's move forward and forget the past."

"It's not that easy."

"I know." There wasn't more she could do for him. She could get him all the help in the world, but unless he wanted to change, he wouldn't recover. She hoped with everything in her that he'd start valuing his life and make the effort to change for the better. He deserved to be happy. They all did.

†

Melissa turned the handle on her front door and pushed it open. The smell of roasted vegetables permeated the air, mixed with the unmistakable smell of her jasmine incense sticks. She smiled. *Ellis is here.* They had spent nearly every evening together for the past two weeks, save the nights Melissa worked. They'd only managed two sleepovers in that time, and it was driving her crazy. As much as they both wanted to spend nights together, Melissa didn't want to overwhelm Justin. *Anyway, it only makes me want her more.* She entered the lounge and grinned. Ellis was sitting cross-legged on the carpet, eyes closed, hands resting on her knees. Melissa had no idea she liked to meditate. She tossed her bag onto the sofa and sat next to her on the floor.

Ellis opened her eyes, turned her head, and smiled. "Hey."

"Hi. You're a welcome sight."

"Bad day?"

Melissa nodded. She laid down and rested her head in Ellis's lap. Ellis sunk her fingers into Melissa's hair and massaged her scalp. "Craig came in. He fell over, drunk, and cut his head open."

"Is he okay?"

"He'll be fine. I finally convinced him to get help."

Ellis bent and kissed the tip of Melissa's nose. "That's good."

"Yeah, as long as he sticks to it. Addiction isn't easy to overcome."

"You love him, don't you?"

Melissa's brows pinched, as she stared up at Ellis. "Of course not."

"I don't mean romantically. You were with him for nearly twenty years. That's a long time. Feelings don't just go away."

Melissa sighed and stared at the ceiling. She gave Ellis's question serious thought. "He was my first love and Justin's father. He'll always be important to me." She looked at Ellis again. "Is that okay?"

"Of course it's okay. I'm not worried you'll go back to him. I'm only concerned he might try to win you back, especially if you'll be spending time with him."

"You don't need to worry. I told him about you."

"You did?"

"Hmm mm. He was shocked, but he said he was happy for me. He knows there is no chance of us getting back together."

"I can't believe you told him."

"Yeah." Melissa rolled away, sat up, and ruffled her hair back in place. "Everyone important knows about us now."

Ellis beamed. "So, no more hiding from the world?"

"Nope."

"So, I can kiss you in public and hold your hand?"

"You can."

Ellis got to her knees and crossed the small gap between them. "Can I shout it from the rooftops?"

"If you like." Melissa shrugged a shoulder and mirrored Ellis's position.

"How about an ad in the paper?"

"If that will make you happy."

"What would make me happy is having you now." Ellis circled Melissa's waist and kissed her. "When does Justin get home?"

"Dad's bringing him back at dinner time."

Ellis glanced at the clock. "So, that gives us about an hour."

"Plenty of time." Melissa stood and brought Ellis up with her, their bodies staying close.

"I'll only need a minute. I've been craving your touch all day."

"Let's get on with it then."

Together, they ran up the stairs. Melissa laughed all the way, as Ellis kept pinching her butt. They didn't have long, but Melissa planned to make the most of it. She didn't know when she would get the chance to make love with Ellis again. She would memorise every touch, every kiss, so she could replay it over in her mind on the nights she was lonely. The one thing she was sure of, Ellis would always be with her, whether that was in person or in her thoughts. She'd found her soulmate, and she wasn't going to let her go ever again.

CHAPTER TWENTY-THREE

Melissa opened her eyes and shivered. She glanced over her shoulder and saw Ellis all wrapped up in the duvet. Over the last two months, Melissa had learned that Ellis was a bed hog. Not that she minded, it was a great excuse to snuggle up to her. Melissa rolled over and found her way under the soft duvet and into Ellis's arms. Ellis's eyes flickered open, and she groaned. Melissa smiled and kissed her shoulder. Another thing Ellis liked to do was sleep in. It was a new habit for Ellis. Ever since she started working for her friend, her hours were more stable. She no longer worked from dawn to dusk, instead, she kept a modest routine. After a few weeks, Ellis was able to allow her body to relax and enjoy the extra time in bed with Melissa, when she stayed over. Last night was the first time Ellis had stayed overnight with Justin in the house. Ellis hadn't been too keen on the idea, but Melissa convinced her it was time they started being a proper couple. Justin had been fine with everything so far, not even minding when Melissa lay in Ellis's lap while they had a movie night. Melissa didn't think Ellis staying over would cause any issues. "I can't believe I get to wake up with you."

Ellis opened her eyes again and hugged Melissa closer. "It's great, isn't it?"

"I wish it could be like this every morning."

"I have an idea."

Melissa pushed Ellis onto her back and rested her chin on her chest, gazing up at her. "What's that?"

"Instead of me moving into your house or you into mine, why don't we get planning permission to knock the walls through to make one big house."

"As awesome as that sounds, I don't think I can afford to do that." Melissa was ecstatic Ellis was thinking of their future together, but there was no way she would have enough money each month to pay for the upkeep of a house that size. She barely had enough as it was.

"You don't need to worry about the money. I have plenty of savings, and my house is paid off. You won't have to spend anything extra."

Melissa shook her head. "I'm not sure I'm comfortable with you spending your money on me."

"Mel, it's just sitting in the bank. I'd love nothing more than to give you and Justin the home of your dreams."

"I *have* the home of my dreams." Melissa kissed Ellis's nipple. "You, you're my home."

Ellis smiled. "I love you, but please think about it."

"I will, but for now, sleepovers it is."

"How do you think Justin will react when he finds out I stayed over?"

"Let's find out." Melissa flung the duvet aside and shoved on her joggers and T-shirt. Ellis dressed at a much slower pace. Melissa couldn't help but smile at the nervous look in her eyes. Once Ellis was ready, Melissa opened the bedroom door and glanced across the hall. "His door is open. He must be downstairs. Come on." She grabbed Ellis's hand and drew her along behind her. They found Justin on his hands and knees in the lounge looking under the sofa. "Morning. What are you doing?"

"I can't find my other football sock." Justin lifted his head and looked over the back of the couch at them. "Oh, hey, Ellis."

"Good morning."

"Coffee?" Melissa asked Ellis.

"Please."

"Have you looked behind the tumble dryer?" Melissa asked Justin, as she led Ellis into the kitchen. "It might have fallen off when I was changing the load over." She set about filling the coffee maker, while Justin went off hunting again. Ellis stayed quiet by the breakfast bar. It looked to Melissa that Ellis was making herself as small as possible. She didn't know why. Justin hadn't batted an eyelid when they walked into the lounge.

"Got it," Justin yelled from the laundry room.

"What do you need it for anyway?"

He came into the kitchen, stuffing the sock into his pocket. "Simon's dad said we can go to the field before pizza tonight."

"That's nice of him."

"Yeah, he always does stuff like that with Simon. He's cool."

Melissa smiled but hated the look of hurt in his eyes. Despite Craig's promise to sort himself out, he hadn't been able to kick the drink quite yet. He relapsed after six weeks and was now trying again. Justin still didn't want to see him, and that was fine with Melissa. She'd stuck to her promise and was supporting Craig as much as she could. It was hard at times, but she wouldn't give up on him. Justin needed his father, and she would do what she could to bring Craig back to him. "What time are they picking you up?"

"In about an hour."

"You'd better get packed."

Justin rolled his eyes. "*I am.*"

Melissa lifted her brows at his sarcastic tone.

"Sorry."

"It's okay." She shook her head and sighed, hating Justin would be a teenager soon.

"I don't think he noticed," Ellis said quietly, once Justin had bolted upstairs.

"Ellis, you're here all the time anyway." Melissa set a coffee mug down in front of her.

"True."

"Or maybe, he doesn't mind that you stayed over."

"Maybe." Ellis grinned and circled her arms around Melissa's waist.

"Honestly, you worry too much."

"I just don't want to make him uncomfortable."

"You don't." Melissa moved forward and pressed her lips to Ellis's. Ellis ran her hands down Melissa's back and cupped her butt. Just as Ellis's tongue touched Melissa's, Justin's voice broke them apart.

"Guys! I don't need to see that."

Melissa's skin heated. For all her assurances Justin didn't mind about them, she now thought maybe he did have a problem after all.

Ellis stood and cleared her throat. "I thought you were okay with us?"

"I am, but I don't want to see my mum kissing someone. It's gross."

"So, you're okay with this? With Ellis staying over?"

"I thought she already did." He shrugged. "It doesn't bother me." He went to the fridge and got himself a can of Coke. "I'll be gone soon. Can you control yourself until then?"

Melissa laughed, while Ellis's face turned deep red. "We'll try."

†

Ellis crossed her arms, as she leaned against the doorframe between the lounge and kitchen. She smiled, as she watched Justin tear into another Christmas gift. The last few months had been the best of her life. Things between her and Melissa were awesome, and her new job as an investment advisor was going well. She kept waiting for something to come along and rip it all away from her, but it never did. Ellis still owned her house, but she spent all her time in Melissa's. Waking up every day next to Melissa was a blessing she never wanted to let go of. Melissa's arm snaked around her waist and Ellis glanced at her. She uncrossed her arms and put one around Melissa's shoulders. "I think we went a little overboard."

Melissa raised her brows. "We? I didn't buy him all that. This is on you."

Ellis grinned and looked back at Justin, who was now ripping the packaging off a set of Nerf guns. No doubt, Ellis would be forced into playing with him. She didn't relish getting her ass kicked, as always. "I've never had anyone to buy for before. I kept seeing things I thought he'd like."

"He's not complaining." Melissa rose onto tiptoes and kissed Ellis's cheek. "Thank you for loving him the way you do."

Ellis kissed her back on the lips. "Thank you for letting me be a part of his life. And yours." She turned and fully faced Melissa. "You've made me so very happy, Mel. I never thought I'd find someone like you. You mean everything to me."

"I love you, Ellis." Melissa's eyes darkened. "Never forget that." She glanced at Justin. "Craig is coming at one o'clock. I can't wait to give you your present."

Craig had done amazingly well in the last four months. He managed to stay sober for all that time and was slowly rebuilding his relationship with Justin. Melissa and Ellis were still somewhat wary of him, but they knew he was doing his best. Ellis hoped he didn't relapse again, but knew it was always a possibility. All she could do was be there for Melissa and Justin if it happened again.

"Didn't you give it to me last night?" Ellis asked, thrilled when Melissa's neck and face tinted pink.

Melissa's voice dropped to a whisper. "It's a two-parter."

"I'll look forward to unwrapping it." Ellis lowered her head, intent on kissing Melissa, when the doorbell sounded. She groaned and stepped away. It was hard to find time for just the two of them. Either work got in the way or family things came up. Ellis was still uncomfortable doing anything with Justin in the house, except kissing when he wasn't looking, and her frustration levels were through the roof. She didn't mind too much; it made their coming together that much more satisfying and passionate. She wouldn't change a thing.

"That'll be my parents."

Ellis took a huge breath and swallowed hard.

"Don't look so worried."

"I'm not."

"Ellis, you freak out every time you see them. I don't know why. They love you."

"I know your dad likes me, but I swear Patricia is plotting to kill me." On more than one occasion, Ellis was sure she saw Patricia shooting daggers at her. Christopher, on the other hand, was nothing but lovable. They found they had a lot in common, and Ellis loved nothing more than she and Justin helping Christopher tinker with his Austin. She felt included in a family for the first time in her life. It felt fantastic.

"That's just the way she looks." Melissa shook her head and took Ellis's hand. "Trust me, if she wanted you dead, you'd be dead by now."

Ellis grumbled and rolled her eyes at what she hoped was a joke. "Great, I feel so much better."

Melissa let out a throaty laugh and tugged her along. "Come on."

Ellis followed willingly behind, not because she was excited to see Melissa's parents, but because she would follow Melissa everywhere and anywhere. Their life together was cemented in their hearts, and Ellis couldn't be happier at finally having the life she dared never dream of.

ABOUT THE AUTHOR
SAMANTHA HICKS

Samantha currently lives in the south west of England with her best buddy, Finley, her springer spaniel. She spends her time writing, drawing, and getting out into nature. Family and friends are the most important things to her, and she finds her inspiration for her stories from those closest to her. Writing has become her greatest passion, and after years of trying to find her confidence, she's finally decided to make a career out of it. She hopes to be doing this for the rest of her life. Sam has a thirst for reading, preferring it to almost anything, and she hopes to one day settle down by the beach.

OTHER AFFINITY BOOKS

_____

<u>Forever Home</u> by Ali Spooner
Nat, Marissa and Maggie survived their first winter by the ocean. Spring brings new growth, friends, and unwelcome visitors to the homestead. Find out how Nat and Marissa's tiny community deal with the hazards and rewards before them, as their homestead continues to grow and prosper. Expect romance, adventure, danger, good fortune, and the odd meal or two, in this sequel to The Bee Charmer.

<u>Disconnected</u> by Annette Mori
Vanna has always felt like something was off with her parents, leaving her feeling oddly disconnected. She decides to move across the country and establish a new and independent life after college. On the way to her new position in Flagstaff, Arizona, Vanna meets out and proud Trey, who loves to flirt.
Trey has never forgotten the beautiful young woman she met briefly and is determined to ensure their paths cross again.
Thousands of miles from home, Vanna finds out more about herself, but not her feeling of being disconnected from her parents. Will Vanna ever form the connection she desperately seeks? Does Trey's determination work out?

<u>Darcy Comes Home</u> by Jen Silver

After twenty-five years Darcy and Angie meet again and from the faintly flickering embers of their forbidden teenage love, a flame erupts. Family complications arise including a reluctant engagement, secret surrogacy, and a persistent ex-wife.

Villagers in Professor Darcy Belsfield's childhood home of Sycamore Haven remember her being sent away to a Christian conversion camp in Canada when her father discovered her making love to her school friend, Angie.

Angie has never married but she does have a past and some unenthusiastic plans for the future. Will the differences in their lives doom the chance of Darcy and Angie discovering if they can build a future together?

<u>Hat Trick</u> by Ali Spooner and K.L. Gallagher

Alexandra "Alex" Hawthorne is on the fast track to the top of one of the most formidable, white-collar, criminal defense law firms in New York. She can ill afford any distractions, especially those with dark-brown eyes, who can rock a power suit while coaching professional hockey players. Not now. Not when Alex is so close to making senior partner. Not after all she has sacrificed.

After a devastating end to her playing career, Janelle Leblanc channeled her passion into coaching and reached the pinnacle of success as the first female head coach in NHL history. Despite her accomplishments, she hears whispers that she was hired as nothing more than a publicity stunt. Janelle's focus needs to remain on the ice if she is to prove them wrong, not on a certain curly haired attorney with the most arresting emerald-green eyes she has ever seen.

Once the spark is lit, their chemistry is impossible to ignore. Can Janelle break down Alex's walls to give them a real chance? Or will Alex's past heartache be too much for them to overcome?

The Lone Star Collection _II_ by Various Authors
Saddle up for a wild ride! *The Lone Star Collection II* has something for everyone! If you enjoy romance, Kris Bryant and Dena Blake have penned hot contemporary stories in *Heat* and *Horseplay*, while *Pins and Needles*, by Julie Cannon, is a historical adventure. Annette Mori also contributes to the romance fare with a beautiful, enduring love story in *Rainstorm*. If you want sizzling erotica check out *50 by 50*, from Renee Mackenzie. What would a collection be without fantasy, paranormal and swashbuckling adventures? *Lured to the Rocks*, a unique work of fantasy by Barbara Ann Wright. In *The Devil's Backbone*, Lacey L. Schmidt spins a thriller about overcoming evil and personal loss. MJ Williamz explores dark passion in *Take Me All the Way*. Del Robertson offers *Return to Me* a classic pirate story, and Yvette Murray tosses in the *Ghostly Galleons*.

Footprints by Ali Spooner
Sandy, the youngest sibling of Gator Girlz, Inc., has

worshipped her older sister Cam all her life and wanted nothing more than to be just like her hero. *Footprints* provides readers with Sandy's story of growing up in the Bayous of Louisiana. When the devastating floods of 2016 impact the Baton Rouge area, Cam and Sandy join the Cajun Navy to help rescue families trapped in the rampant floodwaters. The story also revisits Sandy's victory over Bubba Gump and how Sandy's injuries started her down the path to find the love of her life. Food, adventures, and great family relationships fill the pages of *Footprints*.

Love at Leighton Lake by Samantha Hicks

Tallulah 'Tally' Roberts decides that a few weeks staying in a cabin at Leighton Lake will help mend her shattered pelvis and broken heart.

Caitlyn Matthews works at the lake resort her mother owns, loving nothing better than spending her morning swimming in the lake. That is until she meets Tally. Their attraction is instant, but both are wary of these new feelings with their history of previous relationships.

As they get to know each other, secrets from Caitlyn's past come to light. Caitlyn fears her mother has been lying to her and together they search for the truth.

Love at Leighton Lake is packed full of love, drama, and a cow called Houdini who likes to roam the cabins, much to Caitlyn's delight.

The Others by Annette Mori

As a seer and brilliant scientist, Em convinces her wife, Lise, to prepare for the inevitable conclusion, after the chaos caused by foreign countries attacking the United States. Leaving behind a wake of destruction and a new world order, forcing them to navigate a frightening reality. After ten months in their cozy bomb shelter, they emerge to a world where the vegetation is surprisingly unaffected. Should they band together with other survivors, or try to make it on their own? There are others in this unknown world. On the first day outside of their shelter, they meet members of an alternate society. Are they friend or foe? Change is inevitable. But will they change in ways Em and Lise can live with, or will this altered world change them into something unrecognizable?

Three Mile Cache by Jen Silver

The story is set in Australia circa 1988. When archaeologist Carolyn Wells returns home to Sydney after several months away at a dig in Tunisia, she expects to be reunited with her lover, Detective Inspector Alex Graham. But she soon learns that Alex has been wounded in a hostage incident and is recuperating at a Royal Flying Doctor Service hospital at a place in the outback of New South Wales called Three Mile Cache. Carolyn decides to fly out there and surprise Alex with her arrival. Surprises abound when she gets there. One of the doctors treating Alex has a rather intimate interpretation of a bedside manner. There are

Affinity
Rainbow Publications

eBooks, Print, Free eBooks

Visit our website for more publications available online.

www.affinityrainbowpublications.com

Published by Affinity Rainbow Publications
A Division of Affinity eBook Press NZ LTD
Canterbury, New Zealand

Registered Company 2517228